New York Catholic publication society

Biographical Sketch of Mother Margaret Mary Hallahan, O. S. D.

New York Catholic publication society

Biographical Sketch of Mother Margaret Mary Hallahan, O. S. D.

ISBN/EAN: 9783744660082

Printed in Europe, USA, Canada, Australia, Japan

Cover: Foto ©Raphael Reischuk / pixelio.de

More available books at **www.hansebooks.com**

BIOGRAPHICAL SKETCH.

BIOGRAPHICAL SKETCH

OF

MOTHER MARGARET MARY HALLAHAN,

O. S. D.

ABRIDGED FROM HER LIFE.

————— —— ———

NEW YORK:

THE CATHOLIC PUBLICATION SOCIETY,

9 WARREN STREET.

1871.

CONTENTS.

BIOGRAPHICAL SKETCH

OF

MOTHER MARGARET HALLAHAN.

———◇———

CHAPTER I.

BIRTH AND EARLY YEARS.

MARGARET HALLAHAN was born in London, of Irish Catholic parents, on the 23d of January 1803. Her father, Edmund Hallahan, belonged to a family which occupied a respectable position in society, but, owing to a long series of misfortunes, he himself had sunk in life, and found himself at length obliged to maintain his family by humble labour. The maiden name of his wife was Catherine O'Connor; her family were all pious Catholics, and one of them, Father John O'Connor, was a Dominican, and lived to an advanced age in the convent at Cork. Margaret was their only child, and the idol of her father, of whose indulgent affection she always retained a lively remembrance. She inherited the warm religious instincts of her mother, and manifested them with a certain childish impetuosity, prostrating and putting her forehead to the ground in prayer, and indulging in other exterior

A

demonstrations of piety, which sometimes drew from her mother the warning words, " Little saints make big sinners."

Her education began at the school established at Somers Town by the celebrated *emigré* priest, the Abbé Carron. Here she attended as a day-scholar, and one of her earliest recollections was the affection with which her father was accustomed every day to meet her on her return from school, always bringing her a little cake, or some similar present. Few as are the anecdotes that have been preserved of her child-hood, they are not a little characteristic. She was only eight years old when the Jubilee of King George III. was celebrated, on which occasion her parents took her to St James's Palace, which on that day was thrown open to the public. Most of the visitors who thronged the royal apartments satisfied their loyalty and their curiosity in a truly English manner, by sitting in the king's chair, but when Margaret was invited to do the same, she stoutly refused, though her mother persisted, and afterwards punished her for her refusal, which arose, as she afterwards ex-plained, from a certain feeling that it was only a sham sort of honour, which she could not endure. Moreover, the grandeur of the state apartments did not greatly affect her ; they fell far short of what her lively imagination had pictured as worthy of a king's palace, for at eight years old the child of poverty had already within her ideas of lofty magnificence which were not easily satisfied. Her passionate temper was at that age under little restraint, and on the evening of the same popular holiday, she described herself as " dancing about in a passion, and pulling her own hair," because her parents refused to take her out to see the illuminations.

Her father's death took place in the year following this little incident. Her mother being now left in yet more embarrassed circumstances, the Reverend Mr Hunt, a charitable priest of Moorfields, procured the admission of the child into the Orphanage attached to the Somers Town establishment, where she remained until her mother's death. The whole period of her school-life did not exceed three years, and closed when she was but nine years of age. By that time she had gained the remarkable skill as a reader which she retained through life; but in other respects her school-training was very imperfect. She was never able to master the mechanical art of ciphering, but she acquired a taste for reading, which at a later period she gratified by devouring every book that came in her way. Her lively and impulsive nature did not very readily submit to the strict discipline enforced in the Somers Town Orphanage, and her frequent infractions of the law of silence sometimes got her into trouble. On one such occasion she was kneeling at the outer gate by way of penance, when the Abbé Carron himself entered, and was about to introduce some visitors. Perceiving the confusion of the little delinquent, he good-naturedly signed for her to rise and retire unobserved, then patting her kindly on the head, he said, in a deprecating tone, to her mistress, "You will see, she will be good by and by." If her progress in secular learning was limited during her three years of school-training, she never-theless profited much by the solid religious instruction which she received at Somers Town. It was here that

Margaret's susceptible nature received its first religious impressions, among which must be noted that lively sense of the Divine presence which never afterwards forsook her. She was accustomed to trace this feeling to the effect produced on her soul by a representation of the ever-watchful Eye of God, which was painted in a triangle, after the French fashion, over the high altar in the church. Margaret's childish imagination readily endowed the painting with life ; she believed it to be the veritable Eye of God, and observed, with a sensation of awe, that in whatever direction she moved it appeared to follow her.

Scarcely six months after her father's death her mother followed him to the grave, a victim to the same fatal malady. She died in St George's Hospital; and thus at the age of nine years Margaret was left in the desolation of complete orphanhood. At the same time, a change in the arrangements of the Somers Town Orphanage led to the dismissal of as many of the children as were supposed to have any independent means of support, and among these Margaret was, from some cause, included, although, in point of fact, destitute alike of friends and resources. The good priest who had before interested himself in her favour, however, again came to her aid, and placed her in service, where she appears to have remained for two years. At the end of that time she was, through the kindness of Mr Hunt, received into the family of Madame Caulier, wife to a French emigrant of good birth, who, like many others in like circumstances, had been compelled to embark in trade, and had opened a lace warehouse in Cheapside.

Madame Caulier continued to retain her in her

family for several years, and became warmly attached to her. She failed not to appreciate the rare qualities which were early discernible in her *protégée ;* but at the same time she treated her with excessive harshness. The faults which drew forth her corrections were generally untidiness or careless breakages ; but the severity with which they were visited increased the evil, for Margaret became so nervous, that if she met her mistress when she was carrying anything fragile in her hands, she was almost sure to let it drop from very fear. She never entirely lost the effects of this treatment, so that to the last there mingled with her high and independent spirit a certain character of timidity. She has frequently said that as a girl she never entered the presence of her mistress without trembling, and expecting a sharp correction. She used to wonder how a person otherwise so charitable and devout could show so much severity to a child ; and, deeply sensible of her desolate position, she would say to herself, in the midst of her troubles, " When I take in little orphan children I will do all I can to make them happy ; they shall never have to regret their parents as I do mine."

This conduct on the part of Madame Caulier was far from being the result of any real want of affection. She had the intention of adopting Margaret as her child, and, in a manuscript memoir which she dictated at a later period, she attests the admiration and esteem with which the character of the young girl secretly inspired her. " I knew well enough," she writes, " that she was far fitter to be a queen than a servant." And she adds, that when in doubt on any point she always contrived to get her advice, and generally followed it. She carefully instructed her in all household matters, and nursed her tenderly in her frequent sicknesses ; and it was from her that Margaret acquired the skill she so often afterwards displayed in discharging the same charitable office towards others. Considering her rather in the light of a child than a servant, she would not suffer any of the young people in the warehouse to address her as " Peggy," and evinced her fondness by the care she took in having her well dressed. But whilst thus gratifying her own tenderness, she was careful to screen the object of it from any temptation to vanity, by repeatedly telling her she was an "ugly little thing." Margaret did her best to believe it, but was wont to admit that she did not always feel able to agree with the judgment of her mistress on this point.

Some of the anecdotes related in the memoir spoken of above are too characteristic to be omitted. Margaret was one day sitting in the kitchen with a servant-girl older than herself, who sometimes undertook to give her religious instruction. On this occasion their conversation was on the duty of making restitution. " You know," said her companion, " that if you were to see another steal, and the person who committed the theft did not make restitution, you would be bound in that case to make restitution yourself." For some days after this, Margaret was observed to be unusually thoughtful. At length one day Madame Caulier called her, and giving her a quantity of old newspapers which were lying about the house, told her she might take them and sell them. Margaret took the news-papers, saying to the servant, " Now I will brave

Madame Caulier's anger; I will go and make restitution." Accordingly, having sold the papers, she bought with the money some tea and sugar and a bottle of rum. With these things in her hand, she went to the house where she had formerly been in service, and going down on her knees before the mistress, she said, "If you please, ma'am, I am come to make restitution." "How, Margaret?" was the reply; "I am sure you never did anything that was wrong; what does all this mean?" But Margaret only repeated that she came to make restitution. At last, being pressed to explain herself, she acknowledged that she had once seen a fellow-servant take these articles and give them away, and that having learned her duty in such a case, she thought herself bound to make restitution. On another occasion several things had been missed in the house, and suspicion fell on one of the servants. Margaret was convinced of the girl's innocence, and being much distressed to see her suffering under the unjust charge, she resolved if possible to clear up the mystery. One day her voice was heard vehemently calling out for help; every one ran to the spot, and found her struggling with a man whom she firmly held in her grasp, exclaiming, as they entered, "Here is the thief; Jane is innocent!" It then appeared that for several days she had set herself to watch for the thief, concealing herself for the purpose under a bed, and as soon as he appeared, she sprang out and secured him.

Another incident related by her mistress reveals the germ of that tender compassion which she always cherished for those who had fallen into distress from a better position, and who were solitary and friendless

in the world.   A young relative of Madame Caulier's
had been staying in the house, and whilst there became
seriously ill.   Madame Caulier, who was in the habit
of talking over all her affairs with Margaret, mentioned
her intention of sending this young person home, but
Margaret entreated her not to do so.   " When people
are left to servants, as she would be," she said, " they
often suffer much from neglect;" and she concluded by
begging that the young lady might remain in their
house, promising to take the entire charge of her, and
to attend on her day and night.

These generous qualities of heart were mingled
with the impulses of a strong and passionate nature,
and it was thought necessary, on account of certain
childish faults, to defer her First Communion, which
she made at length on the Feast of the Assumption,
but in what year is not known.   She felt the delay
poignantly, and the great day of her First Communion
left a deep impression on her soul.   She described
herself as being at this time lively and impetuous, and
unable to resist the impulse of " saying everything
out."   She was naturally cheerful and merry, much
fonder of reading than of needlework, somewhat un-
tidy, a fault that was afterwards thoroughly corrected ;
and of a passionate temper, but with such warm instincts of liberality, that, to use her own expression,
she was often " a thief for the poor."   She used to
give away whole loaves to the charwoman, and in
spite of Madame Caulier's severity with her in other
respects, she never made this a subject of blame, for
she was herself most charitable to the distressed.

As time went on, the discomforts of her situation
became so unendurable, that, when not more than

twelve years old, she resolved to escape from them by running away, and seeking another service. She put her plan into execution, and in her simplicity and ignorance of the world, set about to find a situation, knocking by turns at all the doors in one of the streets of London, and asking if any one within were in want of a little maid. In this way she came at last to a hotel, when the mistress, perceiving her forlorn condition, kindly took her in, and kept her to assist in her own nursery, not allowing her to serve the guests. She did not remain here long, for Madame Caulier, alarmed at her disappearance, had her publicly cried, and on discovering her retreat, took her home again, and for a time treated her with greater forbearance. When about thirteen she again entered service, and this time in a Protestant family, where for two years she was unable to hear Mass, and had much to suffer from her fellow-servants, especially from one person who was a professed infidel. On one occasion this wretched man, after declaring, in blasphemous terms, that there was no God, in proof of his words, solemnly called on God, if He really existed, to strike him dead on the spot. In what manner Margaret may have behaved on this occasion we have no means of knowing; but when at another time the same person (as it would seem) ventured to speak disrespectfully of the Blessed Virgin in her presence, her rejoinder was sufficiently emphatic. Having no words ready at the moment with which to reply, she used a weightier argument, and seizing a large plate, broke it over the scoffer's head. She never concealed her religion through human respect, and was remembered in the family by the title of "the little maid that would not

eat meat on Fridays." On leaving this situation
she returned for a time to Madame Caulier, whose
real kindness is sufficiently proved by the fact, that
she always allowed Margaret to consider her house
as her home. But before long she again entered
service in a family where a painful trial awaited her.
The master of the house so far forgot himself as to
offer an insult to the poor servant-girl who should
have claimed his protection. Margaret's modesty was,
however, defended by her own firmness and courage.
Seizing a knife, she threatened to kill the intruder if
he did not at once leave her presence; and the determination of her manner effectually compelled him to
obey. After this she at once returned to Madame
Caulier, and did not again leave her protection until
placed by her in the family of Dr Morgan.

During these years she had no opportunity of
carrying on her education, though she took every
means of gratifying her taste for reading. She always
represented herself as having relaxed at this time from
her habits of early piety, and was accustomed to speak
of this season of spiritual declension, and particularly
of her habits of indiscriminate reading, in terms of
bitter, and probably exaggerated, self-reproach. It
was during the latter portion of her residence with
Madame Caulier that the seeds were laid of that painful affection of the spine from which she continued to
suffer at intervals throughout the remainder of her
life. It was caused, in the first instance, by an im
prudent feat of strength. Possessed of extraordinary
muscular power, she was rather proud of hearing herself called "as strong as Samson;" and when about
seventeen, seeing some men hesitate to lift a great

iron stove, she thought to put them to shame, and carried it unassisted to the top of the house. But this achievement cost her dear ; her back was severely strained, and two years later the injury was further increased by an accidental fall. From that time she became subject to the formation of lumbar abscesses, which caused excruciating agony, and rendered all bodily exertion painful.

It appears to have been about the year 1820 that Madame Caulier recommended her to the service of Dr Morgan, who had formerly filled the post of physician to King George III. He was an invalid, and Margaret, who possessed remarkable skill in the management of the sick-room, was engaged to attend on him in his declining years. At his death he left her a legacy of £50, and she continued to reside first with his son, and afterwards with Mrs Thompson, his married daughter. Under this lady's roof Margaret remained for twenty years, of which five were spent partly in London and partly at Margate, and the remaining fifteen in Belgium. She was intrusted with the care of the children of the family, but she soon won so much of the love and confidence of her mistress as to be regarded by her far more as a friend than as a servant.

Mr Thompson held the office of Secretary to the Mexican Commission, and was at this time absent on an official visit to Guatemala, whither he had been sent by the late Mr Canning, to report on the state of the Central Republic ; and during the two years that elapsed before his return, Margaret was a great comfort and support to his wife. In her devotion to the interests of the family she altogether forgot her own; indeed, the disinterestedness of her character inspired her at all times with a kind of repugnance to receive payment for her services.   How far this feeling was carried may be judged by one anecdote.   Soon after Dr Morgan's death, Margaret being then in his son's house, requested, with some hesitation, that she might be given a trifling sum of money for her necessary expenses.   As it was known that Dr Morgan's legacy had shortly before been paid to her, some surprise was expressed at her being so soon in want of money, and she was pressed to explain what she had done with it.   At first she was unwilling to say, but at length admitted that she had expended the whole sum in Masses for the soul of her deceased benefactor.   She used to relate that once when a gentleman offered her some money, she was so indignant at his supposing that her services had been rendered with a view to remuneration, that she threw the money after him into the street.   Another gentleman having been on a visit to the house, gave her, on leaving, a small sum as a present.   Margaret was unaware of this common custom, and fearing lest the giver might have had some bad motive in making this offering, she ran after him with the intention of returning it.   He had already quitted the house and got into his carriage, but she contrived by running to keep the carriage in sight till it stopped at his door, and not being in time to put the money into his hand, she laid it down on the door-step and returned home.

At Margate, she performed another extraordinary feat of muscular strength.   She assisted at the death-bed of a man, who was a near relative of the Catholic priest.   When he died, finding the poor widow was too timid to touch the corpse, she lifted it alone, and carried it without help to the room where it was to be laid out for burial.

Her first attraction to a more interior and strictly religious life began during her residence at Margate. The person who at that time lived with the family as nurse was Mrs Collishaw, an excellent and pious Catholic of gentle birth, who, having married beneath her own rank, had been cast off by her relations, and reduced to enter service. Margaret often spoke of the strong impression made on her soul by seeing this good friend weeping over her sins. It was by her advice that she sacrificed her passion for secular reading. " I never learnt to know God," she would say, " till I gave up my taste for reading; often I prayed that I might forget everything I had ever learnt, and know but Him alone, and I think He has heard my prayers." So great was the veneration that she felt for her friend, that afterwards at Coventry, whenever she received a letter from her, she used to kiss it, and lay it on her head before opening it. Her religious sentiments were further deepened by a visit which she paid at this time to the convent at Winchester, whither she accompanied one of the daughters of the family whom she was taking to school. It was in the chapel of this convent that she first became conscious of a vocation to the religious life, and from that time she seems to have adopted a method of life, and even a style of dress, indicating that, in heart at least, she had renounced the world. One of her oldest friends thus describes her manner and appearance at this period : —" I was but five or six years old when dear Mother

Margaret used to come to our house with the Thompsons; and all that I can remember is that we used to
hail her appearance in the nursery with delight. The
servants in the house felt the greatest respect for her;
and my brother Francis says, that he well remembers
one of them saying that she was fitter far to be in a
nunnery than a nursery; and how, as a boy, he could
not understand why she always dressed in black, and
wore such a strange-looking cap. We were also much
shocked at their calling her *Peggy,* for our nurse used
to tell us that nicknames were bad words."

The familiar name which Dr Morgan had been
accustomed to bestow on his favourite attendant had
been retained by his daughter's children as a term of
affection. As for the black dress and strange-looking
cap, they had not been adopted without a motive.
Margaret, in her youth, possessed unusual personal
attractions, of which, in spite of good Madame
Caulier's precautions, she could hardly remain altogether unconscious. Even in her later years she
retained traces of that noble beauty and that extraordinary dignity of manner which always left the
impression that she was one of nature's queens.
These personal gifts often drew on her a kind of
admiration exceedingly repugnant to her, and to
which she manifested her dislike with characteristic
impetuosity. When one visitor at the house thought
fit to address her some foolish compliment, she rejected
his advances with so sound a box on the ear that he
retreated, and complained to the mistress of the house
that "Peggy had a heavy hand, and had used it in
return for his civilities." The circumstance of another
person having sought her in marriage determined her

on putting an impassable barrier between herself and the world by taking a vow of chastity. She made it when about twenty-two, "kneeling on a kitchen-chair;" and it was probably after this event that she adopted a style of dress intended as the outward token of her having renounced all prospects of worldly settlement.

One of her peculiar characteristics was a great dislike of strangers and strange places. When, therefore, on Mr Thompson's return to England, it was first proposed that the family should remove to Belgium, and Margaret was pressed to accompany them, she was in great trouble. She thought she should never get reconciled to such a change, and nothing but her affection for the children at last overcame her reluctance to leave England. The removal to Bruges took place in the year 1826, when Margaret, then in the twenty-fourth year of her age, found herself for the first time in the atmosphere of a Catholic country.

CHAPTER II.

LIFE IN BELGIUM.

THE scenes in the midst of which Margaret was now placed were a new life to her. Keenly susceptible to all that was beautiful or magnificent, her soul awoke to a new sense in the churches of Belgium, where, for the first time, she beheld the solemn offices of the Church performed with becoming splendour. New as it was, however, she was so thoroughly endowed with the capacity of appreciating the church ritual, that all in which she now took part, whilst it excited within her a kind of rapture, appealed to instincts of which she had been conscious from childhood. " The first time I heard a military Mass at Notre-Dame," she said, " I thought I should have gone crazy." The house in which the family resided was not far from Notre-Dame, and on the first great feast of Our Lady that was celebrated after their arrival, which happened to be that of the Assumption, she witnessed one of those exhibitions of popular devotion to which English eyes were then totally unaccustomed. When she saw the entire population taking part in the gorgeous procession, she felt like the Queen of Saba in presence of the magnificence of Solomon : "there was no more spirit in her." " I felt," she said, " that I must go to bed and die."

There were at that time but two confessors in Bruges who received confessions in English, of whom one was M. Versavel, under-pastor of the Church of St Walburga, and afterwards confessor to the great Beguinhof, a man of remarkable piety and spiritual discernment, but who bore the reputation of being exceedingly severe in his method of direction. Margaret placed herself in his hands almost immediately on her arrival in Bruges, and remained his penitent for more than fifteen years. In spite of the rigorous discipline to which she subjected her, Margaret was never induced to seek for gentler guidance. If she brought him the same fault twice over, he sharply reproved her, and once kept her eight weeks from Communion. " It was a good thing for me," she said, in relating the circumstance, "and broke many bad habits." She always spoke with gratitude of what he had done for her soul. " I owe everything to him," she said, on receiving the intelligence of his death, as she lay on her own deathbed; "I was just on the turn when I fell into his hands, wavering whether I should give myself to God or the world. I don't know what would have become of me but for him."

The immediate effect of his direction was to re-awaken in her soul that attraction to the religious life of which she had already been partially conscious, and which now made itself so strongly felt as to determine her on making trial of her vocation as a lay sister in the English Convent of Augustinians at Bruges. In compliance with her urgent request, Mrs Thompson obtained for her the first vacancy, but the result was a disappointment, and within a week she was once more installed in her former position in Mrs Thompson's family.

The failure of this first trial of her religious vocation was far from diminishing that ardour in the service of God which had moved her to make the experiment. The manner of life which she now embraced recalls some of those pages in the life of St Catherine of Sienna, which depict that holy virgin discharging the humblest domestic duties, whilst, at the same time, she was constantly seeking for fresh objects on whom to pour forth the treasures of her charity. Unfortunate commercial speculations having straitened the circumstances of the family, and obliged them to reduce their establishment, Margaret's position became every day one of greater labour and responsibility. For many years she discharged the chief part of the domestic service, and by her energy and devotedness sustained the spirits of all around her. For herself, she was supported by higher motives than even her

B

generous affections. She saw in the state of servitude
a hidden grace which would have led her to embrace
it even if not called to it by providential circumstances.
"The state of servitude," she once said, "is a very
hóly state. It is so hidden and ignored, so full of
self-sacrifice that is never considered. God has
appointed it otherwise, or else I should have chosen
it in preference to any other state." These words
reveal to us something of the spirit in which she fulfilled her daily duties, and the religious light in which
she regarded them ; while we gather from a passage
in one of her letters, that neither their number nor
their laborious character were suffered to distract her
from prayer. "I was more recollected," she writes,
"and made more aspirative prayer in the kitchen than
anywhere else. I think Our Lady taught me to cook,
for I always invoked her and my angel guardian when
I was cooking the dinner." Besides her discharge of
these household offices, she nursed more than one
member of the family through dangerous sickness : the
youngest child, who died in infancy, was tended by
her to the last, and baptized by her hands ; and by
her close attendance on its mother during a tedious
rheumatic fever, her own health became seriously
affected. In a moment of urgency she undertook a
journey to England to settle some pressing affairs of
the family, crossing over to Margate one day and returning the next. During the Revolution of 1830,
she was left alone at Bruges, in charge of the children,
whose parents were absent in England, and underwent
much anxiety and suspense during the alarming crisis.

Amid all her labours and anxieties, her generous
solicitude for those whom she loved as her own chil-

dren enabled her to make every sacrifice ungrudgingly. Her bodily sufferings were often acute, aggravated by the severe austerities which she habitually practised. In familiar conversation with one of her religious, she once admitted that she had done much more in the way of penance when living in the world than she had been able to do after entering religion. A friend has described her at this time as frequently washing down the stairs, wearing all the time a rough hair-shirt. The rigour of her exterior penances becoming known to her confessor, he sent her to the Teresian nuns, and desired her to follow their prudent and ex-perienced direction on this point. "They distrusted me at first," she said, "but afterwards they explained to me all their practices." Domestic cares and austere penance did not, however, fill up the whole of her life. Her active labours of charity were on so large a scale as to make her name known throughout Bruges. Considering how humble was her position, and how small her resources, it appears incomprehensible how she contrived to do all she did. But hers was one of those characters that create for themselves channels of action from their own innate force and greatness. Even her imperfect knowledge of the Flemish language was not suffered to be an obstacle in the way of her charities. She used constantly to visit St John's Hospital when residing in that parish, and though unable to converse with the sick, she used to take them cakes, and other little dainties, and was known among them by the name of *The Black Vrouwe* and *The Rich Deba.*[1] She continued her visits to the hospital after removing to St Anne's Quai, walking

---

[1] *i.e.,* Devout woman.

thither daily in spite of the distance, to attend a man-servant formerly in the Thompsons' service. She was also in the habit of begging for some of the poor convents, and used to take fresh rolls to the Poor Clares, and entreat the nuns to eat them. Even the poor ecclesiastical students shared her bounty. A friend visiting Bruges, in the service of an English family, was invited to accompany her on an expedition to the seminary, and wondering what could take her thither, her surprise was not diminished on hearing that she always contrived before vacation time to furnish the students who had no friends with pocket-money or little necessaries. What her own slender means did not supply for these charities, she procured by begging from her friends, both in Bruges and Eng-land. She wrote to one, entreating her to send some cast-off wearing apparel fit for the use of ladies, which she designed for a family of respectability, whose pecuniary losses had obliged them to leave England. "I believe," writes Mrs Thompson, "that while with me, she gave all she had to the poor, and that she spent much time in instructing the ignorant and visiting the sick. Persons also came much to see her." Another member of the family, writing since her death, confirms this account, and declares that as soon as she received any money she gave it to the churches or the poor. Her zeal for the adornment of God's house already suggested wishes which, at that time, seemed impossible to be realised. " When I saw brass lamps hanging in the church of St Gudule at Brussels," she said, " I used to promise our Lord that I would some day give Him silver ones; and then I would laugh at myself, for at that time I had not a penny." She afterwards had a scruple whether she were not bound to fulfil this promise by presenting such ornaments to this very church. As to making any provision for her own future wants, it was a thought that never occurred to her, until M. Versavel, seeing her profuse liberality, obliged her to pay into his hands a portion of her annual wages, which he kept for her in reserve.

Her life of charity was sustained and invigorated by prayer. Every morning she rose at four and heard an early Mass in the Church of St James, where her customary kneeling-place is still pointed out by the people, who, to this day, call it "*Margarita's sweet corner.*" When she read in the life of Marie Eustelle of her being so often found waiting outside the church-doors in the early mornings, the incident recalled many similar recollections of her own. " I have often stood outside St James's Church saying my prayers before the doors were opened," she said, "and happy too I thought myself to be there." Returning home after completing her devotions, she applied herself to her household duties ; and when she had attended to the wants of the family, devoted the remainder of her time to visiting the churches, the convents, or the poor. The extent of her charitable labours, can best be estimated by the lasting memory they have left behind them. "When I visited Bruges, after she first came to Coventry," writes the Right Reverend Bishop Ullathorne, "I found the whole city full of her fame. People of all classes, from the poor to the bankers, came to inquire after her. Her name introduced me to every one. The clergy and superioresses of convents spoke of her with warm interest. I was inquiring my way in the streets of a man of decent appearance, and as he accompanied me, I asked him if he had known Margarita; he told me she used to visit him and be kind to him when sick in the hospital. I asked an old woman who was praying in the Church of St James where Margarita used to kneel; she at once walked up to a pillar in front of the statue of the Mater Dolorosa, and, pointing to a spot behind it, said, in a knowing whisper, 'She used to kneel *there.*' And the people of Bruges spoke not only of her goodness and kindness to everybody, but also of her power of giving freedom of heart to scrupulous persons."

This account is fully corroborated by the evidence of those who were eye-witnesses of her daily habits. Visitors from England, after they had stayed a while in Bruges, expressed themselves astonished at the extent of her influence. The same young friend whose early recollections of her have been quoted in the last chapter describes her pleasure on finding herself introduced to these new scenes under the guidance of Margaret. "My brother Francis," she says, "was at that time staying with the Thompsons, and attending the college, where he was studying languages. We only stayed a month, but during that time I learned to love Mother Margaret, and to esteem her as a saint. Delighted to find myself in a Catholic country for the first time in my life, I wanted to visit every church and convent, and dear Mother Margaret contrived to find time to accompany me. Through her influence I was admitted into the interior at the Poor Clares, the Teresians, and others, for every one respected her. I well remember how she used to call us into her little oratory to sing the Litany of the Blessed Virgin for the conversion of England. One night, being later than usual, we were passing the door of her room when she followed us, and in her gentle tone said, half reproachfully, " What ! going away without saying good-night to the Blessed Virgin ?" Quite ashamed of ourselves, we returned and sang the Litany. I assure you no time in the day did we enjoy so much as those few minutes in her humble little room. There was a simplicity about it all that went straight to the heart."

The room here spoken of deserves a passing word of notice. It contained in a curtained recess Margaret's poor straw-bed, the austerity of which is attested by one of her visitors, who, being one day indisposed, lay down to rest on this couch of penance, which, as she afterwards complained to her friend, did not offer her any great amount of ease. Attempting to arrange it somewhat more comfortably, she was startled by finding under the coverlid a rough hairband, while Margaret was equally disconcerted at the discovery. In another part of the room, on a little table arranged and decorated as an altar, stood her great treasure, an image of the Blessed Virgin. It was given her by M. Versavel, to whom it had been bequeathed by an old woman in Holland, who held it in great veneration, and charged him never to part with it except to some person who would know how to value it. Margaret probably valued it above every other earthly possession, and it was before this image that she was accustomed to invite her young friends to pay their evening devotions. " In that room," writes their mother, " my two sons and eldest daughter, when visiting the family with me, would go, before leaving the house, to say a prayer, or sing a hymn, and sometimes sing Vespers." The eves of Our Lady's festivals were generally chosen for singing Vespers, on which occasions the singers arranged themselves before the altar in choir fashion, Margaret being seated on her bed on one side, and the others opposite on whatever seats they could contrive.

In fact, then, as later, the ruling principle of Margaret's life was prayer. It has been reported, and truly, that during her residence at Bruges she effected the conversion of several Protestants. But she herself declared that the principal means she used for the purpose was prayer. She once acknowledged that she had never been brought in close communication with Protestants without their being converted. "And yet," she added, "I am sure it was not by talking. There was a woman in Bruges whom no one thought would ever be converted. She once lived in the same house with me, and I went nine weeks following to the altar of Our Lady of Dolors for her. I did not speak to her at all, but at the end of that time she was a Catholic." The first of her Belgian converts she had the happiness of receiving many years later into the Hospital of Incurables at Stone, where she made a happy death.

One friend, now a religious in another order, who knew her intimately during her residence at Bruges, remarks that nothing struck her more in her intercourse with Margaret, than her total freedom from human respect. No matter who the person might be, if she deemed it a duty to speak, she was withheld by no human consideration. A Protestant lady lodging in the same house thought fit, on one occasion, to rally her on the subject of religion with unbecoming levity. Margaret replied in terms so forcible as effectually to silence her for the future. Her intensity of feeling was not easily restrained, and sometimes betrayed her into a warmth of language which she afterwards regretted. "And yet," says her friend, "nothing could exceed the delicacy of her conscience on the point of charity. Once fearing she had offended me in conversation, though I had not perceived how, she wrote me an earnest apology, ending with the words of the apostle St James, 'He who offendeth not with his tongue, the same is a perfect man.'"

Her attention was first directed to the Dominican order by the Abbé Capron, at that time third priest attached to the parish church of St James.

He was himself a Dominican Tertiary, and strongly recommended her to enter the Order; but to this step M. Versavel offered a decided opposition. His objections are not known, but he was determined and persistent in refusing his consent, and gave his penitent to understand that her desire was extravagant and unreasonable. It is possible he only acted thus with the view of mortifying her will and exercising her in patience and obedience. For eight years Margaret's entreaties on this point were constantly rejected; she was even forbidden again to return to the subject; but what was refused by man, she only the more earnestly sought from God. With the view of recommending her petition to the intercession of the Blessed Virgin, she determined on making a pilgrimage to Our Lady of Assebroek, one of those miraculous shrines which still attract the warm devotion of the Flemish people.

The parish church of Assebroek stands in a sort of sandy desert about five miles from Bruges; and in order to get there in time to hear Mass and communicate, and then return home before the hour when her domestic services would be required, Margaret had to rise at two o'clock in the morning, and to make a painful foot-journey through the sandy roads in the dark. She persevered in this devotion for nine days, at the end of which time her confessor, without any solicitation on her part, announced to her that he withdrew all his objections to her joining the Dominican order, and that she might do so with his full consent. Her joy was great indeed, enhanced by the feeling that she owed this grace to the intercession of Our Lady. She received the habit on the Feast of the Espousals of St Catherine of Sienna, 1834; and on the 30th of April 1835, being the chief feast of the same holy patroness, she made her profession, in the hands of the Abbé Capron. On this occasion she took a vow of perpetual chastity, and often referred to the transport of happiness which she felt on that day, which she always regarded as the real day of her religious profession. All the bells of Bruges were ringing to welcome in the month of May; but to her heart their chimes seemed to be celebrating her sacred espousals. "On that day," she would say, "I walked on air, it made me comprehend something of what it must be to be in an ecstasy!" The children of the family whom she had so tenderly reared shared in her joy, and testified their sympathy in their own graceful way. They assembled in the hall to greet her on her return from church; the youngest boy having strewed the ground with roses, and prepared a crown of flowers which he insisted on placing. upon her head. She suffered him to have his way, but remarked to one of his sisters, that "it was much as if they were crowning the devil."

Whatever may be thought of the manner of life which we have been attempting to describe, it may be instructive to know in what light Mother Margaret herself was accustomed to regard it. In a manifestation written at the desire of a confessor shortly before her last illness, she speaks of her life in Bruges as being "more like that of devout ladies in the world, praying much, going to as many ceremonies as I could in the church, to the great discontent of those I had to serve; going very often to the sacraments, but not mortifying myself; and giving way to temper and self-will to an immense degree, but all the while desiring to be different, and reading much, which has been my greatest good." To these words we must subjoin the significant comments of Bishop Ullathorne. "These," he says, "were the years of her great combats with her strong nature and high spirit; but whilst this generous soul is accusing herself of *not mortifying* herself, she conceals from us those severe mortifications, fastings, and watchings, and those internal sufferings, through which, as well as by the occasions presented by her duties and her bodily sufferings, she was waging incessant war with nature and its irascible propensities."

After her profession, Margaret redoubled the fervour both of her charities and her austerities. Her ardent temperament, however, was tested and purified by many trials, both of mind and body. She had to encounter severe bodily sickness, and interior suffer-

ing yet harder to bear. Both one and the other were
doubtless part of the providential training of her soul,
and it was in that light that she herself always regarded the continual ill-health by which her powerful
nature was chastened and subdued. The spinal affection already spoken of assumed from time to time an
active form, causing excruciating suffering, added to
which she had more than one attack of fever.

Her interior trials appear to have arisen in part
from that impulse which was constantly urging her to
undertake something for God, whilst, at the same time,
His divine will in her regard was not as yet manifested.
Her sadness and preoccupation were visible to others,
and often elicited the kind remonstrances of her mistress, who would affectionately press her to tell the
cause of her unhappiness.

"I don't know what makes me unhappy," she would
reply; "I feel I want something, but I don't know
what."

The sight of sins and scandals which she was
powerless to remedy also occasioned her a distress
which to those around her seemed altogether unreasonable, and the same kind friend would advise
her at such times not to trouble herself so much about
what she could not prevent, often reminding her that
she could not expect to set the whole world to rights.
Colette, the confidential servant of M. Versavel, also
proffered her homely advice, and tried to restrain the
impetuosity of that ardent nature which longed to
right every wrong with the least possible delay.
Colette's words, full of practical good sense, were
always well received. She had a great affection and
veneration for Margaret, and had the happiness of

afterwards welcoming her back to Bruges at a time when her seemingly impossible dreams had been more than realised. When reminded of the days when she had so often proved a wise counsellor, she shook her head incredulously, and, turning to Mother Margaret's companion, said, with a sort of fond smile, "There never was but one Margarita !"

M. Versavel was often himself the cause of suffering to his penitent, both by the rigour of his direction and by the firmness with which he opposed her commencing any work or embracing any state of life to which he instinctively felt she was not called by God. Her entreaties to be allowed to make another trial of her religious vocation were constantly rejected. "I see," he would say, "that you are intended for *something*, but I do not yet clearly see what it is." He appears to have been secretly convinced that she possessed all the qualities that would fit her to become a religious foundress, and to have been averse to her entering on any course that might hamper her freedom when the moment for beginning her real work should arrive. Events justified the sagacity of M. Versavel's judgment, guided, as it doubtless was, by the Spirit of God ; but at the time the constant thwarting of every proposed plan was naturally felt by his penitent as a painful check.

These mental anxieties reacted on her bodily health, and induced attacks in the head which probably caused her greater suffering than any of her other infirmities.

Towards the latter part of the year 1839, she was seized with illness of a yet more alarming character, and in the belief that her symptoms indicated the

approach of a contagious fever, it was decided to remove her to the Hospital of the Sisters of Charity.
By Mrs Thompson's desire she was provided with a
separate apartment, but even here the accommodation
provided was of the humblest kind. As the patients
were required to bring their own beds, Margaret had
to be carried down-stairs and placed in a conveyance,
whilst the bed on which she had been lying was rolled
up and taken to the hospital for her use. She often
spoke of the desolation of heart she experienced at
this time. "No one would believe," she said, "what
I felt when they placed me in the chair to carry me
down-stairs and took my bed from under me. Mrs
L. was with me, and carried my image of the Blessed
Virgin before me: *that* was my only consolation; I
do believe she used to talk to me at that time." In
the hospital she felt the want of many comforts to
which she had hitherto been accustomed. The room
in which she was lodged was small, the mattress lay
on the floor, and the food was served in the coarse
brown ware used by the poorer classes. But she had
hardly entered before the doors were besieged by
persons of all ranks, among whom the news had
spread that "Margarita" had been carried to the
hospital in a dying state, and who came in crowds to
testify their feelings of sympathy and respect. It
took one person the whole day to open the door to
her visitors, and the concourse was found so trouble-
some to the community, that the nuns at last requested
M. Versavel to put a stop to it.

She remained at the hospital until partially convale-
scent, but did not again return to the Thompsons' family.
Mrs Thompson arranged for her reception into the

house of the Abbé Capron, where two or three pious persons, Tertiaries like herself, then resided. Here she continued for some time, uncertain as to her future plans, but feeling more powerfully urged than ever "to do something for God." Her soul was meanwhile passing through a very crucible of desolation and temptation. Her sense of humiliation under these trials was crushing and terrible. Everything appeared like a dark void; and she described herself as going about from one church to another seeking refuge in prayer from her own pressing thoughts, which would not suffer her to rest.

During all this season of trouble the Epistles and Offertories of the Mass seemed to speak to her soul in an extraordinary manner. "When I read them now," she said, "I cannot see in them what I then saw. They always seemed to be saying, *Do something for God.*" Once, as she was praying in St James's Church, on the Feast of St Catherine, this interior voice became audible even to her bodily senses; she heard the words, *Do something for God,* spoken behind her, and that so distinctly that she answered aloud, "Lord, what can I do?" and looked around to see if some one had not really spoken. She used also to speak of a dream, if dream it were, which left a strong impression on her mind, wherein she seemed to be going over mountains, followed by great multitudes of people. When first she saw the Welsh hills they reminded her of this dream, and she exclaimed, "Oh, how I long to work for Wales! Those hills remind me of my dream in Belgium."

By advice of the Abbé Capron, she at length determined on commencing a religious establishment in

Bruges. The plan seems to have been to have founded a small community of Dominican Tertiaries, living under religious rule, and devoting themselves to active works of charity. Margaret had long since abandoned all intention of returning to England, and had even bound herself by vow not to do so, trusting nevertheless that she might be able to work for the good of her country people in a foreign land. She proposed taking in invalid English ladies, or young persons requiring religious instruction, and with this view she hired a good house in Esel Street. M. Versavel, who had discouraged other projects, entered warmly into this. He not only supplied Margaret with the little fund of her own savings which he had hitherto reserved, but increased it from his private resources, so as to enable her to furnish her house. When her old and valued friend, Mrs Amherst, of Kenilworth, paid her second visit to Bruges, she found Margaret about to take possession of her new abode, and was entreated by her not to forget the new foundation on her return to England. "Come back soon," she said, "and for the love of God bring me some old 'Gardens of the Soul,' Catechisms, and reading-books." "All she wished and prayed for," writes her venerable friend, "was to work for the salvation of souls."

Yet from the first she felt no confidence in the success of this experiment. She continually assured her confessor that "it would not go." Difficulties of all sorts arose to obstruct her progress, and very conflicting counsels were offered her in various quarters. The Bishop of Bruges and some of the clergy proposed her trying a foundation in America, while the Dominican authorities were anxious that she should make her novitiate in a French convent, with a view of afterwards returning to Bruges, and founding a convent of the order in that city. To complete her embarrassment, the temporal assistance that had been promised her was diverted into another channel; ridicule was cast upon her plan; and her best friends seemed to disapprove it. An influential priest actively opposed her, and, God so permitting it, even her own director appears to have forgotten that he had ever given encouragement to the undertaking. All these causes combined to produce in her soul a state of mental distress which surpassed all she had hitherto experienced. She has described it herself in a letter, written many years afterwards to a friend, who remarks on the passage, that "it seems to be a revelation of no ordinary soul, and to belong to an order of things only found in the lives of the saints." "Just before I came to England," she writes, "I had a cross that nearly killed me. I had not a friend. My own confessor turned against me, and denied things he had told me to do. I was so poor, so forsaken, that in going through one of the streets of Bruges, I stopped and put my hand to my head, and looked up to heaven and said, 'O God! where shall I find a friend?' I could not paint the anguish of my soul at that moment. But it obtained for me a freedom of soul unknown till then, and the words of the Following of Christ came into my mind, 'In the cross is infusion of heavenly sweetness,' and these words seemed to convey ease to my tortured brain."

Reduced to actual distress, she endeavoured for a time to support herself by receiving lodgers. But this plan likewise failed, and it was at this critical juncture

c

that she received pressing solicitations from her friend, Mrs Amherst, to return to England, where there was so much need of those who were willing to work for the glory of God. The proposal was one to which Margaret felt a strong repugnance, and she even believed herself bound by her promise to remain in Belgium. M. Versavel, however, warmly supported Mrs Amherst's suggestion, and by his desire Margaret addressed to Mrs Amherst the following letter, which is the earliest from her hand that has been preserved, and will convey the best idea that can be formed of her sentiments at this important crisis :—

"BRUGES, 1842.

"RESPECTED MADAM,—I hope you will excuse the liberty I take in writing to you : it is the wish of my confessor. As you expressed an interest in my regard, he wished me to ascertain from you if there were any probability of my being employed in England in any way for the poor. The reason, Madam, he wishes me to ask this of you is—the Dominicans have been here, and intend establishing a convent here, or at Ghent, in about a year. They wished me to go for a time to Paris to learn the rule, and also to speak French, there being a convent of the order in that place ; but M. Versavel and the Superior of the Jesuits here prefer my going to England, thinking I should be more profitably employed in the service of my neighbour. They would wish to know how or in what manner I am likely to be situated before I give a decided answer to the Dominicans. For me, Madam, you may dispose of me as you may judge fit. I am ready to employ myself in any manner for the salvation of souls, as I am told by those who conduct me that it is the will of God and what He requires of me. I shall feel greatly obliged by an answer in a few weeks. I remain, most respected Madam, yours very gratefully and humbly,

"MARGARET MARY HALLAHAN."

On receipt of this letter, Mrs Amherst opened a communication with the Rev. Dr Morgan of Uttoxeter, who was then in want of a schoolmistress and sacristan, and he was sufficiently pleased with the account he received of Sister Margaret to agree to receive her. Want of means, however, obliging him to give up his design, Mrs Amherst next applied to the Rev. Dr Ullathorne, O.S.B., who had lately been appointed to the neighbouring mission of Coventry. What he heard of Margaret's rare qualities satisfied Dr Ullathorne that she would prove a valuable assistant in all his plans for the good of his congregation, and he empowered Mrs Amherst to engage her services. Before this could be done, however, Dr Ullathorne received the unexpected intelligence of his appointment to the bishopric of Hobart Town, in Australia. He wrote at once to Mrs Amherst, explaining the difficulty, but adding that he hoped to decline the bishopric, in which case he should still be ready to receive Sister Margaret at Coventry.

Mrs Amherst was not deterred by this threatened obstacle from persevering in her design, and the better to ensure its success, she addressed a letter to the Venerable Bishop Walsh, Vicar-Apostolic of the Midland District, in which she strongly recommended that some steps should be taken without delay to secure Sister Margaret's establishment in England.

The persevering efforts of this excellent lady met with the success they deserved. Her recommendation awakened the interest of Bishop Walsh, and he replied to her letter in the following terms :—" The person of whom you speak so highly must not be lost to this diocese ; bring her over to England by all means, and if she does not go to Coventry, I will take her myself." Mrs Amherst accordingly wrote to Margaret, inviting her to her own house until something could be definitely settled, and asking what she would expect for her services from any priest in whose mission she might be established. Margaret replied with characteristic disinterestedness :—" Wherever I go they must board and lodge me. I have clothes enough for five years, and at the end of that time, if I have given satisfaction, they will not like to see me in rags, and will give me new ones." In the meantime, as it now appeared certain that Dr Ullathorne would be allowed to remain in Coventry, he was anxious that Sister Margaret should be established there without delay, as mistress of the girls' school, in which office he trusted that she would likewise exercise a beneficial influence over the young women employed in the ribbon weaving, some of whom belonged to his congregation, while many more, as he had reason to believe, were likely to be gathered into the Church.

On the 30th of April 1842, Margaret crossed from Belgium and landed in England. After a brief visit to her old friend, Madame Caulier, who then resided at Isleworth, she set out for Kenilworth, where Mrs Amherst had kindly prepared to receive her, intending herself to introduce her to the scene of her future labours. After staying a few days at Kenilworth, she proceeded to Coventry, thus entering on the humble commencement of a work, destined, in the designs of God, to be so fruitful in our Lady's Month of May, being then in the fortieth year of her age.

CHAPTER III.

COVENTRY.

THE Catholic mission of Coventry, belonging then as now to the Benedictine Order, had been placed under the care of the Rev. Dr Ullathorne in the November of 1841. The small chapel attached to the mission stood at the top of Hill Street, and had been erected in the year 1807. It was an unpretending brick structure, and already began to show signs of dilapidation. The priest's house was not in a much better condition ; the rooms were small, and scantily furnished, and the walls in many places exhibited alarming cracks. A good schoolroom had been erected close to the chapel by Father Cockshoot, and an efficient schoolmaster was in charge of the boys, but no girls' school had yet been organised. The congregation, though poor and not very numerous, was animated with a good spirit, which led the people to respond with readiness to every measure of improvement set on foot by their pastor. English Catholics were at that time only beginning to recover from a long period of repression and discouragement. Things were indeed a good deal changed since the days when

Margaret and her young companions had encountered
the stones and hootings of the Margate idlers on their
way to chapel; but though important advantages
had been secured to the Catholics by the Act of Eman-
cipation, it was only by degrees that they learnt to
feel their freedom. Many practices and devotions
now familiar to us were introduced with hesitation,
and it was some time before the Church could assume
anything of that exterior order and beauty which is
her natural inheritance. Even after all active persecu-
tion had ceased, Catholics were for many years deterred
by prudence, as well as poverty, from bestowing much
care on the externals of religious worship. But many
influences were already at work, the combined effect
of which brought about much of that beneficial change
which has been witnessed among us during the last
quarter of a century: and it will not be thought too
much to say that the work accomplished by Mother
Margaret, during the twenty-six years that elapsed
from her return to England until her death, contributed in its measure to swell that tide of religious
revival which, like all great streams, is formed and
fed by the confluence of many a slender rivulet.

Yet who could have foretold that any co-operation
in so great a work should have been in store for her
on the day when she first stood in the priest's parlour
at Coventry—to use her own words, " a poor, helpless, friendless, homeless, penniless woman ! "

"I shall never forget my first meeting with her,"
writes Dr Ullathorne, " in the little house I then
occupied at Coventry. She was then in her vigour,
well-proportioned, very erect, and having an expression of dignity and simplicity combined, yet with a

spiritual softness pervading features that indicated her remarkable powers of mind and heart. It seized me with a sense of surprise as well as of gratification. I at once felt that Mrs Amherst's promise that I should find in her a valuable co-operator in my mission was far more than realised. She wore a plain black stuff dress closed to the throat; her hair was cut off her head, and upon it she wore the plainest of Belgian caps, such as are used by the poor. To this, when she went out, she added the Belgian cloak and black chip bonnet and veil. Even then her ankles were so weak that walking out was a difficulty, and more than once she fell down in the street."

The first thing necessary was to settle the precise terms on which she was to enter on the duties of her situation. But when requested to state the salary she would require as schoolmistress, she replied by warmly repudiating all thoughts of being paid at all. In fact, she never could understand how people could endure to be paid for doing anything for Almighty God. "I often think," she once remarked, "what madness it seemed, my coming over to Coventry without a penny in the world. And the best of it was, I did not want them to give me any money. I wonder if the bishop remembers how indignant I was when he asked me what salary I should require for teaching his school. 'Salary!' I said, 'I am come for the sake of Almighty God, and not for money.' Then he said he supposed I should want clothes; but I replied I had plenty. I was so affronted, the rich ladies at first did not know what to make of me." Such was her own account of her first introduction to Coventry, and the incident, so characteristic of her spirit, revealed to her new director that in Sister Margaret he had to deal with no ordinary soul. But he prudently allowed nothing of this impression to appear, and left her to make her own way in the humble duties assigned her.

It had been arranged that she should reside in the priest's house, where her first experiences were far from cheering. She occupied a very small kitchen in company with the old housekeeper, whose jealousy and crabbed temper made her life far from easy. Her bedroom was a poor attic, containing no furniture but a rickety bed and one very old chair. The walls were stained with damp and mildew, and in many places exhibited wide cracks. Her position was desolate enough. She was occasionally invited to the parlour by Dr Ullathorne, who always remained struck after these interviews by her modest reserve, her discreet language, and her gratitude for his proffered kindness. But she was ere long deprived of this comfort and support. Within a fortnight after her arrival at Coventry, Dr Ullathorne found himself obliged to proceed to Rome in order to get the question of his appointment to the Australian bishopric finally negatived. The mission was meanwhile placed under the care of the Rev. Mr Clarkson, the assistant priest, and Sister Margaret was left to find out work for herself, in a place where she was a total stranger. On Dr Ullathorne's return after a few months' absence, he found that she had collected a school of two hundred girls, which she was teaching unaided ; that she had already acquired considerable influence among the young factory women, as well as the weavers who worked in their own houses, and that in addition to her school duties she had found out all the sick poor of the congregation, and was constantly engaged in visiting them. She had likewise prepared a very large class of First Communicants, and had made every preparation for celebrating the great day after the Belgian fashion, with a festal solemnity altogether new in Coventry. Her ordinary manner of life was to rise at five, after which she performed her morning devotions and prepared the chapel for Mass. If there were any very urgent case of sickness she sometimes contrived to visit it before breakfast, but punctually at nine o'clock she was in the schoolroom ; and her exactness on this point was so great that, as she has herself let us know, she made it a matter of confession if she were a minute or two after time. The school closed at twelve and re-opened at two, and the interval was given to dinner, visiting any sick who were near at hand, and preparing for afternoon school, which lasted from two to five. She arranged the school on the plan of that at Somers Town, dividing it into classes taught by monitresses. She always taught one class each day herself, so as to go through the whole each week ; and she used to walk about from class to class asking the angel-guardians of the children to teach them. " I think they must have heard me," she said, " for though I was myself so ignorant, the parents always seemed satisfied, and said the children got on." Between five and seven she found time to say Our Lady's office, and to satisfy other devotions ; sometimes she again visited the sick, in which case one of the young women of the congregation undertook to prepare the schoolroom for the night school, which was open from seven till ten : on Saturdays, when there was no school, she visited the more distant cases, specially in the district known as Foleshill. A certain number of the factory girls lived at Foleshill, of whom the larger proportion were Methodists ; but so great was their attachment to Sister Margaret, that troops of them would accompany her home, singing hymns to the Blessed Virgin all the way. Neither severity of weather nor her own manifold infirmities ever kept her at home when her presence was called for. One winter's night, when she had been detained unusually late visiting a poor woman in typhus fever, she had to return home after dark. A pond without any fence lay in her way, and the ground being covered with snow, she had missed the path. She came home drenched with water up to the waist, and could never say how she had passed this dangerous spot, though she always retained the impression that she had been supernaturally carried through it. On first coming to Coventry she had so completely forgotten English ways, that she asked to be shown the quarter where the "nobles" lived, imagining all the smartly-dressed girls who came to Mass on Sundays, and who were mostly ribbon-weavers, must be of the "noble" class. When she came to understand the state of English society a little better, she was shocked and distressed at the depth of poverty which she discovered. To relieve it, she sold a number of her most valuable books, and could not understand how the kind Providence of God could leave any of His creatures in such necessity, until Dr Ullathorne pointed out to her that without these sufferings many probably would never save their souls. There were at that time many poor creatures at Coventry suffering from frightful incurable diseases, who, on that account, were left destitute of all attendance. One of these was a poor woman covered with sores which bred enormous worms. She could not bear Sister Margaret to leave her, and would make her sit by her bedside for hours together. " I was very frightened of the worms," she said, in relating this circumstance, " and could not help starting when they crawled my way." There was another sufferer in a half putrid state, who was deaf in one ear, so that when the priest had to hear her confession he was obliged to lean over her, and speak into the other ear, regardless of the intolerable effluvium. Another case was that of a poor woman bent quite double in a position that rendered it impossible for her to lie down, or even to sit without support. She had even to be fed by others. When her husband went out to his work in the morning he used to tie her to the bedpost to prevent her falling out of her chair, and then leave her, dependent through the day on the chance kindness of neighbours. Sister Margaret visited this poor woman daily, taking with her such better kind of food as she could procure, and feeding her with her own hands. She found her quite ignorant of religion, and took infinite pains in instructing her. Suffering as she was in body, the invalid was absorbed with delight as the truths of faith opened on her mind. She used to say she could not be grateful enough for being allowed to hear of such beautiful things, and Sister Margaret often declared that the sight of her faith and devotion was such a joy that " it set her up for the day."

She was greatly assisted in her attendance on the sick by some of the young women of the congregation, who attached themselves to her person and delighted in sharing her labours. One of these undertook to take care of a case which was altogether extraordinary. It was that of a woman who had taken to her bed, in the first instance out of pure sloth, but who fell at last into such a state of dirt and disease that no one would go near the house. Miss G., however, hearing that she was dying without help, proceeded to the spot, and finding the house-door locked, made her entrance by the window, undertook the difficult task of cleansing the room and the poor patient, and waited on her with the utmost devotion till the day of her death. All these deeds of charity were amply recompensed. Every one of the sufferers above spoken of were received into the Church, and died happily, their extraordinary sufferings seeming to dispose them for the faith and to procure them unusual graces.

Such was the mode of life on which Sister Margaret had already entered during Dr Ullathorne's absence, and the amount of good which she had effected almost single-handed confirmed him in the impression he had already formed regarding her. At the same time, her difficulties with the old housekeeper came to his knowledge, and blaming her for keeping him in ignorance of what she had suffered, he dismissed the old woman, engaged a girl in her place, and placed the housekeeping in Sister Margaret's hands—an arrangement which continued so long as she remained under his roof. Sister Margaret took occasion of his return to make a Spiritual Retreat under his direction. She entered on it with extraordinary fervour, and during its course made a general confession of her whole life, which cost her many days of great labour and much interior suffering.

In the meantime her influence among the young women of the congregation went on daily increasing. They grew to feel towards her as a mother, won by that singular power of attracting hearts of which so many who approached her were conscious. On this point we can do no better than quote the language of one whose testimony must carry with it the greatest amount of authority. "Over the people, and especially over the young women employed in ribbon-weaving," writes Bishop Ullathorne, "she exercised a spiritual influence in a very unusual degree. I have often asked myself what was the secret of that marvellous influence which she exercised; and I believe that it lay not only in that great, warm, loving soul of hers, that was always going to God, but also in her faith in other souls, in what they are, in what they have latent in them, and in what they are capable of. Then she loved souls so much, and they felt her love." And he adds, that amongst these young persons the name of Sister Margaret soon became "a household word." She succeeded in inducing them to avoid occasions of danger and vanity by modesty of dress, and caution in their demeanour. For herself, she united a wonderful freedom of spirit, and even of manner, with great strictness in all that concerned the keeping aloof from the world. She cherished the religious character which she had assumed by her profession and her vow as jealously as any inmate of a cloistered convent; and even the Protestants of Coventry seem to have understood that the plainly-dressed priest's housekeeper had something of the nun about her. A story is told of some of the young Catholic girls of Coventry persuading her to accompany them one Easter Monday to see St Michael's Church. That venerable relic of Catholic times, the spire of which forms one of the most remarkable features in any view of the city of Coventry, was not at that time shown to the public without a fee, except on the holiday in question. When Sister Margaret and her companions entered the church, the service was going on, and a tolerably large congregation was present. Sister Margaret told them to take her at once to the Ladye Chapel, and there kneeling down, she recited with them aloud the Litany of Our Lady, with the intention of recovering that beautiful building to the Catholic Church. When it was finished, she rose and walked out again, without looking at anything around her, whilst the old beadle exclaimed to her companions, " Why, that's *an old nun!* you shouldn't go about with an old nun !" This story spread far and wide, and got very much misrepresented; but it is a fair example of her habitual mastery of the temptation to human respect.

She had a great horror of that weakness, and in various ways tried to teach her young companions to deliver themselves from its slavery. Once when she was going out to visit the sick, accompanied by her friend, Miss G., she asked the latter to carry a parcel of rather formidable size, containing necessaries for the poor. Miss G. did not altogether relish the proposal, and said she would give a penny to some child who would carry it for them. "No," said Sister Margaret, "I will carry it myself." On this her companion entreated to be allowed to take it, but Sister Margaret was firm in her refusal. "You are not worthy of carrying it," she said, "as you are ashamed of it." She then told her that in her youth she had felt the same false shame at carrying parcels in the streets, and to conquer herself she bought the largest band-box she could find, and carried it down one of the principal streets in London. Probably the relation of this notable example had its effect on the hearer, for she did not refuse to accompany Sister Margaret on a certain expedition to Nuneaton, which demanded no little sacrifice of human respect. The whole distance is now traversed by railway; but a few years ago the journey thither was a more serious affair. No public conveyance plied between Nuneaton and Coventry, and the only plan which Miss G. could suggest was, that they should go with the butcher's son when he paid his weekly visit in his cart. Sister Margaret consented to this, and in due time they arrived at Nuneaton, without any disaster. But when, after despatching their charitable business, the time came for them to return, they found to their dismay that the passengers in the cart were increased to four, by the presence of a young calf which the butcher had purchased, and was about to convey to Coventry. Sister Margaret, whose farm-yard experience was not very extensive, was apprehensive lest the calf should bite, and was only reassured on beholding it safely enveloped in a net. It proved a very harmless companion, and only consoled itself during its imprisonment by sucking the end of Miss G.'s silk dress. The assistance rendered by this faithful and devoted friend, the first com-

panion who joined Sister Margaret's Community at
Coventry, the last who watched by her bed of death,
proved a great support and consolation to her. When
their acquaintance ripened into mutual confidence,
Miss G. discovered, to her surprise, that Sister
Margaret was carrying on her life of incessant and
exhausting labour in spite of bodily infirmities which
would have reduced one of less energetic spirit to
the condition of an invalid. The inflammation in her
eyes obliged her constantly to wear a green shade;
and a distressing eruption covered her whole person,
with the exception of her face, which was never in
any way disfigured, and gave no indication of what
she at times suffered. The scalp of the head was
affected in a particular manner, and at the time we
speak of, the consequent discomfort was increased
from her having hitherto had no one to assist her
with that tender and delicate care of which she stood
so much in need. This care was now effectually
supplied by her new friend, who, with another young
person, equally devoted to Sister Margaret, gladly
relieved her of some of her laborious duties, and assisted her in every work of charity.

Their wonder at the courage which could persevere
in such a daily course as that embraced by Sister
Margaret was increased as they gradually discovered
more and more of the austerity of her life. The
Dominican rule prescribes the wearing of serge
garments next the skin, and though this point is not
obligatory on a secular Tertiary, Sister Margaret
considered herself bound by it; and not being able
to purchase the material in question, she substituted
in its place under-garments of the very coarsest brown

wrapping, such as is used for covering luggage. This mortification was the severer from the exceedingly tender and irritable state of her skin, nor could she be induced by any argument to give up the practice. She spent nothing on herself. Even the clothes which her friends at Kenilworth sometimes sent for her own use were given away as soon as received. The consequence was, that she was often short of actual necessaries, and at last, the bonnet she had brought from Belgium had lost the semblance of a bonnet, and her solitary pair of walking shoes were found to be full of holes. Her two faithful disciples consulted together what should be done in this emergency. They ventured at last to put a new pair of shoes in her room, but no sooner had she cast her eyes on them, than she exclaimed how good God was to send her just what she wanted for a particular old woman, to whom the shoes were immediately conveyed. This mortifying failure of their first experiment a little discouraged them, and it was some time before they ventured on taking any steps for amending the condition of her bonnet. At last, however, with some hesitation, they contrived to produce a bonnet which one of them had made, and entreated her only once to try it on. She consented to do so, and to their extreme joy, the comfort which it afforded to her sensitive head was so great that she agreed to wear it, a result which they regarded in the light of a great victory.

She was in the habit of making little collections among the people for various pious objects, and also begged among her friends for means to relieve cases of distress. Thus, with Mrs Amherst's assistance,

D

she obtained a set of linen for lying-in women, which was lent to the most needy, and became the origin of a useful institution. Moreover, she found means to interest one of the medical men of the town in her charities, who, though a Protestant, was always ready to give gratuitous attendance to any of her sick people. She also received generous assistance from the Carpue family, with whom she now for the first time became acquainted. It consisted of an aged retired priest, who held the rank of canon in the Cathedral of Arras, and who with his two maiden sisters, resided in the extern quarters of the Benedictine convent of Princethorpe.

Sister Margaret occasionally visited Princethorpe, and once, having gone over to attend the Corpus Christi Procession, she made so eloquent an appeal to the Community on behalf of her poor children at Coventry that all were struck by it; and the late Rev. Mother St Geneviéve remarked, that she was sure "Sister Margaret would some day work wonders." This little incident is recalled by one, then a pupil in the convent, who on that day made her first acquaintance with Sister Margaret, and never lost the sentiment of veneration which she then conceived for her. Her influence, indeed, was felt by all who came in contact with her, and a story is told of the success of one of her begging appeals, which will perhaps remind the reader of a somewhat similar passage in the life of St Catherine of Sienna, though, in the present instance, the contribution was less ruthlessly demanded than in the case of our holy Mother. One day after leaving the apartments of the Carpues, she observed that their servant at the turn was wearing a very good dress, which seemed to her the very thing she wanted for a poor woman in Coventry. She therefore addressed the maid as follows: "You have good wages, and I daresay have three or four other gowns up-stairs quite as good as that you have on, which I want very badly for a poor woman who has none; so go up-stairs and change it, and bring it down to me." The maid, quite delighted, complied at once with her request, and Sister Margaret returned to Coventry in possession of the gown.

In addition to her other employments, she was sacristan, and kept everything about the church in excellent order. She possessed great skill in adorning the altar, and as one of her early companions remarked, "could make anything look beautiful out of nothing." The materials at her command were but scanty. When first she came to Coventry the chapel was very imperfectly furnished with requisite linen and vestments. No lamp was burnt before the tabernacle—a circumstance arising from prudence rather than from neglect. This mark of devotion was still but rarely permitted in England, for Catholics felt reluctant to indicate the presence of the Blessed Sacrament to curious eyes, through fear of sacrilege. When Mrs Amherst applied for leave to burn a lamp in her domestic chapel, Bishop Walsh felt himself obliged to refuse her this permission. But, accustomed as she was to the usages of a Catholic country, this omission struck Sister Margaret as a painful want of respect. On Rosary Sunday, 1842, she obtained leave to put a small cut-glass lamp before the tabernacle, and herself bought the first pint of oil for it, praying, as she lighted it, that it might never be suffered to go out. The sight of the lamp seemed at once to raise the faith of the people in the Eucharistic Presence. Some of them wept with joy on beholding it, and gladly brought their weekly pence towards its support; so that Sister Margaret's prayer was fulfilled, and the light she had been the first to kindle was never afterwards extinguished.

The desolation and poverty of God's sanctuary was doubly felt by her after having been so long accustomed to the magnificent churches of Belgium. It was a positive anguish to her when, on the first occasion after her arrival, she beheld the old housekeeper preparing the altar for Benediction, and placing on it the brass candlesticks used in the house and kitchen; and she at once wrote to her friend, Miss Eyre, of Bruges, who furnished her with the means of procuring more suitable altar furniture. Benediction, however, was not at that time often given, and Sister Margaret often went alone before the Blessed Sacrament, and, weeping to see her Lord thus solitary and unhonoured, she would sing through by herself, in the empty chapel, the whole Benediction service—a touching act of reparation such as we have already seen another devout worshipper of the Most Holy Eucharist longing to see discharged in the neglected sanctuaries of England. Another story is told, which belongs, however, to rather a later period. After the building of the new church at Coventry had been completed, the members of the choir thought proper one Sunday to take offence at something, and refused to sing. Sister Margaret, indignant beyond measure at the disrespect thus offered to God, sang through the whole Benediction service alone, at the full pitch of her rich and powerful voice, in the resolve to make some amends in her single person for the shortcomings of the rest.

Even on her first arrival at Coventry, during Dr Ullathorne's visit to Rome, Sister Margaret had taken some steps for improving the condition of the altar furniture, as appears from letters written to Mrs Amherst, who liberally supplied her wants. Her notions on the subject of church decoration, however, were not so magnificent as they afterwards became, and she contented herself with something very far short of the highest Gothic standard. She often related the pleasure she took in the construction of a certain antependium of blue glazed calico, covered with muslin, with which the beholders were amply satisfied, and which was thought rather a splendid affair.

It is probable, however, that the calico antependium was intended, not for the church, but for her school-room altar. Our readers will not have forgotten the image of Our Lady, already more than once mentioned. It need hardly be said, that this image had been brought to England by Sister Margaret, and found an honoured place in her poor room, though she did not immediately venture on displaying it before the eyes of others. But one day, previously to Dr Ulla-thorne's departure to Rome, it was produced in the parlour, and somewhat critically examined by him and Mr Charles Hansom, the architect, then a member of the Coventry congregation. Its various parts were brought out separately, the figure of Our Lady, that of the Holy Child, the silver crown and sceptre. The whole had certainly nothing about it to recommend it in an artistic point of view, and the young architect pronounced it "rude," which made Sister Margaret very indignant. He made amends for this offence by designing a handsome mahogany triptych for its reception ; and in time the triptych, with Our Lady in it, was placed on an altar table in the school-room, and after the night-school was over the Rosary was recited before it. The young women attending the night-school sang some hymns and the Litany of Loretto ; and to these devotions, designed exclusively for the profit of her own scholars, Sister Margaret sometimes added a short spiritual lecture from Challoner or some other pious book.

It must be observed, that the Rosary was quite in disuse at this time among the Catholics of Coventry, and even Sister Margaret's immediate companions thought it a childish sort of devotion, in which they joined chiefly to please her. But the Roses of Mary are never planted without attracting, by their fragrance, the hearts of the faithful. Intended, at first, only for the scholars of the night-school, these pious meetings soon drew a larger attendance. Many Protestants even came, out of curiosity, as they said, to hear Sister Margaret preach, though her preaching consisted only in prayer, singing, and spiritual reading. The school-altar, with its handsome triptych and other adorn-ments, was greatly admired, and its fame spread far and near. Some of the pupils at Princethrope were accustomed to send artificial flowers of their own making for Sister Margaret's image, and at length, when the month of May drew near, she resolved to venture on the purchase of some branch-candlesticks. When the candlesticks arrived, she was terrified to find that their cost amounted to £8. She sometimes took occasion of the schoolroom meetings to appeal to the liberality of those present in behalf of some pious or charitable object, and her appeals, made in very plain and simple terms, were always generously responded to. On this occasion, she turned round to the people, when the Rosary was over, and said, "I have gone in debt £8 for the Blessed Virgin, and I am afraid to tell the Doctor; you must help me out of it." Immediately there were cries of "Here is a shilling, Sister Margaret!" and "Here is sixpence!" and by the end of the month the whole sum was paid. She delighted in making the most of her decorations. One afternoon, having assisted her in preparing the schoolroom for the evening Rosary, her friend, Miss G., was astonished to see her, after surveying the altar with simple glee, take hold of her dress in both hands, and execute a little dance before Our Lady. "What! do you *dance*, Sister Margaret?" she exclaimed. Sister Margaret was a little abashed at her unusual manifestation of devotion having been observed, and explained it by saying, that "she only danced before her Mother."

Meanwhile Dr Ullathorne had begun to form plans for the rebuilding of his chapel, the ruinous state of which was beyond the possibility of repair. It was first requisite to collect funds, and for this purpose he undertook several journeys into different parts of England. Collections were likewise set on foot among the Coventry congregation, the people generously contributing from their slender means. Several of the young women offered themselves as weekly collectors, and among these were the two faithful assistants of Sister Margaret already named. The Rosary evenings in the schoolroom were found to be useful opportunities for bringing the collectors together, and they were now made to assume a more important character. Every Monday evening, after the devotions had been recited, Dr Ullathorne came to the schoolroom, and gave those present a familiar lecture on some subject of interest. After this the collectors paid in their weekly collections, and then was the moment of triumph for the one who brought the largest contribution to the common fund. Besides the considerable sums that were thus raised, these weekly conferences diffused an excellent spirit among the congregation. The instructions which they received embraced a very wide range, and were of an unusually solid and elevating kind. The ceremonies and ritual of the Church were explained in a manner suited to their capacity. Courses of lectures were given on whole books of Scripture, and other more popular subjects were likewise treated. The consequence was, that not only did the Catholics become thoroughly instructed in their faith, but that a tide of conversions set in from Protestantism. The number of converts received in one year was at the rate of one a day, and it used to be said that there was not a street without its convert. The number of communicants likewise largely increased, and the devotion of the congregation became remarked by strangers. Mother Margaret always attributed the success of the work at Coventry to the solid method pursued by the clergy in the instruction of the people. In particular, her experience of the good effected by the instruction of the people in the Church ceremonies, made her always solicitous in urging this point on those of her community who were engaged in teaching. She recalled the interest with which the Coventry congregation listened to some familiar explanation on these subjects from the lips of their pastor, and the practical effects which often ensued. One Holy Thursday, after a beautiful instruction had been delivered on devotion to the Blessed Sacrament, and its teaching enforced by an unusually careful adornment of the Sepulchre, the devotion exhibited by the people was altogether extraordinary. They watched before the Sepulchre with unwearied ardour, and one poor man, who kept a rag shop in the town, remained before it the entire night, standing all the time, without changing his position. Sister Margaret watched him with surprise, and afterwards declared that he seemed like one in ecstacy.

On this occasion, as at other times, the duty of preparing the Sepulchre fell to her. It was one in which she displayed great taste, and it inspired her with peculiar happiness. One of her early companions, describing her skill in this office, adds the remark, that "our Mother always cried on these great feasts, because they were so soon over." She had been used to the long devotions of the Belgian "high days," and it was a pain to her to think how short a time the English people spared out of their day to God.

None took a warmer interest in the work that was going on at Coventry than the Dominican Fathers, whose head-quarters were then fixed at St Peter's Priory, Hinckley, the neighbouring missions of Leicester and Nuneaton being likewise under their care.

The old schoolroom and chapel at Coventry, and all

the life and devotion that centred there, are still fresh
in the minds of many ; and the Rev. Father Aylward,
who was at that time missionary at Coton, has recalled
pleasant memories of the days when Sister Margaret
was devoting herself to the improvement of the young
women of Coventry, and when, delighted to take part
in all that was going on, he would sometimes give his
people an early afternoon service, and then "cart them
off" to join in the processions and other devotions of
their Coventry neighbours.

The task of collecting for the new church obliged
Dr Ullathorne to be frequently absent, and towards
the end of April 1843 he proceeded to Liverpool for
the purpose of soliciting contributions. Before leaving
Coventry he gave permission for the celebration in
the schoolroom of the devotions of the month of May.
This exercise was at that time but little known in
England, though it had been already introduced into
several places by Father Gentili and the other Ros-
minian Fathers. A letter from Sister Margaret, dated
the 2d of May, gives an account of the opening of
these exercises, and contains an allusion to the *Convent*
and *Hospital*, which already found existence in her
hopes.

The foundation-stone of the Church was laid on
the 29th of May 1843. Before commencing the building, Dr Ullathorne, accompanied by Mr Hansom, set
out on a tour through Belgium and Germany, with
the double object of soliciting alms, and of studying
some of the *chefs-d'œuvre* of religious art in those
countries. Letters from Sister Margaret to M. Versavel, the Abbé Capron, and her excellent friends Mr
Charles Eyre and his sister, then residents in Bruges,

secured the travellers a warm reception in that city, where every one was glad to receive tidings of "Margarita." M. Capron talked of paying a visit to Coventry, Mr Eyre was delighted to assist a work in which she was interested, and gave introductions to several English families. He promised, on the part of himself and his sister, to make over to Dr Ullathorne some York insurance shares, which nominally yielded the annual sum of £12, and were supposed to be convertible into about £300.

On returning to England, Dr Ullathorne took the requisite measures for securing their sale. For some time past the shares had paid little interest, and it was hardly hoped that they would fetch the sum which had been named. Many prayers were offered by the associates of the Rosary for the good success of the transaction, and, to the surprise of every one, before the day of sale the shares rose in value, and were actually sold for £700. This sum was contributed to the building, the remaining funds being obtained from the subscriptions of the congregation, from collections in different parts of England, and from the resources of the Benedictine province.

In the February of 1844, Sister Margaret herself paid a short visit to Bruges, in the course of which she obtained means for the purchase of a ciborium, worth about £12 of English money. She collected it from house to house, suffering much in the weary walks. The ciborium was bought in Bruges, and was afterwards recast at Birmingham. It was exhibited at one of the schoolroom conferences, and elicited one of those familiar instructions which created so lively an interest among their hearers.

In order not to interrupt our narrative of the commencement of the religious foundation, which will
occupy the following chapter, we will anticipate the
course of events, and bring together in a few words
all that concerns the completion of the church and
presbytery. The nave of the church was opened for
divine service on the 10th of August 1844, on which
occasion the building was blessed by Bishop Wiseman,
Coadjutor of the Midland District, who likewise
preached. The chancel was not finished until the
year following, and memorable was the day when the
temporary partition that filled the chancel arch was
taken down, and the people beheld, as if by magic,
the beautiful chancel open to their view. The consecration took place on the 9th of September 1845,
Bishop Wiseman and eight other Bishops assisting at
the ceremony.

The work thus happily completed, like most other
good works, found some to cavil at it, and murmurers
were found who expressed their wonder why Dr Ullathorne should have thought of building so fine a
church for a congregation in which "there was not a
respectable person." This observation was overheard
by Sister Margaret, and replied to in characteristic
language. "Coventry Church," she said, "has been
built, not for man, but God, and *He is always respectable.*"

As Dr Ullathorne's plans included the rebuilding of
the priest's house, he resolved, with the approbation
of the Benedictine Superiors, that the new presbytery
should be arranged in such a manner as to be available for the purposes of a small missionary priory.
The proposal was warmly seconded by the authorities

of the Order, and a substantial building was erected, communicating through the sacristy with the church, and containing accommodation for five or six religious. Whilst this was in progress, Dr Ullathorne took up his residence in a house in Spon Street, and here was laid the first germ of Mother Margaret's Community.

CHAPTER IV.

COMMENCEMENT OF A RELIGIOUS COMMUNITY.

It will have been seen, that the idea of some kind of religious foundation had already suggested itself to the mind both of Mother Margaret and her director. The excellent effects of her labours among the poor, and the rapid increase of the work itself, very early gave birth in Dr Ullathorne's mind to the idea of founding a small religious community devoted to works of active charity. The materials requisite for forming such a community seemed to be gathering under his eyes in the persons of Mother Margaret and those faithful companions into whom she was gradually infusing much of her own spirit.

The idea of a commencement of some sort at Coventry had evidently been under consideration before the April of 1843, and in the summer of that year it appears to have taken a definite shape and purpose. A young person, a stranger to Coventry, who was desirous of entering religion, having sought Dr Ullathorne's advice, and heard what was in contemplation, decided at once on placing herself and her means at his disposal. The plan was being slowly matured by prayer and reflection until the moment should arrive for putting it into execution; and as it was felt that the young foundation would need the support and guidance of one already trained in religious life, it was decided to begin on a very humble scale, and to receive the first postulants under Dr Ullathorne's own roof, with the view of transferring them at a future time to a house of their own in another part of the town.

It cannot be denied, that such a plan was somewhat unusual; but it seems to have been one of those cases in which ordinary laws have been providentially overruled; nor was the project carried into execution without the full concurrence, both of the Benedictine and Dominican authorities.

Mother Margaret's strong wish of placing her community under the rule of the Third Order of St Dominic, however, presented some difficulties. The Dominican Tertiaries were at that time unknown in England, and even the English Fathers were not then familiar with their rule. The only convent of Dominicanesses existing in this country was that at Atherstone, the members of which followed the Constitutions of the Second Order, and were strictly enclosed.

But after careful inquiry, and reference to the authorities of the Order both in England and Belgium, it appeared evident that there was nothing new or unprecedented in the attempt to form a Community of Dominican Tertiaries, who, while embracing all the obligations of religious life, enclosure excepted, should devote themselves to the active works of charity.

The Dominican Superiors in England expressed

their willingness to leave the direction of the Institute in the hands of him who had originated it, and the necessary powers for that purpose were conveyed to Dr Ullathorne by the Provincial of the Order. The consent of the Benedictine Superiors was likewise obtained, together with that of Bishop Walsh, the Vicar-Apostolic of the Midland District; and on the 28th of March 1844, the postulant before alluded to having arrived in Coventry, the four took up their residence in the house in Spon Street. One alone of their number possessed any independent means, and that was wholly insufficient for the support of the community. Their only other resources were a small annual pension paid by the father of one of the postulants, the assistance of friends, and the aid afforded by their generous protector, Dr Ullathorne, who placed his house and his purse at their disposal, and devoted himself with unsparing energy to their spiritual formation.

A small room in the house had been cleared and fitted up as a chapel, destined to be the first choir of the new Institute. Small and poor as it was, it had a devout appearance, with its plain wooden altar and tabernacle, the tabernacle-door painted blue and gold, with a figure of the Lamb bearing the Cross—white wooden candlesticks from Belgium, and above, a copy of Vandyke's Crucifixion, which now hangs in the refectory of St Dominic's Convent, Stone. The office of Our Lady was daily recited by the Sisters, at first in English, until they had acquired greater fluency in the pronunciation of Latin. The Blessed Sacrament was reserved in the chapel, and Mass was said there every morning; whilst on certain occasions permission was given for Benediction of the Blessed Sacrament. The correspondence of the next two months affords indications that the Community was gradually assuming more and more of a religious character. The form and fashion of the habit was brought under consideration, and as it was not thought possible at once to assume the white habit of the Dominican Order, a black habit was adopted for a time, under which was worn the white scapular of the Order. And until circumstances allowed of the compilation of a body of constitutions, certain rules and regulations, comprising the most essential laws of religious life, were drawn up for the temporary guidance of the Sisters. Nothing seemed now required save to obtain the formal permission of the Bishop for the clothing of the postulants, and this having been obtained, on the 11th of June 1844, being the Feast of St Barnabas, they received the holy habit in their little chapel from the hands of Dr Ullathorne. The Rev. Father Augustine Procter came over from Hinckley, to be present on the occasion, as representative of the Provincial, nor was anything omitted which could contribute to the solemnity of the impressive function.

The life on which the newly-clothed religious now entered was one of no little labour and hardship. Founded in poverty, that true patent of religious nobility, they had to endure its reality, and not its name. Their food was of the plainest description, and not rendered more palatable by the skill of the Sister who presided in the kitchen. She was but a learner in the culinary art, and somewhat given to experiments. The experiments were not always very successful. Her first pudding was pronounced as hard, that it might have been tossed over St Michael's Tower without being broken ; and having heard that boiled nettles were a very fair substitute for spinach, she once presented the Community with this unusual delicacy, which might have been better relished had not the nettles been old and tough. Fish never appeared on their frugal table; so that on the abstinence-days prescribed by the rule, potatoes formed their principal article of food. Nor were their beds more luxurious than their fare. One of them slept on an old door, and is said to have found the handle somewhat penitential. In the world all had been accustomed to a certain measure of comfort, yet the fervour with which they now embraced their hard rule of life, rendered even its austerities delightful to them. "How sweet everything tastes here !" said one ; "yet what should I have thought of it in my father's house !"

These generous dispositions were fostered by the direction under which they were trained. Two rules were given them in the beginning by their spiritual Father, who desired to form them in a truly heroic spirit :—they were to banish from their vocabulary the words "uncomfortable " and "impossible ;" and his precepts on this head were enforced by his example. Another of his maxims, which Mother Margaret often loved to recall, was, "First put in the Spirit of Christ, and then the spirit of the rule on that." They were thoroughly exercised, moreover, in humility and mortification, and taught the value of labour as an instrument of sanctification. Up to the latest hour of her life, Mother Margaret continued to regard menial labour in a Community as one of its most

E

valuable spiritual elements, and she never departed from the resolution which she formed from the first, of establishing but one grade in her Community, and of subjecting all, without exception, to the holy law of labour.

It was this life, then, of active labour, spiritualised by prayer and a holy intention, on which the newly-clothed Sisters now entered. Their rule of life, however, was so arranged as to enable them, whilst carrying on the work of the school and the visiting the poor, to devote a considerable portion of each day to the exercises of the novitiate, and self-improvement. Mass was generally said in the chapel at Spon Street, which served also as their religious choir, after which, two went to the school, one remained at home and attended to the domestic duties, and the fourth visited the sick, taking as a companion one or other of the young women who still regarded themselves as in some sort Mother Margaret's companions. Among these was Maria Roby, sister to one of the novices, whose ardent attachment to Mother Margaret had led her to determine, in case of her removal from Coventry, on following her wherever she might go, earning her living by the work of her hands. Although the delicacy of her health had led to the preference being given to her elder sister in selecting the first three postulants, she herself earnestly desired to join the Community, and she afterwards received the habit of religion on her death-bed under circumstances which will be hereafter related.

Various circumstances concurred to delay the profession of the Sisters for six months after the year of probation had expired. During this year and a half the little Community struggled on through many difficulties, supported by their trust in the good providence of God, which never failed them. It was remarked that, from the day of the clothing, the weekly offertory doubled in amount. Assistance was often received when most required, and from unexpected sources; but among their most constant benefactresses at this time were the Dominicanesses of Atherstone, and Mother Margaret's early friend, Mrs Amherst of Kenilworth. The following little incident is related by an eye-witness, who has been already named as making her first acquaintance with Mother Margaret in the cloisters of Princethorpe. "I remember, on one occasion," she writes, "driving from Kenilworth to Coventry with Mrs Amherst to see Mother Margaret. Mrs Amherst took with her a basket of provisions, knowing that at that time the Sisters were often in want of necessaries. The Sister who opened the door carried the basket in with her, and we followed. When we reached the sitting-room she put down the basket, saying, 'Here it is!' 'Here is what?' asked Mrs Amherst; and then they told us, that having nothing left in the house, they had just been praying for help, and their prayers were scarcely ended when the bell rang and the basket made its appearance."

Besides the trials of poverty, they were exposed to others from which no enterprise undertaken for God's glory is ever exempt. Critics abounded who treated with contempt an Institute so humble in its exterior; and "Sister Margaret and the *wenches* of Coventry," was the title by which the Community was commonly named. The whole thing was treated as an experiment, which some regarded as absurd, and others as audacious, but which both classes of objectors agreed in predicting could only end in failure. Even grosser calumnies were not spared; and one lady, who felt attracted to the Community, was deterred from joining it by hearing that there was not a single respectable person among the Sisters, and that Sister Margaret herself was nothing but an impostor. Opposition of this kind is perhaps the surest sign of God's blessing, and is precisely that which every religious founder has in turn been required to endure. For the rest, the anecdotes that convey to us the contemptuous expressions of some critics often enough preserve the memory of kinder judgments more worthy of being recalled. On occasion of the opening of Coventry Church, in 1845, a priest, who had not visited the town for some years, came to attend the ceremony. He afterwards called on the father of one of the religious with whom he was acquainted in company with two other persons. He spoke with delight of the progress of religion which he found in the place, of the beauty of the church, and the good that had already been effected by the little Community. One of those present began to speak of the Sisters in a depreciating tone, observing that "they were only a few poor girls." "Then," said the good priest, rising and taking off his cap, "the more honour and glory be to Almighty God, who chooses the weak things of this world to confound the strong!" Eighteen years later, at the opening of St Dominic's Church at Stone, on the 5th of February 1863, it was remarked that the Epistle at the Mass (for the Feast of St Agatha) contained those very words, so applicable to the humble beginnings of the Community.

It was during this time that Mother Margaret made her first acquaintance with Father Gentili, for whose missionary zeal and single-hearted devotion she always retained the warmest admiration. He first visited Coventry in 1844, for the purpose of preaching a sermon, and in the May of the year following he gave a public retreat to the congregation, which various causes combined to render a memorable one. The retreat had been fixed to take place at that particular time for a special reason. As most readers are aware, the city of Coventry is, every third year, made the scene of a procession known as the Godiva procession, which takes place within the Octave of the Feast of Corpus Christi. This exhibition tended so gravely to offend the public sense of decency, that in the year 1845, both Catholic and Protestant authorities attempted to take measures for counteracting the evil. The Protestant Bishop of Worcester addressed a letter on the subject to the city magistrates, and the Catholic priest invited Fathers Gentili and Furlong to begin a mission on the Feast of Corpus Christi, which fell that year on the 21st of May, and to continue it through the Octave. The result has been described in a letter from the Right Rev. Bishop Ullathorne, which appears in the "Life of Father Gentili." During the first three days the efforts of the missioner proved fruitless; very few persons attended the sermons, most being engaged in preparing their houses for the great gala-day; but on Sunday, when the entire congregation was assembled, Father Gentili, on fire with zeal, and grieving at the attachment which they betrayed to their old customs, burst out in such a torrent of remonstrance and reproof, that tears and sobs were heard from every part of the church. He continued to preach three times a day during the remainder of the mission, and on the day of the procession, few, if any, of the Catholics attended it. He was particularly anxious to prevent the children of the congregation from witnessing so demoralising an exhibition. "He promised them," says Bishop Ullathorne, "that if they would remain with him he would give them more amusement than they would find in the streets." He kept his promise as well as they kept theirs; for he interwove his instruction with such a chain of stories and dramatic pictures, told and represented in action, and in a style so winning, so amusing, so ludicrous, and so awful, by turns, as the subject shifted or its feelings changed, that older persons stood astonished, and the children were out of themselves —sometimes subdued into awestruck silence, whilst at other times they broke out into a rapture of mirth. It was one of those hours that are never forgotten throughout a long life.

During the remainder of the mission the church was crowded, both by the Catholics of the congregation and by strangers. Father Gentili reverted to the subject of the late procession, and reminded his hearers how, at his suggestion, they had prayed for the rain to put an end to the unseemly festivities, and how their prayers had been answered, as had indeed been the case. He then delivered one of his famous discourses on devotion to the Blessed Virgin, and concluded with these words: "You have had the procession of your lady, and now we will have a pro-

cession of Our Lady. The one shall expiate the other."
Such a thing as a procession of Our Lady had not been
witnessed in Coventry, or probably in England, since
the overthrow of religion. But Father Gentili was
not the man to be withheld by any feeling of timidity
or human respect, and he found a most hearty co-
operator in the person of Mother Margaret. With her
assistance a bier was prepared, and on it was fastened
her own image of the Blessed Virgin, adorned with
lights and flowers. When all was ready, and Father
Gentili beheld the spectacle which recalled, in so lively
a manner, the practices of a Catholic country, the image
of the Virgin Mother, decked with its gala wreaths,
and surrounded by young girls dressed in white, he
was like one in an ecstasy, and poured forth one of
his inspired strains of eloquence on Our Lady, as
" Cause of our joy." On that and the two successive
evenings, a solemn and beautiful procession was made
round the church ; and the crowds who came to see
the sight, filled not only the church and churchyard,
but even the adjoining streets.

This event was one which Mother Margaret always
recalled with peculiar delight. She loved to think
that the image which she regarded with such devout
veneration should have been the first to have been
publicly carried in England since the reformation ;
and among all the circumstances of her life, there
were few on which she looked back with feelings
of more unmixed happiness than this public act of
reparation offered to the Mother of God.

By the close of the year 1845, all obstacles to the
profession of the Sisters were removed, and December
8th, the Feast of the Immaculate Conception, was

fixed on for the ceremony. The formal consent of the Right Rev. Bishop Walsh was given in a letter, dated Nottingham, November 28, 1845; whilst to obtain that of the Dominican Provincial, Dr Ullathorne proceeded in person to Leicester, where he was then residing. The circumstances were recalled by Mother Margaret, twenty-two years later, as she lay on the sick-bed from which she never rose. "It was just such a day as this," she said, "bitterly cold, with frost and snow on the ground. The Doctor had to go to Father Nickolds, at Leicester, to get his consent for the professions. He went on the outside of the stage-coach, for there was no railway then, and came back frozen through. The three Sisters were put into retreat immediately on his return. As for me, that day, I walked on air. I was so delighted to find that all was settled, after the many difficulties we had had; and on the Immaculate Conception, too, the very day I had set my heart upon. I have just been reminding Sister Rose of it; how I had to decorate the church, and go to the Sisters, and then run away and cook the dinner, all by myself, for they were in retreat. At five in the morning, I had to renew the vow of chastity I had taken before, and to take the vows of poverty and obedience in the hands of Father Aylward, and then to get the church ready for the ceremony." The Rev. Father Aylward on this occasion acted as the representative of the Rev. Father Provincial; Father Augustine Procter, then Superior of St Peter's Priory, Hinckley, was also present, and the form of protestation read aloud by Mother Margaret is still preserved, written by his hand.

To Mother Margaret it was a day full of consolation, one on which the foundation-stones were securely laid of the spiritual edifice which God had designed to raise. Whenever she recalled the thought of that day, or spoke of it to others, she failed not to dwell with a kind of rapture on every circumstance which could most strongly prove that God, and not man, was the founder. "This is the way I see it," she said, not long before her death; "that Almighty God would do the work Himself, and so He chose out the lowest instrument He could find, that no one else should have any part in it. You see He chose a sinful woman, a sickly woman, a woman without family, without friends, without education, and without reputation. If He could have chosen anything viler He would, but He could not,—so the work is His from beginning to end." And in after years, when doubts were occasionally expressed as to the stability of the Congregation, which some persons regarded as likely to die with her, she was accustomed to reply in the same strain: "If the work were *mine*," she would say, "no doubt it would die with me : but as it is God's work it will stand.

CHAPTER V.

REMOVAL TO BRISTOL.

THERE was a saying current among Mother Margaret's religious children in after years, that each new foundation was purchased at the cost of a life. The profession of the first four Sisters, which must be considered, in one sense, as the greatest of all her foundations, was not left exempt from this tribute, and the

life which was in this case demanded was one which
Mother Margaret held especially dear. Maria Roby,
her devoted companion in so many labours, has already
more than once been mentioned. Although her sister
had been the first to receive the religious habit, Maria
ardently aspired after the same happiness ; and while
circumstances obliged her to postpone her wishes, she
continued to render the Community all the services
in her power, and to assist them in visiting the sick.
She also lent her aid in many domestic occupations ;
and during the month of December 1845, she was frequently at the Priory, whither the Sisters had now removed from Spon Street, helping in the completion of
a black velvet funeral pall, on which the religious were
at work. The pall was finished by the 30th, and
being stretched out on the ground, Maria by a sudden
impulse lay down, and desired the Sisters to spread
the pall over her, saying, as they did so, " I wonder
for which of us this pall will first be used." The next
day she was seized with an apoplectic fit, and in a few
hours expired. The immediate cause of this seizure
is supposed to have been the distress occasioned by
something that had been said which seemed to check
her hopes of joining the Community. Her desire of
embracing the religious life was so well known, and
her association with the Sisters had been of so close
and affectionate a nature, that, although she remained
insensible, it was determined to give her the habit.
This was accordingly done, and as one of the Sisters
observed, " She would rejoice when she opened her
eyes in the other world to find herself a novice of St
Dominic."

A prayer written in pencil was found a few days

afterwards in her desk, wherein she recommends her vocation to the intercession of the Blessed Virgin, and entreats her, "if such be the will of Almighty God, to obtain that she may soon leave this world to seek our Lord where He is to be found, among the sick poor, to attend upon them and comfort them in their afflictions." When laid out in the habit before burial, crowds came to see her, and to attend her funeral. She was laid to rest in a vault in front of the Ladye Chapel, and such was the respect and emotion displayed by those who witnessed the ceremony, that some persons present observed, no peeress could have had a greater funeral.

At this time the Community included, besides the four professed religious, another of Mother Margaret's friends, who, even before her conversion to the Catholic Church, had been accustomed to visit the sick with some of the Sisters, and had been greatly struck by the example of self-sacrificing charity thus brought before her. She resided with them at first as a visitor, and then as a postulant, and received the religious habit in April 1846. They may also be said at this time to have laid the foundation of their first orphanage. A poor Irish woman, whose husband was absent in Ireland, died of fever, leaving four children altogether destitute. Unwilling to send these poor orphans to the workhouse, Dr Ullathorne made an appeal on their behalf to the congregation, who agreed to provide for one boy, while the other boy and two girls were taken charge of by the Sisters. On this occasion the good-hearted people of Coventry showed an admirable spirit of charity. They contributed provisions for the support of the orphans, and more than

one poor man came to the priest offering to adopt one
of them for the love of God—one of those who made
this generous proposal being himself the father of
seven children.

Mother Margaret, however, was not disposed to
yield her treasure into any one's keeping. When the
three children were delivered over to her charge, "you
would have thought," writes one of the religious, "that
she had had the whole world given her." It was the
first opportunity which had yet been afforded her of
exercising that tender charity towards orphans which
in her might almost be called a devotion. Those who
witnessed the reception of the Coventry orphans relate
the delight with which she set to work to improve
their appearance, and how the slender resources of the
Community were made to furnish them all with a good
suit of mourning. The children remained with the
Sisters for some time, the priory-loft being turned into
a dormitory, until, to Mother Margaret's great grief,
their father sent for them to Ireland, and she had to
give them up.

Meanwhile, as the Community promised to increase,
it became necessary to consider what steps should be
taken for establishing them in a residence of their
own. It was proposed to purchase some house in a
suitable part of the town, and adapt it to the use of
the Community. This plan, however, was never one
which Mother Margaret favoured. "I cannot *buy* a
house," she would say; "I want to build one. I
should like to have a proper convent with square
cloisters."

The plan to be adopted was still under discussion
when events took place which changed the future

prospects of the little Community, and seemed for the moment to threaten their dissolution. The Vicariate-Apostolic of the Western District had become vacant in the October of 1845, by the death of Bishop Baggs, after he had scarcely filled it for two years. Dr Ulla-thorne was nominated as his successor, and his conse-cration took place at Coventry, on Sunday the 21st of June 1846, the same day on which Pius IX. was crowned Sovereign Pontiff.

The Benedictine authorities, on whom the care of the mission now devolved, proposed (as we learn from a letter of Mother Margaret's) that the Sisters should continue at Coventry, and even offered to rent a house for them in the town if they would remain. The Do-minican Provincial was equally desirous that they should settle at Leicester. Mother Margaret felt, how-ever, that the foundation was still too young and un-formed to be left entirely deprived of that paternal care which had hitherto, under God, been its main support. It was therefore determined to remove the Community into the Western District, where it might still enjoy the guidance and protection of him who might truly be regarded as its founder. The nuns of Atherstone, who had always shown a most sisterly in-terest in all that concerned the Coventry foundation, offered to receive the religious within their own con-vent until accommodation should be provided for them in Bristol.

Their hospitable invitation was in part accepted, and on the 10th of July, two professed religious, one novice, and one postulant, left Coventry for Atherstone, where they remained for six weeks, joining in all the Community exercises. It was a sad and desolate time;

Bishop Ullathorne had removed to Prior Park almost immediately after his consecration, and, left to herself, with her little band dispersed and homeless, Mother Margaret began to realise the difficulties and responsibilities of her new position. She was leaving the scene of fruitful and happy labours for a dark and uncertain future, and the first letter she wrote after the Bishop's departure was headed by the words, " God alone, God alone, God alone ! " She never afterwards laid aside the use of these words, which have been adopted as the motto of the Congregation. " It was the circumstances which made the motto," she used to say ; "for with me, at that time, it was truly God alone ! "

Kind and liberal friends, however, were not wanting to the Community at this critical juncture. Among the Benedictine Fathers, who had been present at the ceremony of Bishop Ullathorne's consecration, was the Rev. Father James Dullard, chaplain to the Benedictine Nuns of the Perpetual Adoration, then established at St Benedict's Priory, Rugeley, but who had formerly resided at Cannington in Somersetshire. The Rev. Mother Mary Clare Knight, the venerable Prioress of this Community, retained her interest in the Western District, and her brother, Mr John Knight, besides possessing a considerable sum left at his disposal on behalf of the missionary fund of the district by his late brother, Charles, was understood to be desirous of contributing to the same purposes from his own means. Father Dullard, who was aware of these circumstances, and who from the first moment of his introduction to Mother Margaret had conceived a strong admiration for her character and sympathy with her designs, advised her to make known the position in which she was placed to the Prioress of St Benedict's, Rugeley, who, as he assured her, had it in her power to assist her establishment in the Western District. In consequence of this advice, Mother Margaret drew up a formal statement of the position of the Community, its objects and present prospects, in the form of a letter addressed to the Prioress. A warm-hearted and generous response reached her by return of post, and at the suggestion of Mother Mary Clare, her brother, Mr John Knight, determined on presenting Mother Margaret with the liberal donation of £500, for the purpose of assisting her in establishing herself in the Western District. This donation was not, however, received until the January of the ensuing year.

By the end of November 1846, the little Community, now six in number, had succeeded in hiring a house in Queen's Square, Bristol, of which they took possession on the Feast of the Immaculate Conception. The anecdotes of this period sufficiently attest that their poverty was something more than nominal. But poverty is generally felt as a light trial by a young Community ; and the temporary make-shifts of a new foundation, such as using a crate for a chair, and sleeping in a china-closet, were inconveniences easily endured in the midst of the joy of reunion ; while the fact of being for the first time under their own roof, gave them a sense of freedom and independence which lightened every hardship. Nay, their very poverty made each new benefaction which they received an exquisite joy. No treasures purchased by their own wealth could ever have afforded them the same delight as they derived from an unexpected and most munificent present, which they received at this time from the Franciscan Community at Taunton. It consisted of a box, containing, besides clothes for the poor, church-linen and vestments, candlesticks and lamps, with a handsome ciborium and chalice, in short, everything necessary for the service of their chapel. When this box was opened by Mother Margaret and Sister Mary Gertrude Roby, they both sat down and cried for joy and gratitude, "never expecting," as they said, "to have such beautiful things for their own."

The house in which they found themselves established was gloomy enough, and its cheerfulness was not increased by the reputation which it enjoyed of being haunted. Its former occupant had been a surgeon, and rumour affirmed that the remains of subjects whom he had dissected were buried in the cellars, and that the house was haunted by their ghosts. More serious anxieties than those suggested by the ghost stories began, however, to overshadow the future. Bishop Ullathorne had to proceed to Rome on the affairs of his diocese, and for the first time Mother Margaret found herself left with the entire care of the Community in her own hands. Her distress was augmented by the failing health of Sister Mary Gertrude Roby, whose religious spirit and prudent character had marked her out, in the judgment of her superiors, as qualified for the post of novice-mistress. Her threatened loss was doubly felt at this time, when the Community was rapidly increasing in numbers. Within three weeks of their taking possession of their house, four new postulants were received, one of whom belonged to the number of Mother Margaret's first followers at Coventry, whilst a second, in addition to other qualifications which rendered her most welcome to the Religious, brought a considerable accession of temporal means, so that after her profession (which took place on the 24th of January 1848) the Sisters became possessed of a certain fixed income, and were relieved from some of the pressing anxieties which up to that time embarrassed them.

Three of the postulants were clothed on the 17th of January 1847, just before the departure of his Lordship for Rome. "That day," writes one of the Religious, "was the last on which Sister Mary Gertrude Roby took her meals in the refectory." The foundation of Bristol, like that of Coventry, was not to be made without the sacrifice of a life. Her disease, which was consumption, had been augmented by anxiety and fatigue, and by the long separation from her beloved Superioress, which came on her at the very moment when her health was beginning to fail. She devoutly breathed her last on the 25th of February, and was buried in the private cemetery of the Visitation Convent at Westbury.

The work undertaken by the Religious, as soon as they had established themselves in their new home, was not a little laborious, considering the small number yet professed. A room in their own house was given up for the purpose of a poor school, and some time in the following year the poor schools attached to the Church of St Mary's on the Quay were likewise placed under their charge. The first step towards carrying out Mother Margaret's long-cherished plan of the Catholic hospital was taken so early as the January of 1847, when three infirm patients were received under

F

her roof, two of whom lived to be removed to St Mary's Hospital, Stone, where one survived until the year 1866.

Admittance was likewise obtained to the Bristol Infirmary, which was regularly visited two or three times a week, the Sisters being also constantly engaged in visiting the poor at their own houses. In all these duties Mother Margaret at that time took a leading part. "She was most active in the schools," writes one, at that time a novice in the Community, "encouraging the Sisters and keeping order, and her active mind was a great support. She also frequently visited the poor in their own houses, and often amused us by relating some of her adventures in the noted locality called Pipe Lane."

Besides these external works of charity, the more laborious task of training the Religious in regular community-life had to be carried on in the face of many difficulties. Often did Mother Margaret afterwards acknowledge how tenderly the providence of God had been manifested in the way in which her Community was gradually built up and developed. Those who formed its foundation-stones were precisely those best qualified for the severe and laborious life to which they were called. Their devotion to her person, and their intimate knowledge of the heroic life she had led among them at Coventry, inspired them with an ardour which enabled them to overcome all the obstacles of poverty, and the discouragements of a period when the outline of religious life indeed existed, but when all its details had to be gradually filled up.

Mother Margaret was, nevertheless, keenly alive to the disadvantages under which her novices laboured, owing to the want of more regular instruction. The need was felt of a more perfect knowledge of the Rule and Constitutions. None among her present companions were qualified for the task of bringing to light each part of the Rule, or of training the novices in the recitation of the Office, the practice of the ceremonies of the Order, and other points of regular discipline. Neither was such an office the one for which Mother Margaret's own genius was best adapted. Her soul, creative in its conceptions, generally needed the hand of another to carry her designs into execution. She was herself so conscious of her own insufficiency for the task, that she constantly prayed for some one who would be able to bring all things into shape, or, as she expressed it, "who would settle the Latin and the music;" and she used to say to her Sisters that "the right person had not come yet, but she would come in time." Meanwhile, she managed as well as circumstances would allow; and a great amount of mental labour and anxiety devolved on herself. The Office was the first thing that required attention. At Coventry it had been recited in English, but this was only intended to continue until the Religious should be competent to undertake the recitation of the Latin Office, and they now began reciting it in the language of their Church. A paper is preserved, written at this time, in Mother Margaret's handwriting, containing directions for the ceremonies, as prescribed by the Dominican Constitutions, for the use of the novices. On some points she was uncertain, but where such was the case, nature gained little from the doubt, the question being generally decided in favour of what was most austere. Thus for the first three years the Religious stood during the entire Office, not being aware of the rule which prescribes that each side of the choir should sit alternately during the chanting of the psalms. It is truly surprising, considering the circumstances of the Community, and the absence at that time of any English books on the rule, that so large a portion of it should have been thus early brought out and reduced to practice. The essentials of religious life were all observed. The chapter of faults was held regularly, and so strict was the discipline enforced among the Religious, that, to use the expression of one of them, " penance was their daily bread." " We were never spared, in or out of chapter," writes another, " but constantly exhorted to fervour, being often told by our Mother that she would rather work with one fervent Religious than with a hundred who had not the right spirit."

Bishop Ullathorne's absence from his diocese was not prolonged beyond Palm Sunday ; but his short stay in Rome was productive of several important results. Previous to leaving England, he had been furnished with letters from the English Provincial to the Master-General of the Dominican Order, praying that Bishop Ullathorne might be appointed Superior, in perpetuity, of all the English Religious Sisters of the Third Order.

" Everything requisite has been done for the establishment of the Sisters of Penance," he writes ; " and, at my request, the General has written a letter to you ; and though I did not even mention the subject, he supposes in the letter that any other Communities established in the District will be under your general direction. The Holy See has given me a Rescript, with power to establish *all* approved Orders, and as many convents as may be required, in answer to my especial application for *your* convent, so that I return home provided in all those matters." In his farewell audience with the Holy Father, a special blessing was also asked and obtained for the Dominican Community.

The Bishop's return was followed by the profession of the eldest novice, who had accompanied the Community from Coventry, the ceremony taking place in the Church of St Mary's on the Quay. The selection of the public church for the celebration of the ceremony was necessitated by the narrow limits of the Community Chapel, which consisted of a very small room, communicating through glass doors with another room, into which seculars were admitted three evenings in the week, when the Rosary was recited in common. About twenty or thirty persons generally assisted at this devotion. The propagation of the Rosary was, of course, the chief instrument used to increase among the people a solid devotion to Our Blessed Lady, and a knowledge of the mysteries of the faith. But it was not the only means by which Mother Margaret manifested her zeal on this point. When she first came to Bristol no image of Our Lady was to be seen in any of the Catholic churches or chapels, nor had the exercises of the month of Mary as yet been introduced. They were first performed in the Church of St Mary's on the Quay, in the May of 1847, by the Rev. P. O'Farrell, O.S.F., at Mother Margaret's petition. She lent him the French " *Mois de Marie,*" from which the meditations were taken, and sent over to Ireland for an image of Our Lady to be publicly exposed during the month, for which she paid

£3. She also induced an artist in Bristol to make a mould from Deger's well-known statue, and paid him £16 for doing so, no inconsiderable sum, considering the then straitened circumstances of the Community.

From this mould a vast number of small statues were cast, such as have since become very common, though at the time they were quite a novelty, and so many of these were sold that the artist realised a handsome profit. Another devotion which Mother Margaret was active in propagating was that to St Philomena, by means of whose oil many remarkable cures were at this time effected. One of these cures was that of a young person who had been two years confined to her bed, but who, after using the oil, recovered so entirely as to be able to join a religious Community. A little girl, under the care of the Sisters, who suffered so intensely from inflamed eyes as to be quite blinded, likewise recovered after the first application of the oil, and never again suffered from a similar cause. She had been received into the convent in consequence of a promise which Mother Margaret made to Our Lady, to take seven orphan children in honour of the Seven Dolours. In time the number of orphans received far overpassed the promised seven, for it was difficult for Mother Margaret to shut her heart to the claims of destitute children. Her sympathies were excited on the first Whit-Monday after her establishment in Bristol by the sight of the Protestant schools, who, as usual, assembled and walked in procession with the clubs, passing through Queen's Square on their way. She observed how much they seemed to be enjoying themselves, while the poor Catholic children, for whom no such holiday was provided, were running after their more fortunate neighbours to see what they could not share. "Next year," she exclaimed, in the fulness of her heart, "I will take care that the Catholic schools are equally cared for!" And, as we shall see, she failed not to keep her word.

In the August of 1847 she was attacked by malignant typhus fever, which she caught visiting a poor family who were laid prostrate by the disease. The moment she entered the room in which they were, and inhaled the pestilential atmosphere, she felt she had taken the infection. Nevertheless she remained until she had discharged her duties to the sick, and then returned home, where the fever she had taken soon manifested itself in so alarming a form, that her life was despaired of. "In the height of the fever," writes Bishop Ullathorne, "she told me, 'I shall not die, I have not yet done my work.'" It never occurred to her to suppose for a single moment that the continuance of the Community depended on her single life; but she desired at least to leave behind her such an outline of her general design as might serve as a guide to those into whose hands its direction would fall. In the midst of her sufferings, therefore, she exerted herself to draw up such a sketch, the original sheets of which, stained with her blood, were unfortunately destroyed, but the copy, made at her desire, continued for some years to be used for the instruction of the novices.

CHAPTER VI.

CLIFTON.

MORE than a year had now passed since the settlement of the Community in Bristol, and they were still
unprovided with a permanent home.   The house in
Queen's Square had never been intended as more than
a temporary residence, but it was not until October
1847 that any decision was taken as to their ultimate
plans.   This decision was in part brought about by
circumstances connected with the Catholic Mission at
Clifton.   The ground at present occupied by the
buildings of St Catherine's Convent was at that time
the burial-ground attached to the chapel and priest's
house, whilst the site of the present cathedral presented a most desolate spectacle.   The whole property
had been purchased some years previously, at an enormous cost, by Father Edgeworth, a Franciscan, who
began the erection of a large church in the Italian
style, which was raised to a certain height when unfortunate pecuniary embarrassments obliged him to
suspend further operations, and the property came
into the hands of the Newport Bank, to which he was
a debtor.   Bishop Ullathorne was at that time most
anxious to provide a church which might serve the
purposes of a cathedral, and he agreed to purchase the
whole property for the sum of £3000.

The portion of ground occupied by the chapel and
cemetery appeared to offer a desirable site for the proposed convent, and was accordingly purchased by the
Community for the sum of £1000.

Mr Knight's donation of £500 had been made for

the express purpose of being expended on the purchase or erection of a convent, and it furnished one half of the purchase-money of the property. The thousand pounds which formed the only remaining capital of the Community furnished the other half, leaving £500 towards the erection of the necessary buildings. Early in Lent 1848, the Community removed to Clifton, but the accommodation in their new home proved exceedingly limited. The chapel-house contained two sitting-rooms and seven bed-rooms, or rather cells, four of which were over a portion of the chapel, and were ranged on either side of a narrow passage, at the end of which was a window looking into the chapel below. Besides the Community, which now consisted of six professed Sisters, together with several novices and postulants, there were the three hospital patients, and one little boarder; another inmate being added to the household soon after their instalment, in the person of a poor woman dying of cancer. A room over the sacristy, and the organ-loft, were arranged to accommodate some of these objects of charity, and a house was hired in Berkeley Place, where a certain number of the Religious were received, one of the rooms serving as the middle school. The pro-cathedral, meanwhile, rapidly progressed, but until it was completed the convent chapel continued to be used for the purposes of the mission, and the passage looking into the chapel served the Religious as their choir. A side-altar was erected in the chapel, on which was placed the image of Our Lady, a circumstance not altogether acceptable to some of the congregation. In May, Bishop Ullathorne, at the request of the other Bishops, proceeded to Rome with the view of obtaining the Hierarchy, the Very Rev. Dr Hendren, O.S.F., holding the office of Vicar-General during his absence. When Whit-Tuesday came, Mother Margaret did not forget her resolution to provide a holiday for the Catholic schools. The unfinished buildings at the pro-cathedral were given up for the day to the use of the children, and arrangements were made for receiving two hundred, who walked processionally up Park Street with banners flying, one of these being a banner of Our Blessed Lady. This was considered by some a most audacious proceeding, and gave rise to many murmurs. "Mother Margaret and *her doll*" were spoken of in severe terms; and even good Dr Hendren could not resist telling her that she was "a very daring woman." "I thought he meant it as a compliment," she said, in repeating the story, "for at that time I knew so little of the real feeling of English people, that I thought every one must be as pleased to see Our Lady as I was myself." From this time the meeting of the Catholic schools continued to take place yearly, until the great increase of numbers rendered it impossible, but the procession with banners was not again attempted.

Before beginning the building of the convent it was settled that Mother Margaret should pay a short visit to Belgium, for the purpose of soliciting alms, and providing some of the requisites of a religious house not easily procured in England. During her absence, news was sent her that the image of Our Lady had been removed from the chapel in compliance with the prejudices of some among the congregation. The intelligence moved her more than the loss of all her worldly possessions would have done, and she expressed her indignation in no measured terms. "I have been in many passions on Our Lady's account," she used to say, "and when they turned her out of the chapel, I told some of them *they* might stay away if they liked, but that Our Lady should never be turned out." The image was replaced immediately on her return, when the chapel ceased to be used for the service of the mission.

Meanwhile, fresh and unexpected trials were in store for the Community. During the last visit of Bishop Ullathorne to Rome, it had been determined to remove him from the Western to the Central District, and in the beginning of August 1848, he left Clifton, and took up his residence at Birmingham. The blow was doubly felt by Mother Margaret at a moment when, in addition to her other cares, she found herself involved in the troubles of building, a matter in which she was then altogether inexperienced. The entire charge of the Community now devolved on her, for though his Lordship continued to act as Ecclesiastical Superior, the active part he had hitherto taken in the government of the Community was necessarily diminished by his removal to another diocese.

At this time of trouble and desolation a new friend and benefactor was given to the Community in the person of the Rev. Frederic Neve, who, soon after his ordination and appointment to the mission of Clifton, became chaplain and director to the convent. On the 22d of September 1848, he made his profession as a Tertiary of the Dominican Order in the hands of the Provincial, and received the necessary powers for erecting the Confraternity of the Rosary. "It would do you good," writes Mother Margaret, "to see our little chapel now on Rosary-nights. We have our Divine Mother in it, and things in our own fashion. Many have already been received into the Confraternity." The custom began of a short instruction being delivered by the chaplain on Rosary-evenings, and this attracted many hearers. The preacher's first discourse was on the subject of humility, and he enforced his lesson by begging the prayers of the people to assist him in his work. In "those fruitful days," as one writer calls them, the little chapel was always crowded, and the only place which the Religious could occupy was the passage before mentioned, where they heard Mass through the window.

Bishop Ullathorne had been succeeded in the Western District by Dr Hendren, who proved himself a kind and sincere friend to the Community. Sadly as she felt the loss of Bishop Ullathorne, Mother Margaret's respect for the episcopal office moved her to give his successor a festive welcome, as she had seen done in Belgium on similar occasions. She even exerted herself to make him an offering out of the slender funds of the Community, for the service of the diocese, in acknowledging which he condescended to say: "It is I, rather, who should make this offering to you ; *for the evening services at your chapel are sanctifying my people."* One of the first acts after his appointment was to give permission for Benediction of the Blessed Sacrament at the convent chapel on certain feast-days, and Mother Margaret writes of this, in a kind of rapture—" Bishop Hendren has signed the book ! I feel richer than if I possessed £1000 ; for if with time we can have all these devotions, it will save thousands of souls. I have no other wish, will, or desire, but to extend God's reign upon earth. We have told the poor people that the chapel is theirs, and that they must be at home in it."

If Mother Margaret's anxieties were at this time increased by the weight of temporal cares, it must also be owned that the proofs of God's bounty and providence which the Community daily received were sufficient to inspire them with confidence. One notable answer to prayer occurred in the autumn of this year. After the chapel at Clifton had been given up to the use of the Religious, they formed a portion of it into their choir; but their poverty did not at first admit of their procuring stalls. Mother Margaret, however, could not rest satisfied till the choir was properly furnished; and, after debating for some time whether she should venture on so large an order at a time when she had not a sixpence to spend, she determined to run the risk, and to leave it to Providence to supply the means. The stalls were accordingly ordered, at a cost of £30, which in those days was a sort of fabulous sum, and many were the prayers offered up that, when they arrived, the money might in some way be found to pay for them. On the very day that they were set up in the chapel a letter came by post enclosing the exact sum. Another story, belonging to this year, will perhaps raise a smile in those who are not accustomed to the notion of providential interference manifesting itself in such homely details. When Christmas approached, Mother Margaret was anxious to regale her children with better fare than ordinary: she wished much to give them a Christmas turkey, but did not feel quite justified in buying one. She therefore told them that if they wanted a turkey they must pray for it—a command they in all simplicity obeyed. When Christmas Eve came, a ring was heard at the bell, and one of the Sisters exclaimed, in joke, " That is the turkey !" She ran to open the door, and found that a man was actually waiting outside with a turkey in his hand that had been sent as a present. She carried it in high glee to the Community-room, and the Sisters were still amusing themselves over the incident, when another ring came, and another turkey, and a little later a goose, and so on, till they found that they were not only supplied with a Christmas-dinner themselves, but were able to give one also to their children and old women.

In the April of 1849, the Community received an accession of four members. Two of these were sisters whose vocation was decided during Bishop Ullathorne's visit to Rome in 1847.

Previous to this last addition to their numbers, the Religious had been making a Novena to St Theresa for new subjects, and had specially been praying that some might join them capable of assisting the services of the choir. Their prayers were granted, and on her return home Mother Margaret soon discovered that the Sister who was "to settle the Latin and the music" had been sent to her at last.

The main part of the convent was meanwhile rapidly advancing towards completion, and the Religious took possession of it in the month of July. The bell, which had already been solemnly blessed by Bishop Hendren, was suspended in the bell-tower, and the *Angelus* began to sound over Clifton thrice a-day. The cloisters connecting the convent with the chapel were begun in the autumn of the same year, and completed through

the generous assistance of the Rev. F. Neve ; the staircase communicating with the present orphanage being
excavated at tremendous risk to the safety of the
entire building. Thus by degrees the convent assumed
a regular form, and the Community continued at the
same time to increase in numbers, which latter circumstance, while it rejoiced Mother Margaret's heart, filled
her with many anxieties. "My head is tired with
thinking," she writes, " and my soul is oppressed with
sadness, when I look round and see fifteen souls committed to my care, and I without knowledge or ability
to guide them. I feel very anxious about their spiritual direction, and wish that more of us were thoroughly formed. I feel the loss of your paternal care
more than ever ; so many *white heads*, and only myself
to guide them."

The year 1849 had been one of internal development, and promised to be followed by one of external
expansion. Many proposals were received for establishing the Sisters in various parts of England ; and
at one time the liberal offer made by the Dominican
Fathers of resigning to the Community the chapel
and land occupied by them at Chilvers Coton, about
five miles from Hinckley, appeared to point out
this spot as the probable site of the future Novitiate
which Mother Margaret purposed locating in the
Central District. Coton was in the immediate neighbourhood of Weston Hall, where Mr De Bary had
now fixed his residence, and it was at no great distance
from Coventry.

Many causes, therefore, combined, as it seemed, to
attract Mother Margaret to this part of the country,
whilst, at the same time, her desire daily increased to

fix the Novitiate House in some more retired spot
than Clifton. "I think," she says, in her correspondence with Bishop Ullathorne, "that were you now
with us, you would judge it quite necessary that we
should have a place where there is not much work,
that we may be able to train the novices to a more
spiritual life, and that they may have time to learn
the Rule, Constitutions, and Office. As it is, they are
set to work directly, and have not time to be trained;
always giving out, and taking nothing in, which in time
would be the destruction of all spirituality. If you
make them truly spiritual, they will become fit instruments in God's hands to work for His glory." Her
idea of the Central Novitiate was, that it should be the
model-house of the Institute, and she therefore desired
that, whilst enjoying the advantage of a retired situation, it should include every institution of charity
which could be carried on within its own enclosure. Her notion of spirituality, and even of retirement, never excluded the idea of *labour.* She
often loved to quote the words of St John of the
Cross, "Work, suffer, and be silent," as embodying
the essentials of religious life. It is thus she expresses herself on the subject at this very time : "It
is no use persons coming to us who are not willing to
suffer everything for the salvation of souls. They
must have a heroic spirit, and be ready to bear heat,
cold, fatigue, and every other inconvenience. It is
easier to *say* that we delight in mean and abject employments, than it is to do them. We have had experience of this, and all would prefer to wear a hair
shirt or a chain, than to clean the kitchen, wash, iron,
or cook ; though God has commanded all to earn their

bread in the sweat of their brow. This is quite lost
sight of, and is almost looked upon as a disgrace. Yet
it is certain that Our Lord, in working as a carpenter,
must have fulfilled the command, and Our Blessed
Lady had no servants to wait on her. The more I see
of human nature, the more I feel certain that humble
and laborious employments are the best mortification,
the shortest way to obtain true humility, and to make
us have a proper feeling of charity towards the laborious and the poor. We can ill give lessons to others
of things we have not ourselves experienced."

She desired, therefore, that the Novitiate House
should be a school of mortification and the interior
life ; but, at the same time, that all such charitable
institutions should be annexed to it as would give the
novices an opportunity of becoming practically trained
in those heroic duties in the service of their neighbour,
which formed so essential a part of the life they
aspired to embrace.

The year closed in the midst of these hopes and
projects for the future, with which, however, both
humiliations and crosses were mingled. The busy
tongue of gossip did not spare the rising Institute, and
all the world did not understand the principles that
guided Mother Margaret's conduct. What most perplexed the curious public was her lavish expendi-
ture on all that concerned the service of God, at a
time when they had good reasons for believing that
the Community was enduring many of the straits of
poverty. They argued, that if Mother Margaret were
really in want of money, it was strange that she should
burn so many candles in the chapel ; and they never
dreamt that at the very time when remarks of this

G

kind were in circulation she was writing to her Sisters on the subject of their money difficulties, "Do not burn one candle less in honour of Our Lord, or His Blessed Mother; we must be sparing to ourselves, but not to God." Yet she was far from being indifferent to hostile criticism; we might even say that she was at all times keenly sensitive to unfriendly strictures which betrayed a less generous standard of principles than her own.

"I cannot explain the state of my soul at present," she writes; "I feel I have much to do for God, and I wish to do it, and I have at the same time such a desire of solitude that I would run into any obscure place to be alone with God. There are so many remarks made about our active duties; some think that what we do is to get a name; and when we decorate our little chapel there are also unkind remarks. I can say, with truth, I have not the least sensible satisfaction in these things. For before a feast the body is very weary, and the soul very depressed, seeing that when we have done our best we have done nothing for so great, so good a God. I have more feelings of discontent than anything else. Indeed, when I see least I see most, and in seeing nothing I see all things. Whatever exterior works we do, I hope it is purely for the glory of God and the salvation of souls."

Meanwhile, plans had been formed for establishing a filiation at Bridgwater, in Somersetshire; whilst, at the same time, the earlier project of founding in the Central District was not laid aside. About Easter, Mother Margaret proceeded with one companion to Staffordshire, for the purpose of examining some of the localities proposed for this latter foundation. She visited Hinckley and Longton, and paid a short visit to St Benedict's Priory, where, for the first time, she became personally acquainted with the venerable Mother Prioress. She also visited Weston Hall, where the zeal and piety of Mr and Mrs De Bary were producing some remarkable results. Both were professed Franciscan Tertiaries, and from the period of their conversion to the Catholic faith, they gave themselves up to the service of God with the entire devotion of Religious.

They lived at Weston Hall in a certain style of holy and primitive simplicity. A room in the upper part of the house was arranged as a chapel for the use of the mission which was served by one of the Dominican Fathers from Hinckley; whilst the great Hall was converted into a poor-school, which Mrs De Bary taught herself. There was an odour of antique piety about the whole establishment which charmed Mother Margaret's heart; and she often described her delight in seeing the crowds of country people who gathered there on Sundays, their hobnailed boots making free with the oak staircase, and all their voices heartily united in singing the plain-chant Mass. After that time she frequently visited Weston Hall in the course of her journeys to and from Staffordshire, and always met with the same affectionate welcome.

"Every one in the house," writes one who formed her first acquaintance with Mother Margaret in the course of these visits, "seemed to feel the joy of her presence, and the people would stop and linger about the house to catch a sight of her. Mrs De Bary's affection for her was that of a child for a mother. In her last sickness, when so ill that all other letters had to be read to her, she would always read Mother Margaret's letters herself, and her greatest pleasure was to talk about her. I well remember her last attempt to write to her; it was the last time she ever sat upright."

Nothing definite regarding the Staffordshire foundation was decided at this time; and it was arranged that the filiation at Bridgwater should first be tried. As usual, Mother Margaret had to pass through a crucible of interior suffering before beginning this new undertaking. "I am more depressed than I can express this last week," she writes, in a letter alluding to the preparations that were in hand; "I see only the naked cross, without anything to support nature. I am glad to be alone to give vent to what I feel. Make me a saint, my dear Father, cost what it will! I never have, nor do I expect, rest in this world; but, with your help, I hope to get eternal rest. Ask the Holy Ghost for me, my dear Father, that I may only think, speak, and act by the influence of that Divine Spirit."

The Bridgwater foundation was dedicated to Our Lady of Good Counsel, a beautiful picture bearing that title, by the German artist Seitz, which had been indulgenced by the Sovereign Pontiff, having been presented for the chapel of the new convent by Spencer Northcote, Esq. It was opened on the first Sunday in July, 1850, but this first filiation of the community was not destined to take root. The Religious continued there only until the April of 1851, when the difficulties which arose in the way of their making a permanent establishment in the town, added to the necessity of providing for the more important foundation in Staffordshire, obliged them to withdraw. When the convent was finally broken up, the picture of Our Lady of Good Counsel was removed to Clifton,

where it was placed over Our Lady's altar in the convent
chapel, which was undergoing some important alterations. Hitherto the stalls of the Religious had occupied the body of the chapel, and their position was
consequently very exposed. It was now proposed
to convert into an up-stairs choir that portion of
the house which projected into the chapel, at the
same time raising the roof and enlarging the sanctuary,
and the proposed alterations were accordingly begun
in the month of September 1850, two wings of the
cloister being meanwhile given up to serve the purposes of church and choir.

CHAPTER VII.

FOUNDATION AT LONGTON.

IN the autumn of the same year which had witnessed
the establishment of the Bridgwater Community,
Mother Margaret found herself called upon to com-
mence a far more important foundation in Staffordshire. Longton, in the Potteries, had been selected by
Bishop Ullathorne as the site of the convent which
he desired to see established in his diocese. A large
and densely populated town, it is situated in the
midst of what was once a fine open country, which
the hand of man has sadly disfigured. Undermined
in every direction by coal-pits, which in some places
approach so near the surface as to render the houses
above them insecure, and to allow of the vibrations
from the underground excavations and explosions
being distinctly felt, and lit up at night by the grim,
glaring furnaces, which impress the spectator who

first beholds them with a sensation of awe, Longton, with its sister towns in that strange district, presents a feature of English society of which the refined and luxurious classes know but little.

The house which had been taken for the Sisters was rented from the Railway Company. It had been built, at considerable expense, some years previously, in a style rather unusual for the neighbourhood, and bore the title of "The Foley." Mother Margaret had not seen it when, on the 23d of October 1850, she left Clifton for Staffordshire attended by one companion. Its forlorn aspect, and the general appearance of the town, struck Mother Margaret's heart with a sense of extreme desolation. Everything looked black and dismal, except the furnaces, the constant glare of which kept her awake at night, and reminded her, as she said, of the infernal regions. "The Foley," with its smart cornices, was empty and dirty. The autumn rains were flooding the cellars, and rendering the black soil so slippery that, as she described it in her first letter to Clifton, they were in danger, each time they went out, of breaking their legs. This letter bears traces of having been written under the first unfavourable impressions, and its portraiture of Longton is far from prepossessing.

But as time wore on, Longton, in spite of many discouragements, yielded its harvest of consolation ; and, ere a fortnight was over, Mother Margaret was beginning to pray for larger means, "to moralise a people with scarce an instinct of God," and to cherish hopes of one day raising saints, as she expressed it, out of the Longton mud. During her stay in Staffordshire she spent a few hours at St Benedict's

Priory, and also visited some of the neighbouring missions, the poverty of which caused her a keen distress. At Stoke-upon-Trent she found that the school was held in the chapel, and that the Blessed Sacrament was reserved in a pewter ciborium. The emotion which this caused her was the immediate cause of an illness which lasted some months. "My throat swelled," she said, "and I felt choking." With her heart still full to overflowing, she wrote to her Religious at Clifton : "We went yesterday to the Chapel at Stoke; and oh, my Sisters! I cannot tell you what I have felt since! A total want of all things! Our Lord and God in a *pewter* ciborium, gilt a little on the inside! and not one decent thing in the place. How can we expect the people to be converted? They have nothing to attract them; and how can they believe us when we instruct them in the Real Presence? They may well doubt the faith of Catholics—the Lord of heaven and earth in *pewter* for the love of us, and His creatures using silver for the meanest purposes: I am almost wearying my beloved Spouse to give me money. We must do something for this place." And, in fact, with the generous assistance of the Community of St Benedict's Priory, whence this letter was written, the most pressing wants of the Stoke chapel were afterwards supplied; although, at the time when Mother Margaret was begging for this mission, in which she was no way personally interested, she had still everything to provide for her new foundation. In the same letter she speaks of the kindness of the nuns in lending her a chalice for Longton, "till we have one of our own."

Mother Margaret returned to Clifton after an absence of three weeks. It had been hoped that St Catherine's Chapel would have been finished in time to have been opened on the Feast of the Immaculate Conception, but as this was not the case, the Blessed Sacrament was on that day exposed for adoration in the chapter-room, then used as a choir. Its sacred presence, so unusually near, inspired Mother Margaret with extraordinary devotion, and she owned to one of her Sisters that in a transport of fervour she could hardly restrain herself from rushing to the altar and clasping Our Lord in her arms.

On the 26th of December, the Feast of St Stephen Protomartyr, the alterations of the chapel being completed, it was solemnly consecrated by the Bishop of Clifton, and dedicated to the Holy Rosary and St Catherine of Sienna. Mother Margaret's feelings on this occasion can be guessed by those only who know the spirit in which she regarded the rites and benedictions of the Church. The possession of a consecrated church was in her eyes a gift, a privilege, a special means of grace, to be numbered among God's choicest favours. The following year, when the decoration of the chapel was completed, and the whole of the interior beautifully painted, she poured out her heart, not in a letter, but in a prayer, which is still preserved in her own handwriting.

It was whilst these decorations were in progress that Mother Margaret one day took occasion, in the absence of the workmen, to examine everything, and the novices were summoned to accompany her.

Every one admired the jewel-like effect of the painting, but her quick eye perceived that all the gold had been placed on the *outside* of the sanctuary-arch, facing the people, and that there was none on the inside, which faces the altar, and is out of sight from the body of the chapel. She was much displeased. "If those men had *faith*," she said, "they would never have stuck all the gold on the side that faces the people and put none on the side that faces Our Lord !" About the same time she wrote : "Our little chapel will be very beautiful ; but, my dear Father, I shall never be satisfied, for when I look at it, I think how poor, how mean it is, for our God with us. I wish I were rich, that I might cut out Solomon's Temple !"

At the close of the year 1850, the Community numbered fifteen professed Religious, two novices, and six postulants. The last day of the old year had been marked by a memorable circumstance ; the black habit had been laid aside for. ever, and henceforward the Religious assumed their proper livery, the white wool of St Dominic.

The rapid extension of their work gave rise meanwhile to the discussion of an important question, and for the first time elicited from Mother Margaret a strong expression of her opinions on the subject of education. The Sisters were now conducting the Clifton poor-schools, a middle pension-school within their own convent, and other schools at Bridgwater ; whilst at Longton it was evident that schools of every kind would form their principal means of usefulness. They had hitherto worked on independent of all aid and all inspection ; although the advantages to be derived from Government support were continually urged on Mother Margaret's attention, and probably the hardest things ever said of her were occasioned by her resistance on this point.

The following extract from a letter, written about this time, will give some insight into her sentiments on the subject:—" I cannot but think that *Old Harry* has something to do with this great school movement. In the end it will turn out a hindrance to Religious teaching the poor. We know the pride and vanity of England ; how most people run after anything new ; and where money is the object, they become worshippers directly. I think you will find that when the Religious have prepared their pupil-teachers, these will take precedence of their mistresses. I fear it will be in England as it always has been ; mind and body will be taught, and the poor soul (the only precious part of man) will be left in ignorance. I do not know what I am writing about, but I have asked Our Lord so many times to let me see it in the true light, and I always have the same impressions. I say, again, perhaps I am too stupid to understand what I am writing. I wish we had schools to teach humility and love of the Cross —the only lesson our Divine Master, the Eternal Wisdom, has wished us to learn of Him."

Her paramount care was for the education of the *soul*, a thing she instinctively felt would sooner or later be sacrificed by any national system ; and who shall say that on this point her instinct did not guide her aright? But she was not on that account indifferent to the education of the *mind*, although in regard of the poor she considered that it should have its limitations; and she held fast to the old-fashioned notion that a knowledge of needlework may do a poor girl more useful service than a knowledge of grammar.

On the 6th of January 1851, a little colony of Religious left Clifton for Longton, where Mother Margaret's first care was to convert the drawing-room of the Foley into a very devout chapel. As soon as it was arranged, she applied to the Bishop for permission to have the Blessed Sacrament reserved ; for, she says, " I never feel courage till we have our Lord in the house." This was granted, and the Rev. J. Dixon was appointed chaplain to the convent. Preparations were immediately made for beginning a middle-class pension-school in the house ; the stables were turned into a poor-school, and a night-school was also opened, in which the Sisters very soon had the consolation of receiving nearly eighty girls, who were employed during the day at the pottery-works. The chapel being open to the people for Mass and evening services, they resorted to it in such numbers as to fill not only the chapel, but every available standing-place in the hall and staircase. Mother Margaret's letters to her Sisters at Clifton, written in the first effusion of zeal, overflow with her ever-expanding desires to do more for God and for souls. "*Pray, pray !* my dear children, and be ready to make any sacrifice to save souls and advance God's Church on earth. See how little He makes Himself for ungrateful man ! Pray much for the Potteries : I have put them in a particular manner under the protection of our Holy Father. . . . I think our Lord sends me from place to place to stir me up."

The slender numbers of the Communities, and the paramount importance of first providing for the necessities of Longton, obliged her to refuse many applications made about this time for filiations in other parts of England. " How wonderful are the ways of God with His unworthy creatures !" she writes. " We are asked for in all places. Dr —— said he would go down on his knees if we would go into his district. The work begun with such poor materials begins to flourish in spite of all the knocks it has had."

From this time her daily course of labour began to include that constant and minute correspondence with her absent children, which increased with the multiplication of her convents, until it gradually withdrew her from almost every other work. The prodigious extent of this correspondence can only be roughly estimated, but the letters preserved amount to a surprising number. They present a true portraiture of the soul of the writer, and are as many-sided and as remarkable for that mixture of elevation and simplicity, which made one of her friends truly remark—" Mother Margaret was a *wonderful* woman, the most extraordinary combination of the natural and the supernatural that ever lived." From the sublimest ideas, expressed in the sublimest language, she could turn to the homeliest practical details. If the loftiness of her style on spiritual matters reminds you of St Catherine of Sienna, no less does the terseness of her shrewd remarks recall St Theresa. Perhaps the most remarkable feature in Mother Margaret's epistolary style, however, was the facility with which she adapted it to the individual character of each one whom she addressed. With some she was pithy and laconic, and, if perfectly at her ease, would convey her direction or her reproofs in a certain axiomatic language that forcibly reminds you of St Theresa. At other times she was tender, expansive, eloquent. Her letters addressed to her Communities on different Feasts might be cited in proof of this, but her private correspondence with her religious children is often couched in a style of singular beauty. "I fear you will have had a good share, my beloved child," she writes to one, "in the trials in which our Beloved favours His chosen ones. Why do I use the word *fear?* They are the best gifts of God ; each trial is a proof of His watchful love. *He must be very, very near us when we feel the thorns with which He is crowned.* It is a time of harvest when we get alone with God. Then love gains strength. The more we know, the more we desire to know and love this God of love—our one, our true, our only Lover !"

In reading some of her letters to her children you would think you had opened a page of the Canticles. "I must not forget you, although you are so little. Little as you are, I wish you to grow less and less, that your Divine Spouse may have the joy of saying to you, 'Come, my little one, my love, my dove, come, and grow great in my kingdom.'" A chantress is in anxiety lest the Holy Week services should not be rightly performed for want of proper singers. "Leave all to God," she writes to her ; "do your best, and be resigned. Keep close to your Divine and suffering Spouse. He had no soft music to still His pains. His music was the wicked cries of the multitude. Oh, how condescending of our loving God to allow us in some way to soothe His sorrowing heart by the expression of our love ! For I know,

my child, that you do love Him, and I love Him too.
Cold as the feeling is, He will accept it : so let us
love, be humble, and take all things with tranquillity."
Occasionally her most sublime and touching effusions
of heart terminate in some familiar little trait of
maternal tenderness. " Let God alone be your refuge
and strength," she writes to a local superioress, on the
eve of a great feast of the Order. " A few minutes
spent before the most Adorable Sacrament will obtain
you more light than any counsel of creatures. God
bless you all, my children, and make you all like our
sainted ancestors. Mind you have rolls for breakfast
to-morrow, and a good recreation in the afternoon."

This last quotation may possibly scandalise some,
as addressed to a Community of Sisters of Penance.
We will risk its insertion, however, having heard one,
who had a good right to judge, declare, after perusing
these letters, that nothing in them struck him so
much as these expressions of indulgence towards a
far-off colony of her children, who, as she well knew,
needed to be cheered amid the black mud of Longton.
We will venture on even a more startling extract, or
what may possibly seem so in the eyes of the world.
Who that knew Mother Margaret can have been
insensible to her spirit of hospitality ? It was, like
her faith, on the true antique model. She had a real
delight in entertaining guests, and making them at
home, and—shall we add it ?—in providing them
with a good dinner. As to priests, she felt she could
not do enough to secure the health and comfort of
those who laboured day and night in the service of
the Lord. So when she heard that some of the
Fathers were going on a visit to Longton, she writes

at once—"on hospitable thoughts intent"—"Get a large piece of beef, and a leg of lamb for their dinner, pease and potatoes, and a good bread and butter pudding, and a fruit pie; and get them some good beer." And on another occasion, "I hope Sister ——— has thought of making some mince-meat. You must have some mince-pies and plum-puddings for Christmas; and give Father ——— something good sometimes, and a good supper at night."

However, not to leave the reader under the impression that the rolls for breakfast and Christmas puddings may be taken as a sample of her ordinary directions in the matter of creature comforts, we will close these passing extracts with some of a different character, the tenor of which was of far more frequent repetition. When the Lenten Indults of the year 1866 appeared, granting the faithful some increased dispensations, she wrote to all her convents, "The new dispensations make no difference to us: all we have got to do is to fast and pray the more." "The nearer we keep to all our rule prescribes the more God will help us. A *relaxed* house is my greatest dread. I would rather see you all die of hard work and austerity, or pestilence." At the close of a Lent she writes, "It is a joy and a comfort to me to know that all my dear children have been fasting, and abstaining, and keeping to all the austerities of the Order. It is some reparation for the sensuality of the day. Thank God we *work* hard, *pray* hard, and *live* hard; may it be so to the end!" "Abstinence never hurt any one; if our heart is in our work, what does the food signify? Let the body die and go to heaven." She was no friend to that over-solicitude for health which is the canker-worm of generosity, and the cloak of a subtle self-indulgence, but made continual war upon it, often reminding her Religious that "no one would die before their time ; and that if they died of over-work or fasting, what better could they desire?" It must be added, however, that in cases of real necessity no one granted dispensations with a freer heart than Mother Margaret, whose tenderness towards the sick was unvarying.

Meanwhile events were taking place of considerable importance to the Dominican Order at large, and the English province in particular. The Passionist Fathers having withdrawn from the mission of Woodchester, the church built there through the munificence of W. Leigh, Esq., was, at the recommendation of Bishop Ullathorne, offered to the Dominican Fathers, who had by this time established themselves there. They were now in expectation of receiving a visit from the newly-appointed Vicar-General of the Order, the Most Reverend Vincent Alexander Jandel, who was nominated to that office by his Holiness in July 1850. He immediately began the visitation of the Provinces, and rumours were now afloat that he might any day be expected in England. It was of course desirable that Mother Margaret and her religious Sisters should take the opportunity of soliciting his protection ; and a letter was consequently drawn up in her name and addressed to his Paternity, giving a brief sketch of the origin and progress of the Community, its object and rule. A kind reply to this letter was received on the 8th of July, and on the 13th of August his Paternity arrived at Clifton, the whole Community, headed by the Chaplain, receiving him at the door of the convent, and conducting him processionally to the Choir, where he delivered a short address in French.

It had been determined to request his Paternity to give the habit to two postulants, then preparing for their clothing, and as he was necessarily obliged to leave Clifton the following morning, the ceremony had to be performed after the evening service. Arrangements for the purpose were therefore made with extraordinary celerity, and the members of the Confraternity of the Rosary who attended that evening were not a little taken by surprise on entering the chapel to find it transformed into a temporary choir, and to be informed how very interesting a function was about to take place.

The Father-General left Clifton on the morning of the 14th, and proceeded to Hinckley, where, in concert with the Very Rev. Father Aylward, he drew up a petition to be sent to the Holy See, in which, after stating the powers and jurisdiction over the Religious Sisters of the Third Order, which by advice of the English Fathers, he had delegated to the Bishop of Birmingham for life, he prays for a confirmation of these powers, in the name both of himself and of his Lordship.

The Papal Rescript, granting the prayer of this petition, *salvis juribus ordinariorum*, is dated August 31, 1851.

The joy caused by these events was damped by Mother Margaret's daily increasing indisposition. In fact the state of her health at this time caused her Community the gravest uneasiness. From one of her own letters we gather that she was dreading an attack

H

on the brain, that painful sores had opened on her head, arms, sides, and knees, and that the doctors insisted on perfect freedom from business as affording the only chance of cure. Fears were entertained lest her malady should result in softening of the brain; and her weakness was so extreme, that when she thought herself unobserved she would drag herself through the cloister, holding by the window seats. At length she consented to try the effect of sea-air, and by the advice of her medical attendants she set out, on the 18th of August, for Bangor. On her way thither she stopped at Holywell, where she unexpectedly met with F. Aylward, who was staying there, and who accompanied her on her first visit to St Winifred's Well. But for him she would probably never have found courage to have entered those icy waters; indeed, the doing so seemed a rash experiment, for she was at that time suffering from erysipelas, which, being driven in by the shock of the water, might well have proved dangerous. But he bade her have courage, telling her he would go to the chapel and pray for her whilst she was bathing. The effect of the bath was decidedly favourable; she felt no bad results from the suppression of the eruption, and that night had the first uninterrupted sleep which she had not enjoyed for many months; indeed, for six weeks previously she had been suffering from complete *insomnia*. Her gratitude for this favour was of the warmest kind, and she determined, on her return from Bangor, to pay a longer visit at Holywell, for the purpose of making a Novena to St Winifred, and taking the baths during each of the nine days.

She accordingly returned to Holywell, and began

her Novena on the 8th of September, the Feast of
Our Lady's Nativity. The sight of the ragged and
suffering pilgrims from all parts of England, Ireland,
and even America, crossing themselves and praying
aloud ere they entered the healing waters, and of the
crutches and other votive offerings suspended among
the antique tracery above the empty niche, by those
who had come there maimed and diseased and had
departed sound, was a consolation to her faith. "To
see such things in *England!*" she exclaimed; "it is
like a Catholic country." "You must come here, and
look at this wonderful well," she writes to a friend;
"if it is not miraculous, it is at least one of the wonderful works of God. I could look at it for ever;
but at present you cannot be there for many minutes
for the quantity of people of all sorts, Protestants as
well as Catholics, with all sorts of diseases. And yet
they will not believe its real cause; they say it is
wonderful water, and that is all: I am almost in a
passion with them!" She revisited Holywell on two
other occasions, being both times accompanied by one
of her Religious, who writes as follows: "I had the
happiness of twice accompanying our dearest Mother
to St Winifred's Well. I remember the first time she
entered the water she was very timid; but she immediately made the sign of the Cross, and prayed with
such faith and fervour that it moved all who saw her.
Once when we were there a poor paralytic woman
was brought to the well; it was beautiful to see our
Mother kneeling by the well praying aloud to St
Winifred for the cure of this poor creature. I could
not help thinking, at the time, how like the scene
before me was to what we so often read of in the

Gospels." After her first visit to Holywell, Mother Margaret endeavoured to propagate the devotion to St Winifred by every means in her power. She induced many persons to visit the holy well, or to use the moss or water of St Winifred—among others, the Most Rev. Master-General, who, in his last visit to England, made a pilgrimage of thanksgiving to Holywell ; and when the church at Stone was in course of erection, she had one of the side chapels dedicated to St Winifred, and caused a little font to be placed in it, which is kept constantly supplied with water from the well, and is often resorted to by the people.

From Holywell Mother Margaret proceeded to Staffordshire, visiting St Benedict's Priory, on her way to Longton. This journey had been undertaken with a particular purpose. The Father-General, during his stay in England, had expressed his wish that the Novitiate House might be transferred to the diocese of Birmingham. This had always been Mother Margaret's intention, and preparatory steps had even been taken for establishing the Novitiate at Longton. But experience proved that Longton was altogether unfit for the purpose. It presented a great field for active labour, but was not the place in which to train young Religious. As Mother Margaret pithily expressed it, " They would *hear* nothing but sin, and *see* nothing but mud." Moreover, every effort that had been made to procure land in this neighbourhood had failed, all being in the hands of great proprietors, who refused to sell an acre. An offer, however, was made about this time by Mr James Beech, of an acre and a half of land situated at Stone ; and this circumstance finally determined the establishment of the Novitiate House in that locality. Stone, although within an easy distance of the whole Pottery District, is itself a healthy country town, free alike from smoke and potsherds, and not densely peopled by a factory population. The offer was therefore gratefully accepted, and Mother Margaret went over from Longton to inspect her new possession.

On this occasion she was accompanied by Bishop Ullathorne, as well as by several of her Religious. "I well remember," writes the former, "her delight on first visiting this property. She saw at last a space in which to expand. It was in October, and the apple-tree now standing before the window of the room she was wont to occupy was richly laden with fruit. A basketful was taken to Clifton, as a specimen of the produce of their future home." This apple-tree was threatened with destruction when the builders came upon the ground, but was happily spared, and always bore the name of "Our Mother's Tree." The birds that resorted to it became in after years the object of her special benevolence: they were fed by her in the winter, and protected from wandering cats in the summer time. The tree, moreover, has another and a sweeter association. In the Corpus Christi processions, the last station has always been made at an altar erected beneath its branches. It was Mother Margaret's favourite station, and she desired that the antiphons sung there should always be in honour of the Blessed Virgin; for she associated it in her mind with two verses from the Canticle of Canticles: "As the apple-tree among the trees of the wood, so is my Beloved among the sons: as the lily among thorns, so is my Beloved among the daughters." [1]

The establishment at Stone was not by any means intended to supersede that at Longton, and Mother Margaret frequently visited the latter place, to direct and encourage the work of the Religious.

These visits often gave her opportunities of personally exercising her apostolic zeal. At Clifton much of her time was taken up in the parlour, and she was forced almost entirely to resign to her Sisters those labours among the poor in which she had hitherto taken so active a part. But at Longton she came in closer contact with the working-classes. The facility she possessed in reaching and touching a soul was as remarkable as her method. There was no circumlocution about it—she at once went straight to the point. The wife of one of the factory class, who had made a little money and risen from the ranks, came once to the convent at Longton, where she wished to place a child at school. She was a Protestant, and wholly destitute of education, and, ringing at the bell, she asked to see "the Lady." Mother Margaret went to the door, and heard her statement, that she and her husband "had no learning," but that they wished their daughter to have some learning, and desired therefore, that she might be received in the pension-school. The conversation was accidentally overheard by one who has narrated the incident. Mother Margaret waived for the moment the question of "learning," and asked her visitor, "Do you go to any place of worship?" "No, ma'am." "Does your husband?" "No,

_____
[1] Cant. ii. 3, 2.

ma'am." " Do you know that you have got a soul,
and that you must take care of it ? " " Yes, ma'am."
" Then bring your husband with you, and come and
see me again. I want to talk to you, and I 'll take
your child." The result of this conversation is not
known, though probably enough it ended in a conversion. This was her general style of opening the
siege. She did not deal in controversy, but she
seized the attention of her hearers, and put before
them in strong, simple terms, God and the soul,
heaven and hell,—the truths of eternity. An artisan
from Birmingham once came to Stone to finish some
work in the church, and Mother Margaret, after
settling what was to be done, fixed her eye on him,
and asked him if he were a Catholic. The man
answered he was not. " What do you do for your
soul—I suppose you know you have got one ? "
" Well, ma'am, I suppose I have." " Do you ever go
to church ? " " I can't say I do." When they had
got thus far, the Sister who was present, seeing the
turn the conversation was taking, thought it best to
retire, and went to dinner, leaving Mother Margaret
and her catechumen together. Presently she entered
the refectory with a glowing countenance, and whispered to the Sister, " Go and take that man a Catechism and a ' Garden of the Soul,' and give him the
address of a priest in Birmingham." The Sister
obeyed, and found the poor fellow kneeling before
one of the altars, weeping like a child. All his
John Bull reserve had vanished. " No one," he
said, " ever seemed before to care whether I had got
a soul."

At Longton she was content to spread all nets to

catch souls. One of the Religious wrote to her at Clifton, asking what they were to say to the factory girls as to the lawfulness of going to *dancing* houses; she replied as follows: "You must teach the people to leave their sins, and do penance for them. Never encourage them to go to any of those places. We must pray and do penance for their sins as well as our own, and draw down the blessing of God on this most wicked country." But she well knew that souls must be drawn "by the cords of Adam." So she permitted the girls to assemble for little tea-parties from time to time in the field attached to the convent, and these meetings, which afforded them an innocent recreation, quite made up for those which she required them to abandon.

After taking possession of the ground at Stone, an additional piece of land with some cottages on it was purchased by the community. The cottages were turned into a residence for one or two of the Sisters, who came over from Longton, and took charge of the poor school at Stone during the week, returning to Longton for Sunday. Mother Margaret's correspondence at this time is full of plans regarding the new foundation. "I have a convent in my head," she writes, "but I fear no person will ever understand it." Her feelings of fear regarding the new undertaking which lay before her find expression in several letters. "I have been suffering from great depression," she says, "and anxiety about temporal things. I try to think that all is right, and am convinced our Lord will accomplish His own work, but it is an interior martyrdom. It always is so when I have to act, trusting in Divine Providence alone;

and it is just as it should be, for our good God knows it is best for me to work without any consolation." This letter was written in the March of 1852, and in the August of the same year the first stone was laid of St Dominic's Convent.

CHAPTER VIII.

ST DOMINIC'S CONVENT, STONE.

THE year 1852 was memorable in the annals of the Community as one of expansion. The commencement at Stone of another convent, with all the attendant anxieties of building, would at all times have been a sufficiently grave undertaking; but how completely it was in this case a work of faith and obedience may be judged from the fact, that at the time the contract for the new works was signed, the expenses of the building at Clifton was not yet defrayed. At this moment Mother Margaret was greatly perplexed where to find the necessary funds for defraying the new expenses to which she had pledged herself. It was after consulting on the subject with one of her Religious that she came to her with a beaming countenance, exclaiming, " I have thought of what I will do ! " The Sister to whom she spoke waited for an explanation, fully expecting to hear that she was going to beg or borrow of somebody. But that was not Mother Margaret's way. " I will make Our Lady a present of two children on her Feast ! " she said ; and the two children were accordingly received. Nor was she disappointed in her hopes of thus winning the blessing of Heaven : for in no year did the Community receive a greater increase of members and of means than in this. The rapid accession of postulants raised the numbers at Clifton to twenty-two, and as the convent had only been built for twenty, they had already outgrown its limits. In the month of May his Eminence Cardinal Wiseman came to Clifton for the purpose of preaching a charity sermon on behalf of the Convent of the Good Shepherd, and during his stay he paid a brief visit to St Catherine's. He was received at the door with every solemnity, and conducted to a chair of state prepared in the Cloister, where all the Community in turn knelt and kissed his ring, and received his blessing. He afterwards met the Religious in the Community-room, and entertained them with his accustomed affability.

In the spring of this year, also, began a closer intimacy with the Fathers of the Birmingham Oratory, who were at that time involved in the troubles of the Achilli trial.

The result of the trial is known to every one, and was felt by Mother Margaret, as by all Catholics, as a disappointment ; but few events in this world are unmixed evils, and the frequent correspondence with the Birmingham Oratory, which grew out of this business, ripened the acquaintance which Mother Margaret had already formed with its respected Superior (Dr Newman) into friendship,—a friendship she cherished to the latest hour of her life, and to which she was accustomed to give expression with her characteristic heartiness and simplicity.

During the Novena of the Immaculate Conception four sisters were in retreat for their clothing and four for their profession; qualified in Mother Margaret's pithy style, as "all with good wills, and not two of them alike." "I look round with surprise," she adds, "and think of the grain of mustard seed. We must think how to spiritualise all these young ones." And what, it may be asked, was her method of spiritualising those under her care? To answer such a question precisely would require lengthy treatment; but glancing over her letters, and calling to mind the general tenor of her instructions, we should be disposed to reduce her system of religious training to two heads— the exact observance of the Constitutions of the Order, and the practice of an interior life. She valued the first like a true daughter of St Dominic; and in her later years particularly, her letters overflowed with exhortations and prayers, that the rule might everywhere be observed "to the letter." But still more did she value an interior spirit, without which even the most rigid exterior observance is but a body devoid of soul. "I wish you would, in a particular manner, pray for my soul," she writes; "for, in the midst of this multiplicity of works and women, I fear lest, through my remissness, much may go wrong. They want more spiritual food than I can give them; for I feel more than ever, that unless the religious women of the present day are more led to an interior and spiritual life, many, many evils will arise. If the head and the body are always at work, and the heart left untrained and untaught, self will be the object, and not God. Do pray, and work with us, that God, and God alone, may be our aim."

God alone—this was the key-note of all her teaching. The words flowed from her pen and from her

lips on all occasions; there is hardly one of her
spiritual letters in which they do not recur. "Let us
pray, let us love, let us live for *God alone.* Let a holy
jealousy take possession of us, keeping all our thoughts,
words, and works for *Him alone.*" Truly, if any were
to ask in what Mother Margaret's idea of the interior
life consisted, no better answer could be given than
the words of her favourite motto—*God alone.* She
meant by it the surrender of the whole heart, and the
whole intention; the single eye directed to God as a
motive; the single heart open to embrace Him as its
end; the single will and purpose to live for His service,
and to seek His glory before all things. Much as she
cared for the active works of charity, they were, after
all, but the husk; there was a spirit that must animate
them, or she prized them very lightly. How often
did she remind her children of this, and warn them,
lest, through want of a pure intention and guard of the
heart, they might be labouring all the day, and have
nothing really to offer to God at its close! How often,
in her homely impressive language, did she urge on
them to sanctify their work with prayer, raising their
hearts to God by means of some simple ejaculation as
they went about their ordinary occupations! She was
even jealous lest exterior works, however useful, should
be over-valued, so as to steal away the heart from God,
and was not altogether dissatisfied if sometimes the
Religious engaged in the schools met with mortifying
disappointments. "I am glad of it," she remarked on
one such occasion, when the half-yearly examiners expressed dissatisfaction at the state of certain classes;
it will teach you that your Sisters are *nuns* not *school-
mistresses.*" Sometimes she herself gave her children

a practical lesson of mortification on this head. Entering a poor school one day, she desired a Sister who was teaching a class to question the children before her. The subject was Bible history; and one of the questions being, "Where did Abraham come from?" a small boy called out, with some satisfaction, "From Mesopotamia." "What a big word!" said Mother Margaret: "now I'll ask him some questions;" so she asked him if he liked plum-pudding for dinner, and more to the same effect, and then left the class. The next time she came the children were repeating by heart the Latin hymns of the Blessed Sacrament, and were getting through them rather at a rapid rate. She sat down and asked them how much they understood of what they were saying, and then gave them a beautiful instruction on these hymns, and the reverence with which they should be recited. "It made me feel," writes the Sister who relates this anecdote, "how little I understood of the real spirit in which these children should be trained."

It would be impossible to give all the anecdotes that might be quoted on this subject, or the manifold ingenious ways she took for purifying the intention of her children over their active work. When once, however, she was satisfied that the heart was free, she had no further solicitude—they might work, teach, play, sing, draw, write, read, and the more the better: she required only that it should be *all for God*. A precious maxim of hers has been preserved by a Religious of another Order, to whom she uttered it: "If God is in your heart, your work will never drive Him out of it." But if she saw in any a disposition to over-estimate the *work* of the Community before its *sanctification*, she hastened to apply a remedy. Here are her words to a local superioress, whose zeal she sought to restrain: "All excitement springs from ungoverned nature. God is found in peace and silence, and one prayer from a contrite, humble spirit will do more than a great deal of talk. Our sisters have not too much time to give to God and to their own souls. I want no more active work for them than to do properly what they have begun. Let them all have time to study what belongs to their Rule and Constitutions: it is by that they will be judged."

From what has been said, it will be readily understood why Mother Margaret so often repudiated the character of an *active order*, attributed, in common parlance, to her Institute. "She wisely held," says Bishop Ullathorne, "that such a combination of the active with interior life as her Congregation presented was as well adapted for contemplation, in favour of those whom God calls to it, as any enclosed house would be." Speaking to the juniors and novices in 1864 of the temptations which some young persons get in active orders, who think that if they were in a purely contemplative convent they would have more time for prayer, she says, "A sentence of St John of the Cross has struck me more than anything I have read for a long time. It is this—'Work, suffer, and be silent.' I assure you I look upon it as our motto. It has been such a help to me wherever I have been since. Contemplation does not mean kneeling down and saying long prayers, but it means the union of the soul with God. Who ever reached a higher degree of contemplation than St John of the Cross? And yet was there ever a more active saint, labouring from morning till night to gain souls? You see then that those who lead most active lives can be contemplatives; and, indeed, I hope and feel that many of our Sisters have already attained to a high degree of contemplation." The Superioress of another Community having once asked her the secret of the unity which prevailed in her Congregation, "My Sisters," she replied, "are all so busy, they have no time for sin and selfishness. I like to see them go to bed thoroughly tired." But though she valued the active work of the Community, both for its own utility and as a means of promoting the sanctification of those engaged in it, she could not endure that it should be regarded either by the world or by her religious children themselves as the main object of her Institute. Hence, in the translation of the Constitutions made for the use of her Congregation, she would never allow any point of religious observance to be sacrificed for the sake of work. She dreaded that kind of activity which in one of her letters she characteristically describes as, "all *go*, and *do*, and no food for the soul." Certain points, which chiefly regarded the arrangement of hours, were regulated so as to suit the convenience of those engaged in active duties, but neither in the austerity nor the obligation of the rule would she admit of any mitigations. For several years, indeed, the Office of Our Lady was substituted for the Divine Office, which latter was only recited on greater feasts; but the number of these feasts went on annually increasing, and provision was distinctly made in the Constitutions for saying the Divine Office exclusively, whenever circumstances should permit.

In the matter of prayer she was not an advocate

for enforcing one system to be taught in the novitiate to the exclusion of any other.

She desired that all freedom should be allowed to each one's attraction. "If one word suffice for your prayer," she writes to a young Religious, "keep to that word, and whatever short sentence will unite your heart with God. He is not found in multiplicity, but in simplicity of thoughts and words. We meditate to find God, but if our soul goes to Him immediately we put ourselves in prayer, we need no images, for we have the reality. I never could reason or make an imaginary scene in my life, and that is why the Exercises of St Ignatius do not suit me. Whilst I was trying to form a scene, I could ask for grace and mercy for the whole world, and for myself too. We are not all formed alike, and God is glorified by the variety of His creatures, so that, however holy one practice may be for one soul, it would not lead another to God, and yet all are good and holy. If our dear Lord lives in the centre of the soul, (as He really does), what need have His spouses to look for Him elsewhere? There He is, to hear and to grant all we ask; again, when we are before our God in the Adorable Sacrament of the Altar, *what need we anything else but to look and ask?*"

One little expression in the above beautiful extract recalls the occasion which first made it familiar to her. A little tract on devotion to the Sacred Heart was once put into her hands, in which occurred the following words, being, in part, a translation from St Catherine of Sienna:—"*There He is*, all God, all man, hidden under the whiteness of a little piece of bread." She read it just before the celebration of the

Forty Hours, and a few days afterwards returned it to the Sister who had given it to her, saying, "I have something to thank you for. Your '*There He is*' has never been out of my head all the Forty Hours. I have never once entered the church without saying to myself, 'There He is, there He is!'" and as she spoke, the tears were in her eyes. It became one of her favourite ejaculations; and one day, long afterwards, when leaving the choir where the Blessed Sacrament was exposed, she touched the same Religious on the arm, and indicating the altar by a quiet gesture, whispered to her, as if in confidence, "There He is!"

It would doubtless be presumptuous in us to attempt to describe the nature of her own prayer—she used to say of herself that she could never put into words what passed between her soul and God—but one thing may safely be affirmed, namely, that it bore the same character of *simplicity* which stamped itself on all her acts. Speaking to one of her religious children of the difficulty she found in manifesting her interior, as required to do by a director, "I cannot understand or analyse myself," she said; "and I often tell our Lord, that if I could do for Him what He can do for me, *I would love Him with my whole heart, and be perfectly humble.*" Possibly the facility she found in directing her own heart to God prevented her from thoroughly estimating the obstacles which some find in this exercise, and their consequent need of systematic help. How completely prayer had become like second nature to her we gather from an admission which she lets fall in one of her written manifestations. "Aspirative prayer," she writes, "is

I

to me almost as natural as to breathe, and God is ever soliciting me to closer union with Him." A Religious, a convert to the faith, once speaking to her of the difficulty of acquiring Catholic habits, told her amongst other things, how long a time it had taken her to acquire the *habit* of always raising the heart to God the first thing on waking in the morning. "What!" said Mother Margaret in a tone of wonder, "don't Protestants do that? *Why, child, what else could you have thought of?*" She had been gifted from a child with an extraordinary and abiding sense of the presence of God; and one was sometimes disposed to think that her prayer resolved itself into a continuous act of that most Blessed Presence. A Religious who knelt near her in choir has said that one day she heard her softly murmuring to herself, during the time of meditation, the words, "O beautiful God!" and that the ejaculation and the tone in which it was uttered supplied her own heart with devout thoughts as she listened. She told another of her children that when before the Blessed Sacrament her prayer often was, "Lord, make them all saints!" Or again, "Lord, deliver me from all human respect, double dealing, and servile fear."

Nor, whilst speaking of the simplicity of her prayer, and of her instructions on that head, can we omit one little word of hers on the subject of the Divine Office. A Sister having asked her to give her some instructions how to say it, Mother Margaret looked at her with some astonishment. "*How* are you to say it, child?" she replied; "why, say it as well as you can, to be sure." And when the Sister continued, "But what ought I to think of in saying it?" she replied, "I know nothing about all that variety of ways ; *I just stand up before God and say it in His presence as well as I can.*"

This love of simplicity ran through everything. She could not bear those little subtleties of self-love which she was wont to denominate " faddles." It mattered not what turn the weakness took, whether it were love of notice, desire of sympathy, affectation of manner, or the fancifulness so common in the weaker sex, it met with little mercy at her hands. She did not even like the assumption of religious gravity, especially if she detected in it the least savour of conscious mannerism. She liked to see every one easy and natural, after her own cast and character, and was no advocate for fashioning the exterior of an entire community on one model. A religious demeanour, indeed, she highly valued, but one which springs from the mortification of nature, not the dressing of it up. "I never like you less," she said to a young Religious, " than when you are trying to be *extra good.*"

The idea of a religious life which she presented to her novices, was one in which love of the Cross held a prominent place. "The end for which you have entered religion," she writes to one doubtful of her vocation, " is to become quite a new creature, and to be entirely transformed into Christ crucified. The cross and humiliations of Jesus must be your only aim. You are elected to be the spouse of Christ crucified, to follow Him in hunger and thirst, in nakedness and poverty, nay, even to death ; for I hold out no other inducements to you but the cross of Christ, my beloved Spouse ; if His cross and His love will not content you, I have nothing else to offer." A life devoted to the active works of charity can hardly fail to be fruitful in occasions for exercising the virtues of mortification and love of the Cross; but, more than this, Mother Margaret retained so much of the antique spirit of Christianity as heartily to love the practice of exterior mortification, and to believe that without it the spirit of interior mortification is liable enough to expire. On this point both her instructions and her example were a continual protest against that false and effeminate spirituality which professes to sanctify the spirit without mortifying the flesh. She preferred those practices of penance which humble both flesh and spirit, but discouraged such as afford any lurking-place for self-love or ostentation.

There was one branch of mortification which she often pressed on her Religious, and wherein her example was even more efficacious than her words. It was the courageous indifference to petty ailments, the cheerful endurance of weak health and bodily fatigue. She did not like them to show signs of pain by contractions of the face. With an earnestness not sometimes without its touch of humour, she would seek to make them ashamed of the small self-indulgences to which feminine natures are so habitually inclined, and which she included under the comprehensive term of "faddiness." How truly heroic was her own lifelong struggle with disease and suffering, few, perhaps, even of her own children, were fully aware. In one of her letters she speaks of her repugnance to letting the younger Religious know anything of her infirmities. "All this," she says, " is good for the soul, and it is a strange pleasure to say to our Lord from time to time,

'You, and you only, know what this miserable car-
case goes through.'" The remark was made by a
priest during her last illness that Mother Margaret
had taught her children how to work and how to
pray, and that now she was teaching them how to
die; he might have added that another of her lessons
had been to teach them *how to suffer*. One anecdote
on this head may suffice, in which this victory over
nature rises to the sublime. A Sister, feeling herself
indisposed in the morning, went very early to our
Mother's cell for the purpose of asking leave to absent
herself from the morning office. Entering softly and
unobserved, she found her standing erect, and engaged
in washing the wounds which at that time covered
her whole person, praying aloud, as she did so, for
strength to get through the duties and fatigues of the
day. Struck with awe at the touching spectacle, and
ashamed of her own pusillanimity, she withdrew without making her presence known, and went to choir
with the rest.

One of the prominent features in her system of
spiritual training was her constant inculcation of solid
piety in preference to anything of private or senti-
mental devotion. One scarce knows how to convey
any notion of her teaching on this point, from the
very fact of its energy and abundance. What she
cared for was to get the root of *faith* firmly implanted
in the soul, well knowing that once there, it would
not fail to put forth the blossoms of devotion. The
tendency to reverse the process, and to make piety
consist in certain devout practices,—nay, even in the
mere frequentation of the sacraments, was an abuse
she found no words strong enough to condemn. It

was what she called "shim-sham piety." In the same way she set little store by feelings. "Take no notice of feelings," she writes, "they always deceive us, and lead us wrong; keep to the one principle—to seek God and to serve Him, in darkness or in light, and to have but one intention—God's will, and God's work."

She could not bear that a Religious should betray inexactitude in any of the appointed ceremonies through a liking to indulge in private devotion. "It is not your own satisfaction you are to seek," she would say; "if it is a distraction to you to hold a candle, think you are our Lord's candlestick for the time." Nor could she endure that any private devotion should be preferred before the Liturgy and Office of the Church. She writes in great satisfaction at the conclusion of one Holy Week, "We have had the services correctly, and to the letter. All has been done as it should, not one thing for fancy." One might say that she thought better of a person's piety if they made the sign of the cross reverently and exactly, in the right time and manner, than if they performed a hundred devotions out of their own heads. In the schools she insisted that all the necessary points of Christian doctrine, and the practices of obligation, should be taught in preference to what was simply pious and attractive, and any departure from this rule strongly roused her indignation.

Among the instruments of spiritualising a religious Community, to which she attached the highest importance, must certainly be numbered the possession of regular conventual buildings.

In her opinion, something of the religious spirit evaporated in a house which did not reflect that spirit in its exterior arrangements, and where many rules and ceremonies, in consequence, are apt to fall into abeyance. Hence her solicitude, at any sacrifice, to complete every office in the Mother House, that it might serve as a model for the whole Congregation; and that Religious attached to younger foundations might return thither from time to time, to reinvigorate their religious spirit by a more exact practice of the Constitutions.

Of these Constitutions something must now be said. At the time to which we have brought down our narrative they were rapidly approaching completion. Their compilation was exclusively the work of one Religious, whose delicacy of health gave Mother Margaret reason to fear at one time that God was asking of her the sacrifice of a life most dear and precious. Happily these fears proved groundless, and the necessity of withdrawing her from the work of teaching enabled her to devote herself with less interruption to her laborious task. The contents of each chapter were first scrutinised by Mother Margaret, and then submitted to the approval of the Bishop of Birmingham before being incorporated in the work. They are exclusively drawn from the Constitutions of the great Order. With the exception of a few explanatory foot-notes of minor importance, the work contains not one word drawn from any private source, and the precise authority for each paragraph is cited in the margin. The volume already printed contains only the first part of these Constitutions; the second part awaits the approval of the Most Rev. Master-General. This approval, as well as that of the Bishop of Birmingham, is appended to the printed volume.

It had been determined that the removal of the Novitiate to Stone should not take place until after the annual Retreat in July 1853, and that the same occasion should be selected for delivering the Constitutions to the assembled Religious before their separation. Great efforts were therefore made to get the book completed and out of the printer's hands by that time.

The Retreat opened on the 7th of July, and was given by the Rev. Father Augustine Maltus, O.S.D. The Constitutions did not arrive until after its close, and by a somewhat singular coincidence, on the 22d of July, the Feast of St Mary Magdalen, one of the chief patronesses of the Dominican Order. After Vespers, the Religious being all assembled in choir, his Lordship, the Bishop of Birmingham, delivered them a beautiful and touching address. The book of the Constitutions was then delivered to each one of the professed, and the following day the dispersion of the Sisters began.

Mother Margaret and three professed Religious went first, to prepare for the reception of the Novices who followed with their Novice-mistress a few days later. Only a small portion of the convent and cloister were yet built : a large piece of ground was staked off where the church was intended to stand, and where the builders were already making their preparations. The Sunday Mass was still being said in St Anne's Chapel, and on the space now occupied by the choir, sanctuary, and priest's house, stood a small house and a row of cottages, of which the house and two of the cottages alone were as yet in the possession of the Community. As to the convent, it was, of course, very incomplete. The first step, so soon as the workmen were out of the house, was to convert the present Community-room into a temporary choir, whilst the only completed wing of the cloister was assigned to the use of the congregation, and sufficed at that time for their numbers. There were plenty of inconveniences and make-shifts, but these only afforded matter for amusement and merriment ; and whatever might have been the anxieties of the elders, to the light-hearted Novices it was a happy time. A letter accidentally preserved from one of their number has recently brought to mind some of the incidents of those poetic days, when there was no gas and very little crockery, when the Novitiate was in the hands of the workmen, and the Novices attended their daily instructions under the trees in the garden ; when studies were pursued with tolerable success on an old box in one of the lavatories, and when every room in turn was tried as a refectory. And every room above ground having proved a failure, the Community had at last to retreat to certain apartments in the basement story, playfully denominated the *dungeons.*

On the 4th of August, the Feast of our Holy Father St Dominic, the first stone of the church was laid with due solemnity. The first Mass celebrated within the convent walls was the Pontifical High Mass, sung in this day by his Lordship, the Bishop of Birmingham. The Rev. F. Trenow was appointed chaplain to the convent and missionary priest ; and from this day the Chapel of St Anne's ceased to be used by the congregation, and was exclusively given up to the purposes of a poor school. The congrega-

tion was at this time bnt small; and some persons
who saw the dimensions of the proposed church,
questioned the prudence of erecting a building of
such proportions for so humble a congregation. It
soon, however, began to multiply. "I was almost
happy this evening," writes Mother Margaret, "seeing
so many poor Irishmen, with their heels out of their
stockings, praying at the other end of the cloister."
When Easter came the communicants numbered
eighty, an increase which was thought extraordinary
at the time; but the progress of the congregation,
however consoling, brought with it some inconveniences. On week-days the Community had their
choir to themselves, and a most devotional choir it
was; but when Sunday came, there was an end to
cloistered retirement. The congregation gradually
overflowed the narrow limits assigned to its use; and
the women and children had to be accommodated
within the stalls of the Religious, and in every available quarter.

On Rosary Sunday, 1853, the Confraternity of the
Holy Rosary was formally erected at Stone. The
modest list of names that day enrolled on the books
has since swelled to a thousand, and the congregation
at this moment is estimated at about fifteen hundred
souls.

One trouble at this time was the state of the community at Longton. The house was so dilapidated
as to be hardly habitable; pools of water stood on the
floors, and, owing to the excessive damp of the chapel,
it became at length impossible to reserve the Blessed
Sacrament. As no other house could be procured in
the place, and as the owners refused either to sell or

to repair the Foley, it became necessary to withdraw the Religious, with the understanding that the legacy left by the Rev. Mr Hulme should be devoted as soon as possible to another foundation in the Potteries. On the 29th of January it was publicly given out at the Sunday Mass that the Community were about to leave, and that after the next day Mass would be said in that chapel no more. The people were much distressed; some, even of the men, sobbed aloud ; " Now the Sisters are going away," they said, "there will be nobody *to blow us up*." Most of the Religious were transferred to Stone, but two remained in the house till the first week in February to superintend the removal of furniture, and whilst there, were fast snowed into their dreary residence, so as to be unable to open their doors until a passage was cut through the snow with no little trouble.

The nave of the church was now fast approaching completion, and the 3d of May 1854, the Feast of the Invention of the Holy Cross, was fixed on as the day of opening. The nave alone was built at this time, a kind of temporary sanctuary being arranged in front of the chancel arch, which was closed in with masonry. One of the aisles was boarded and curtained off from the rest of the church to serve provisionally as a choir for the Religious, and this choir they continued to occupy for the space of nine years.

The opening of the church took place with all the solemnity possible ; and the presence of the Fathers from Hinckley, who had been invited with eleven of their young postulants, all wearing the habit of the Order, gave the ceremony a truly Dominican aspect. The Pontifical High Mass was sung by the Bishop of Birmingham, the sermon being preached by the Very

Rev. Dr Newman, who came over from Dublin for the
occasion.   After the conclusion of the ceremony the
Community assembled to receive the congratulations
of his Lordship, who was pleased to express the singular happiness he felt in witnessing the beginning of
this new work.   He recalled the old days at Coventry,
and his words emboldened Mother Margaret to make
a request.   She was very desirous that the evening
service should include a procession of Our Lady ; but
she did not feel quite sure how far his Lordship would
agree to the proposal.   At last, however, she ventured
to make it with a mixture of simplicity and timidity
that was all her own.   "My Lord," she said, "don't
you think Our Lady would like to take a walk round
the church ? "   Not only did she obtain the permission
she desired, but the Bishop consoled her heart by
following the holy image in full pontificals, and himself singing the usual prayers.

It may be proper in this place to give a short sum-
mary of the after-progress of the convent, to which additions continued to be made up to the winter of 1856,
when further progress became impossible, until possession could be obtained of the row of cottages which
occupied the site of the present chapter-room and
guest-house.   As the owner refused to part with them,
the only resource was prayer ; and innumerable were
the Rosaries and Novenas offered for this intention.
Whilst further progress was suspended at Stone, how-·
ever, fresh works were being elsewhere undertaken.
The acceptance of Mr Hulme's legacy, now reduced in
various ways to the sum of £1600, rendered the foundation of a convent somewhere in the Potteries a
matter of obligation.   Stoke-upon-Trent, a town about

six miles from Stone, was selected for the purpose; and in 1856 were begun the nave of the Church of Our Lady of the Angels, the priest's house and schools, and a very small portion of the adjoining convent. It was taken possession of by a small Community in September 1857; and many were the hardships which for years fell to their lot.   They slept in a common dormitory; and their Community-room served by day the purposes of a middle school.   For a choir, indeed, they were well provided in a gallery constructed for the purpose; but their temporary refectory and kitchen had to be approached through a wooden communication which was not impervious to wet.   It was not until the year 1866 that the addition of another wing to the convent supplied the Religious with necessary accommodation, enabling their numbers to be increased, and the convent to be erected into a Priory.

In the meantime further progress was being made at Stone.   In the August of the year 1857 the property before spoken of was purchased, though at an exorbitant price; and the cottages were, for a time, adapted to the purposes partly of a middle pension school, and partly of an hospital.   The latter charity may be said to have first fairly begun in 1856, when the sum of £2000 was left to the Community, by a benefactor who wished to be unknown, for the purpose of commencing the hospital.   It was judged most prudent, and in accordance with the wishes of the donor, to appropriate this money to the support of hospital patients, rather than to the erection of a building, or the purchase of land; and in March 1856, a house was therefore hired in the town, whither were transferred one or two infirm women, who had hitherto been maintained at Clifton, other patients being also received, whose numbers gradually increased.

After possession had been obtained of the cottages in August 1857, the hired house was given up, and the hospital patients were moved into them; but the accommodation thus provided being quite insufficient for their increasing requirements, it became essential to provide them another home. A tavern adjoining the convent garden seemed precisely what was wanted, but the obstacles that stood in the way of its purchase were even greater than in the former case. The Community may be said to have compassed this property with their prayers and processions, as in old time the people of Israel went about the walls of Jericho. Again and again were the fifteen mysteries of the Rosary recited processionally during fifteen successive days; and at last, in the summer of 1860, the unexpected death of the proprietor caused the property to be put up for auction, and, to the surprise of all concerned, the Community became the purchasers for the sum of £1500. Under ordinary circumstances it would have been a very perplexing question how this sum could have been procured. In this case, however, the precise sum of £1500 had recently come into the possession of the Community, and that in a totally unexpected manner. It was not bequeathed by any benefactor, but was property belonging to a member of the Community, though she had long given up any hopes of recovering it, and had been received as a novice with the understanding that such was the case. Just before her profession, however, which took place about this time, the affairs were brought to a most unlooked-for termination, and without any litigation or vexatious dispute, the Community found themselves possessed of the exact sum which enabled them to complete their long-desired purchase.

The hospital patients were at once transferred into their new quarters, and, at the same time, the commencements were laid of a new charity which arose out of the following circumstances :—News was one day brought to Mother Margaret that a poor Irishman had died in Stone, leaving five little boys quite unprovided for, the eldest being twelve years old, the youngest an infant. The mother was sick in the Stafford Infirmary, and not expected to recover. All five children were about to be sent to the workhouse, but Mother Margaret could not bear the thought of this, and though a little perplexed at the fact of their being boys, she resolved to take them all. Her first idea was to hire a house in the town for them, but as nobody was willing to let one for the purpose, the convent premises were examined, and a very small building discovered on the recently-acquired property, the lower room of which had been turned into a stable. The horse was at once dispossessed, and located in the coal-cellar, the room cleared and cleaned, and the five little boys established there under the care of a woman from the hospital. Their mother being sufficiently recovered to leave the infirmary afterwards joined them, and this was the beginning of St Vincent's Orphanage, which now numbers forty inmates, and occupies an entire row of cottages opposite to the convent.

Whilst these undertakings were still in hand, Mother Margaret was at the same time engaged in establishing other more distant foundations, of which we shall speak hereafter, and in dispensing charities on her own munificent scale. No wonder that strangers who beheld such things drew the conclusion that Mother Margaret must possess some boundless fund of wealth, and that they felt incredulous when assured that the only wealth of the Community was obtained by prayer. "There is nothing like prayer," was one of Mother Margaret's favourite sayings, and her life was its justification. More than one narrative of an answer to prayer has been already given; we will here add another taken down at the time from her own lips. It must be premised that in the year 1865 the Community had agreed to purchase a piece of ground on the other side of the road, which they then trusted would serve as a site for their Hospital and Boys' Orphanage. They were, however, utterly without the necessary means, and, as usual, Our Lady of the Rosary had been incessantly invoked, and the Fifteen Mysteries recited again and again. The result shall be told in Mother Margaret's own words :—

"I had a letter from a lady who was an annual subscriber to our Hospital, saying that she was coming to the convent for an hour or two, and wished for a private interview. I had an early dinner, and when she came I felt very frightened to go to her. She began to talk, and almost the first thing she said was that she meant to withdraw the sum she had annually given to the Hospital. My heart began to sink; but after a little more talk she said, 'I am thinking of giving you instead, £1000 at once.' I could not tell you what I felt. I began to cry. She said, 'Will you accept it?' I said, 'I can only tell you that at this very time we have £1500 to pay for the ground we have purchased, and, except to God, we did not know where to turn for the money.' But that was not all. As if to show clearly that it was the Fifteen Rosaries, she said that she wished us to undertake a certain charity for her, which no one was to know, and that she would give £500 additional for that purpose, which she would send on the Feast of St Theresa, making in all £1500. She said, 'How do you get the means for all you undertake?' I answered, 'You ask me how we get it, and don't you see how God has sent you here just at this moment to give us the very sum we want?' She went away; and Mother Sub-prioress came, anxious to know the result of her visit. I said, 'I should like Sister R. and Sister A. to come too.' Then I told them all; and we all sat and cried together. And, as if to finish it, instead of waiting till the Feast of St Theresa, she sent the money on *the Eve of Rosary Sunday.*"

CHAPTER IX.

HER FAITH AND DEVOTION.

WE have hitherto been engaged in tracing the exterior features of Mother Margaret's life, and the providential guidance by which she, whom we have seen in 1814 a friendless and destitute orphan, was led, step by step, to become the re-foundress in England of one of the ancient Institutes of the Church. And having reached this stage in her history, it may be well for a while to suspend our narrative, and introduce the reader to a closer acquaintance with Mother Margaret

K

herself, as she was known to her Religious children and her more familiar friends.

Even apart from the gifts of grace, she had many of those natural qualities which infallibly raise the souls that are endowed with them above their fellows. She possessed in a remarkable degree that magnificent physical organisation which so often accompanies great moral force; and the life-long bodily infirmities from which she suffered, while they tamed and chastened her animal nature, never impaired its vigour.

This *strength* of soul, which at once made itself felt, led some superficial observers to call Mother Margaret's a *masculine* character; but this was a singularly erroneous judgment. Those who really knew her were well aware that her strength was far more from the heart than the head,—that even her intellectual gifts, her quick perception, and rapid judgment, were all essentially feminine; the manly powers of deduction and reasoning were developed in a far inferior degree. "She was," said one who best knew her, "the veriest woman I ever knew."

But the natural force of character of which we have spoken was blended in her with another kind of power, the source of which was not in herself. She might have said, with the Psalmist, that God was "the strength of her life." As one friend well expressed it, "She was *full* of God." It inspired one with a kindred devotion only to hear her pronounce, in her rich, full tones, the words, "Almighty God." God was the very atmosphere of her life, an atmosphere she made sensible to all who approached her. God's glory, His interests, His side in every question, was what she first considered, and His holy Name was ever on her lips. " How good God is ! " was her exclamation all day long. Everything that occurred was so simply and immediately referred to God, that her companions could not but live, as she did, in His continual presence. If it rained, she would say, " How good God is to send the rain ! " if it was fine, " How good God is to send the sunshine ! " If she had anything to give away, " How good God is to give us the pleasure of giving ! " Or if she had completed any great undertaking for the glory of God, her thanksgiving was more in detail. " How good God is," she would say ; " first He gives you the desire to do something for His glory, then He gives the means, and after all He rewards you for doing it, as if it had not been His own work from first to last ! " How greatly she longed to be with God, and how often such longings broke forth into words ! " Lent is past," she writes, " and so flies all time till we are in our true home in the bosom of God. Oh, happy, blessed thought ! To be with God for ever and ever ! To be with Him who is our life, our light, our love ! The cross soon passes, and the glorious resurrection comes." On her death-bed she could not refrain from sometimes expressing a regret that the last hour was so long delayed—" not," as she once said to her medical attendant, " on account of my sufferings, if they were ten times worse : it 's to see Almighty God, that is what I long for." If she heard of any act of dishonour to God, it touched her to the quick. After hearing the narrative of a shocking act of sacrilege and blasphemy against the Holy Trinity, committed some years ago in one of our military colleges, she caused the Athanasian Creed to be recited in English every Sunday after Mass, as an act of reparation.

This continual sense of God, in which faith and love had an equal share, explains the ardour she always manifested in all that regarded His worship, and the profuse munificence with which she adorned His sanctuary. She would have lavished the wealth of an empire, had she possessed it, in the decoration of His temple and tabernacle. " When our Mother had to provide anything for the church," said one of her earliest companions, " it was as if she was ordering for some prince of boundless riches, *to whom all the bills would be sent in.*" Her last charge to the Religious who succeeded her in the government of the Congregation was, " Never forget the Church of God; let that always come first." Hence it was that, as we have already said, she was so ready to answer appeals for help from poor missions, and that she gave away vestments, copes, albs, and altar linen so liberally, that the value of her gifts, if reckoned, would have amounted to many hundreds. Nothing moved her so much as the least semblance of meanness or stinginess in what appertained to God's service; whatever was given to Him was to be the best that could be given. When the high altar of this church was being put up, though she was then far from well, she went to watch the workmen, and see that everything was done properly. The brick foundation for the altar having been put up in a rough coarse way, she sent for the head workman, and desired that the masonry should be carefully finished, plastered, and whitewashed. The man looked a little surprised, and said he would see about it. " But it must be *done*, sir," she said in a positive tone; "you will make it all as good inside as out, and better, if anything. I'll have no rubbish inside God's altar." She looked disgusted and disappointed when she found that the marble portions, instead of being formed of solid blocks, were only stone covered with thin slabs of a more costly material, and went away saying, half aloud, "I suppose one can't help it, but I wish it had been solid!"

Nothing displeased her more that any remissness or negligence in necessary preparations relating to the Blessed Sacrament, nor was it any excuse in her eyes if the omission proceeded from being absorbed in prayer, whether at Meditation or Mass. That was not her idea of recollection, which she would say did not consist in being absorbed in self, but should always leave the soul vigilant for every duty. On one occasion, when she had observed some hurry and confusion among those engaged in preparing the altar, she administered a severe reproof. "Our Mother cried, and so did we," writes one of those who relate this incident. "I do not remember her words, but she reminded us of the deference that was shown in every movement before an earthly sovereign, and contrasted it with the way in which we had been moving before the throne of the King of kings."

Another time, when there had been but a poor attendance at one of the Processions of the Blessed Sacrament, the indifference of the people struck to her very heart. "You may well feel the indifference of man to our good, our loving God," she writes; "there was not a man to carry the baldachin this morning: we had to get a boy from the school to carry the Cross. All running after the pounds, shillings, and pence. I never can feel the English have right faith, they are so cold and tepid. As our dear Lord's spouses, we ought to make up for this coldness to the best of our power. Never, never can we comprehend the generous love of our good God; it is as incomprehensible as our coldness and forgetfulness of this wonderful Mystery. Let us love, let us love with our heart, mind, and strength." When writing on this subject she hardly found words in which to pour out her heart. "The world is cold," she writes, "because it knows not Jesus; but for us, who know Jesus, who are loved by Jesus, who are fed and clothed by Jesus, and to whom Jesus communicates Himself nearly daily in the Sacrament of His love, what can we do, what ought we not to do, for this dear, this loving, this Divine Jesus! . . . May you ever increase in devotion, love, and faith to this Gift of gifts—the adorable Sacrament of the Altar, our hidden God, our Spouse, our Life, our All. . . . Drink deep during this holy Octave of this furnace of Divine love; and ask of your hidden, solitary God, the spirit of recollection. . . . How cold are Catholics' hearts become! Did we think and feel as we ought towards this Divine Mystery, some would surely die of love. It humbles us to think we can do so little, and love so little a God whose very essence is love!"

The following letter was written to one of her convents on the Feast of Corpus Christi:—

" GOD ALONE.
" J. M. ✠ D. C.
" *June* 13, 1851.

" MY VERY DEAR SISTERS AND CHILDREN IN JESUS,—I cannot let this Feast of *Love* pass without wishing you all to reap the fruit of this holy Octave, in which we commemorate the boundless love, the wonderful humility of our God with us. I wish I could obtain for all of you a sense of what you are in possession of, in dwelling with Jesus, the Beloved of the Father, the Joy, the Happiness, the Beauty of Heaven; for we have, in our Lord and God, the most beautiful of the sons of men residing with us in our poor, mean tabernacle. To you, my dear Sisters, who have the honour, the happiness to be His chosen spouses, how will you spend this Octave? Will you spend it in coldness and indifference? Will you not leave the creature to find your Creator, and make some reparation for the coldness and indifference of ungrateful man, who is wholly unworthy of the gift he possesses? Let it be your chief pleasure and re-creation, during this holy time, to spend it with Jesus your Spouse, the *only solitary* in the House. And to you who are aspiring to become the spouses of the immaculate Lamb of God, how diligent ought you to be in your continual visits to Him, to beg Him for every grace you need, to prepare you for so high, so holy a dignity. Remember our enemy is watching to rob us of this most precious favour; he makes the way dark, dreary, and miserable; but you will be victorious if you are faithful in giving all your spare moments to Him who lies hidden, solitary, and silent for the love of you. How often does His divine Eye and Heart turn towards the choir door, to see which of His chosen ones will pass one hour with Him! Believe me, my dear Sisters, if you are faithful in going before Our Lord with all your doubts, difficulties, and troubles, they will soon vanish, and you will advance

rapidly in the way of perfection. Pray often and
fervently during this Octave, that all may know, and
love, our good, our merciful, our loving God; that His
temples may be rebuilt, that His priests may be holy,
that He will vouchsafe to convert our unhappy
country to the true faith; but, above all, ask that
those who are chosen from the rest of the world,
particularly you who belong to the same, may be
faithful to the end in loving, serving, and adoring
Him, in the Most Holy Sacrament of the Altar. I
should weary you all before I should be weary of
speaking of this Mystery of Love. God give you
many blessings during this holy Octave.—Your unworthy Mother in Jesus,   " MARGARET,
                          " *Of the Mother of God.*"

The anguish which she felt in beholding the poverty
and squalor that is often suffered to surround the
tabernacle of our God Incarnate, can hardly be expressed in words. What struck her most on her return to England was the poverty of the altars,
particularly in private chapels. Visiting at a great
house, she was questioned by the ladies of the
family as to what she thought of England after her
long absence in a foreign country. " Well, ladies,"
she replied, " if I must say the truth, what has struck
me most in England is to see you using mahogany for
your closets, *whilst you keep our Lord in deal !* "
Until the foundation of Stone, she trusted no one
but herself to decorate the altar on the greater festivals, and after the increase of occupations obliged her
to allow that duty to devolve on others, she always
superintended the office of Sacristan, and gave special

directions for the celebration of each festival. If the material decoration of the Throne of God had this importance in her eyes, yet more was she solicitous regarding everything that concerned the worship which was offered before it. Her religious children were accustomed to say that of all the saints there was none she resembled so much as King David. His royal munificence, his forgetfulness of human respect when he danced before the ark, his delight in singing with voice and heart the praises of God, and the exuberance of his holy joy in rendering Him the best of all things— something of all this was to be seen in her. She often expressed her devotion by saying she would like to *dance* before the tabernacle, and used to say that Father Faber had spoken the right thing when he said that on Corpus Christi *one could not stand still.* There was a thrilling exultation in her manner of chanting the Divine Office. On one adoration day in particular, when, the Community being small, there were few Religious in the choir who could sing, a priest who was present remarked that he should never forget the tone of Mother Margaret's voice, it was so clear and joyous; "and yet," he added, "you could tell from the very sound that there was not a thought of self in it; it was truly a creature singing the praises of her Creator." She burst into tears quite overpowered at first hearing the *Tantum Ergo* sung by all the people in the churches of Rome, and she never visited her convent at Stoke, without expressing her delight at the hearty way in which the congregation there joined in the public singing. One Sunday, when there had been Exposition of the Most Holy Sacrament, she came from the choir after service was over, quite overpowered. "O my dear child!" she said to the Superioress, in her own simple phraseology, "it more than repays me for all that has been done in this place to hear these people singing the praises of God; *and to see those big men go down on their two knees!*"

In speaking of a subject which is literally inexhaustible, it is hard not to be diffuse; but one feature in Mother Margaret's holy zeal for God's worship must not be omitted. It was her *liturgical* spirit. This was one of the points in which she reflected rather the antique piety of past ages, than the tastes and habits of the present day. We have heard some Catholics condemn, as preposterous, the notion that the Offices of the Church were ever intended for popular use. Such was not Mother Margaret's spirit. To her there were no words like the words of the Church, no music and no language like that which the Church has sanctified. She tolerated the use of English hymns and devotions for the people, but they were opposed to her taste, and she strenuously maintained the principle of training Catholics to take part in the Church Office in preference to every other devotion.

For herself, her delight in the ritual of the Church was often too deep for words. "This Holy Week," she writes, "we have had all the proper things for the first time, I mean the font and the paschal candlestick. I suppose, as we grow old, we get into second childhood, for I could not sing the *Gloria* for tears, I hope, of gratitude to God for all His mercies to us, and above all, for being a true child of the Church. The blessing of the candle and the font are quite soul-inspiring. You would wonder who could live out of the Church, or not love its ceremonies."

Her letters addressed to the Religious of her various houses on the various festivals, if collected, would fill several volumes. We will quote a few passages, for the purpose of exhibiting her deep sympathy with the devotion of the season, and the fervid language with which she sought to kindle a like devotion in her children. "Another Advent!" she writes. "How good God is, year after year, to remind us of what we are to do to prepare for Him. If we read the epistle of to-day, it tells us we are to *put on the Lord Jesus Christ.* What a work for Advent! to become another living model of our Spouse Jesus! Here you see, my beloved children, St Paul has cut out our work for Advent, "Put ye on the Lord Jesus Christ." Do it, dear spouses of Jesus, do it with all your heart, soul, mind, and strength. Put on in deed and in truth the spirit and works of your Divine Spouse; He sees, and knows, and notes down every thought, word, and act of His beloved spouses." At Christmas, she writes: "Everything in the Church at this Holy Season preaches to us the Nativity of our dear Lord, the Versicles, the Hymns, the Antiphons, all excite us to prepare the way of the Lord. . . . Surely we ought to be the most perfect, the most loving of all His creatures! For us He is born; for us He lies helpless in the manger; for us He weeps, and our dear Mother Mary weeps with Him too, in union with her Son, for the sins of the people. Dry His tears, my dear Sisters, by the fervour of your love, by the sincerity of all your devotions, and above all, by the practice of the three vows of religion which you have pledged to Him. . . . Let us take our heart in our hands to the crib of our infant Jesus, and show Him all its wounds

—all that is an obstacle to the reign of His pure love
in our souls. . . . Let us listen to the sweet voice of
inspiration that sounds from the stable, the crib, the
manger, the straw, the beasts, for everything there
preaches to us."

The Feast of the Circumcision always drew from
her the most impassioned words regarding the Most
Precious Blood, to which, like a true daughter of St
Catherine, she bore an extraordinary devotion.   In
Lent and Passion-tide she ceased not to direct the
thoughts of those around her to the practice of penance, and the cultivation of a tender devotion to the
Passion of Jesus. "Never do I go before God," she
writes, at the beginning of Holy Week, "without
begging Him that His generous outpourings of His
Most Precious Blood may be for the sanctification of
you all.   For what will all these great mysteries avail
us if we do not apply them to ourselves, and so im-
bibe the graces and blessings that flow from the
sacred wounds of our bleeding Bridegroom? But if
Jesus is a Spouse of blood to us and for us, let us not
cause that blood to flow again by opening the wound
of His sacred side (the wound of love by excellence)
by our imperfect thoughts, words, or looks.   Did we,
dear Sisters, see Jesus hanging on the cross with all
His wounds open, and the cold bleak wind blowing
into them, our first thought would be what we could
do to comfort Him.   Let the same feeling animate us
now; let us endeavour to console and bind up the
wounds of our Lord and God. . . . I hope you will
all do your best to honour the Passion of Christ by
some acts of penance. The sins of the world would
call for this even if the love of our crucified Lord did

not excite us to it. Would to God we could crush our proud sensual nature, and live and die on the cross!" And then when the Easter sun has risen, she writes as though her soul were overflowing with the Paschal joys: "This is the day that the Lord hath made! let us rejoice and be glad! The Church, like a tender mother, tells us when to mourn and when to rejoice; and now it is her will that we should be joyous with a holy joy—a joy such as is felt in heaven, where the angels see their God and our God face to face. May all your hearts beat with this true joy, my very dear children; for there is no joy in the world, in its ways or manners."

What can we say on the subject of her devotion to the Church? She verily saw in it the spotless Spouse of Christ: she lived in its round of fasts and festivals, she gloried in its triumphs, she made its sufferings her own. "What times these are we live in!" she writes. "It makes me heart-sick to hear the things that are said of God and His Church. It makes me wish more than ever to say the Divine Office, to bind us more closely to God and His Church. It seems as if we ought always to be in prayer."

Her devotion to the Church and its ministers naturally took its highest expression in her devotion to the person of the Sovereign Pontiff. The true daughter of St Catherine, she, in this as in so many other respects, reflected and reproduced her spirit. She saw in the Holy Father only "the Christ on earth." How numberless were the prayers, Novenas, processions, and days of adoration, offered in her Communities for the needs of the Church!

In the months of September and October, in the

year 1866, when the affairs of Rome appeared hastening to their crisis, she ceased not to exhort all her
children, as the daughters of St Catherine, to "offer
everything for the Pope and the Church." She bade
them, as they went about the house, use as their constant ejaculations the words, "O Lord, help the
Pope, protect the Church!" and teach the same to
the children.

"Some of you," she said, "are always praying and
thinking of yourselves: that is all self-love. Be more
generous and pray for what is of more consequence.
As children of St Catherine, whose precious relics we
have with us, it is our special duty to pray for the
Church."

The emotions of delight and veneration with which
the personal presence of the Sovereign Pontiff filled
her soul will best be described in speaking of her visit
to Rome; but from that time she generally mingled
some words of familiar affection with her expressions
of sympathy and respect. At such times she would
say, "We are true *Papists;* there is no doubt of that;
and I thank God for it!" There was nothing she had
a greater horror of than any sort of timidity or human
respect on the part of Catholics when called on to
profess their faith. The spirit of polite compromise
with heresy was in her eyes treason, and she treated
it as such. "In our days," she once said to her Religious, "the worst enemies of the Church are not
heretics and persecutors, but half and half Catholics,
'*rotten* Catholics,' as Dr Milner used to call them, who
are willing to come to a compromise with heresy and
want to teach the Church—they think themselves so
wise; and my prayer for them is that God would

make them fools. Let all who have to do with the children instil into them a great love to Holy Church. Do not use half measures yourselves; be bold and open in your profession of loyalty to the Church; let us have no compromises. When seculars question you, let them plainly understand that out of God's Church there is no salvation; that if they are not Catholics they will be lost, unless they are in invincible ignorance. And if they ask you who founded the Protestant religion, tell them ' the devil;' I never give any other answer, and I hope, please God, I never shall." Her loyalty to her Order was part and parcel of her loyalty to the Church—it had the same tone, the same deep and heartfelt intensity about it. "Thank God on your knees every day of your life," she once exclaimed, "that you are members of an ancient Order—an Order of Saints, an Order that has never been tainted with heresy!" Her letters are full of such passages. " Pray," she writes, " that we may have the true spirit of our Holy Father; without that, it were better we ceased to exist." . . . " *Let us all aim to be Catherines.*" Indeed, we might sum up her whole teaching by saying, that the spirit she sought to form in her Community was the spirit of St Catherine of Sienna.

One other of Mother Margaret's devotions remains to be spoken of, the one which is perhaps most commonly supposed to have been predominant in her soul, the devotion to the Blessed Virgin. And truly it would be difficult to overstate the warmth and breadth of that devotion to the Mother of God, which held the closest place in her heart, next to her love of God Himself. She never could speak without emotion of the favours, the protection, the tender and maternal care which she and her Community had received from this best of mothers. If she tried to do so, her words poured out mingled with her tears. " Who has obtained all these things for us ? " she writes ; " Mary, our beloved, our thrice loved Mother. Praise her, bless her, love her, confide in her, and you will be light with the light of God, and full of joy. . . . You have all a double reason to honour and bless our Immaculate Mother, for she is really the cause and instrument of all we have in every way ; she is truly the 'Cause of our joy.' . . . Never, never could I put into words all her bounty and goodness to us. . . . I know not what to say when I go to pray, but this one word, how good, how wonderful is God ! May He be blessed for ever, and our Immaculate Mother, who has done these great things for us." She constantly impressed on her children that in the foundation and growth of the Congregation, every grace, from first to last, had been received through the intercession of Mary. In 1862, when the cloisters of St Dominic's Convent were finally completed, she had a solemn procession of Our Lady round them, as an act of thanksgiving to her for all she had done. Her words on this occasion have been preserved, and were as follows :—

" It is, of course, fit that we should open the new cloister by a procession in honour of Our Lady, as it is her gift. I cannot attempt to put into words what I feel about the Blessed Virgin on this Feast of her Immaculate Conception : it would be impossible. It is hardly credible to look back and see what has been done since this day seventeen years by one poor woman, without a name, without a family, without a sixpence, without a penny, with no help, no friend, except God and His Blessed Mother. As to this Convent, she has laid it stone upon stone. Therefore, not for one or for two, but for all of you, to-morrow ought to be one continued act of thanksgiving for the favours obtained through our dear Blessed Lady. And what Our Lady desires of you is, that you should all be in your measure, *Marys.*"

It was her invariable custom to keep all the Feasts of Our Lady by what she called "giving her a present." Sometimes it was a new vestment, or other church ornament, sometimes an orphan received gratis. In speaking of Our Lady, all the childlike simplicity of her nature came out without restraint. She would call her the most endearing names, and say how much she would like to dance before her. "I hope I shall be saved," she said one day; "I think the Blessed Virgin will not let me be lost, it would be very unkind of her if she did. I made a bargain with her that I would work for her, and she was to take care of my soul; so I go on and do what I have to do, and leave my soul to her."

It is not to be told what pain she endured when any of the ordinary phraseology of Protestant disrespect to the Mother of God reached her ears. Every one will remember the delirium of Protestant bigotry . which broke out all over England on the appointment of the Catholic hierarchy. No Catholic could at that time drive through London without having his eyes and ears shocked by some blasphemous inscription or disgraceful cry. Cars containing effigies of the Pope, the Cardinal, and the great enemy of souls were

L

paraded through the metropolis as in the days of Shaftesbury, and the effigies were afterwards committed all together to the flames. In the city of Exeter, the emblem of our Redemption itself was added to the bonfire which was lighted before the gates of the Bishop's palace. But it was reserved for the Protestants of Bristol to conceive the idea of a yet more horrible exhibition. The proposal was made to dress up an effigy of the Blessed Virgin *and flog it* through the streets of the city. It is indeed difficult to imagine how a thought so utterly revolting could have suggested itself to any, even nominally, Christian mind, were it not evident that these outbreaks of popular fury often bear the signs of an infernal inspiration. But when the tidings of what was contemplated reached Mother Margaret, it nearly killed her. She wrung her hands as in agony, and turning her face to the wall, exclaimed repeatedly, "I shall die, I shall die; O my Mother, I shall die!" In a letter written at the time she expresses her anguish, and adds, "I must go out and rescue her, I fear I shall not be able to restrain myself." And she urged some of the Catholic gentlemen to take the law into their own hands, and "to go out and fight for the Blessed Virgin," wondering how any could be so tame-spirited as to keep at home. Happily, however, the outrage was never perpetrated, and England was at least spared so black a disgrace. And indeed the malicious designs of the rioters were in other respects also frustrated in a remarkable way. A mob gathered near the convent one day, and were venting their ill-will in cries and abuse, when a gentleman stepped out of the crowd and proposed to them to pull it down, offering £30 to any one who would begin the work. But instead of increasing their excitement, his words had the effect of allaying it, and not so much as a stone was thrown at the windows.

Her devotion, *par excellence*, was the Rosary. She loved it as a true Dominican should, considering it the most powerful of all prayers with God, and the most acceptable of all offerings to His Holy Mother. What has not the Rosary obtained for her and her children? It has been that prevailing prayer to which recourse has been had in all necessities and in all trials, and never without result. The Fifteen Mysteries, recited daily and processionally for fifteen successive days, this has been the instrument for effecting all which the world has been pleased to call wonders. People who knew the humble origin of the Community, and the comparatively short space of time which it has taken to expand to its present dimensions, would sometimes come to Stone, and express their surprise at all that Mother Margaret had done, and ask *how* she had contrived to do it; and she might have replied by pointing to her Rosary. One such visitor, a bishop, after going over the church and convent, said to her, "Mother Margaret, what a wonderful woman you are; you must have a mine of gold down there," pointing to the ground. "Oh no, my Lord! nothing down there," she replied, "but I have plenty *up there!*" pointing towards heaven. "Our Blessed Lady is my gold mine; it all comes from her."

During her visit to Belgium in 1856, a magnificent carved oak statue of Our Lady of Victories, exhibited in the town hall of Bruges, attracted her admiration, and, to use her own expression, she "invited her to Stone," though well aware that the cost of such a work of art was far beyond her means. Some years afterwards, however, this statue was brought to England, and, through the munificence of a generous benefactor, was presented to the Community. Mother Margaret's delight was absolutely child-like; Our Lady had accepted her invitation; and when the difficulty of locating so large a piece of carving in the church of Stone caused some to suggest its removal to Stoke, she answered decidedly, "No, on no account; it was to Stone I invited her, and to Stone she has come." As it was found impossible to find a place for the image in the church, she began to pray, "that she might know where Our Lady would like to go." She wished much to build a chapel for the purpose, and went about repeating to herself, "Wisdom hath built herself a house, she hath hewn out seven pillars." At last St Anne's Chapel, in the garden, was assigned as the temporary resting-place of Our Lady of Victories, until such time as the contemplated sanctuary could be reared. The designs for this sanctuary, as they existed in her imagination, were superb indeed. All was to be marble: there was to be a "Gothic dome" rising over the canopy; the sanctuary was to be on the top of a mountain overlooking the whole of Staffordshire, and fifteen little chapels of the Rosary Mysteries were to be on the sides of the mountain. All England was to come there in pilgrimage; it would be a great act of reparation for all the insults offered to the Mother of God. Such were the bright day-dreams she loved to paint in hours of recreation, nor was she easily damped by the question of possibilities. "We have not got a mountain," observed one of her hearers, but she instantly silenced that difficulty, and replied, as though surprised at the objector's want of conception, " Well, child, *I suppose we can make one !* "

The thought of this cherished plan never left her mind, and in a letter written on the Feast of the Assumption, 1864, she says, " I hope before many years are over we shall see the pilgrimage to Our Lady of Stone opened on this glorious festival. I can think of little else but this building, and seeing numbers come to honour Our Divine Mother." The nearest approach to a fulfilment of this day-dream was on an occasion linked with the sad memory of her own mortal illness. During the whole summer of 1867 her evidently declining health had caused the Religious in all her convents to offer unceasing prayers for her recovery, and their solicitude was shared by the children under their care. On the 16th of October 1867, the children belonging to the middle school of **Stoke** proposed making a pilgrimage on foot to Our Lady of Victories for the recovery of Mother Margaret's health. The proceedings of the day are best described in Mother Margaret's own words : " To-day," she writes, " a *real pilgrimage* began to our Lady of Victories. The children of the pension school at Stoke, some of our own Religious, and some others, thirty in all, walked all the way from Stoke, saying the Rosary aloud, and singing the hymns of Our Lady. Our orphan boys went about three miles to meet them, and some of the Religious from here. No one made any remark, but carriages and horsemen stopped to look at them. They said the whole Rosary four times over, and no one spoke a word. Each child brought a good-sized candle in her hand all the way to offer to Our Lady. I am sure our dear Blessed Mother must be pleased *to have nine miles of prayer.* It was all offered that I might get well. I ought to be grateful for this. So you see our pilgrimages have begun : may our dear Lord bless them for the sanctification of the people ! "

This, however, was the first and last of the Stone pilgrimages, such demonstrations, in the existing state of public feeling, being judged by Superiors indiscreet.

CHAPTER X.

COMMUNITY LIFE.

FROM the subject of Mother Margaret's faith and devotion, we pass to speak of her daily life within her own Community. One of its main features will have become sufficiently apparent by what has been already said. It was from first to last a life of incessant *work.* Making every allowance for her strength of organisation and ardour of temperament, it must still be confessed that the burdens she imposed on her suffering body were such as nature alone could never have found the courage to bear. Rarely, if ever, did she permit herself a single dispensation, and, unless laid low by such an attack of positive sickness as could not be disguised, she continued to assist at every Community exercise, and to discharge even the least ceremony of the choir with an exactitude that often cost her dear.

She was always the first to rise in the morning, and the first to appear in choir. For some years she always called the rest of the Community, and when at last she consented to resign this office, she continued to show the same alacrity in hastening to the presence of our Lord. After the Divine Office was substituted for the Office of Our Lady, Mother Margaret continued daily to recite Our Lady's Office as well, choosing this morning hour for the purpose, and rising earlier in order to secure herself the necessary time.

Her example in choir was one of the most precious lessons she has left to her children. The Divine Office was, as she often said, her refreshment and her delight, and no one could behold her discharging the choral duties without feeling that it was so. However weary or suffering she might be, she seldom absented herself from choir. Her voice, so rich and full of volume, was always heard in the psalmody, clear and distinct above every other; and her manner of reading the morning and evening meditations was such as positively to rivet the ear. She read slowly and expressively, with a majestic simplicity which gave its full force to every word, while it was as far as possible removed from what is commonly called *fine reading*. She contrived to infuse a new meaning into the most ordinary and familiar words, and in fact it was in her method of rendering these that her extraordinary power as a reader chiefly appeared. This gift of hers was the more remarkable, as it did not show itself if she undertook to read any ordinary book aloud; and of this she was herself perfectly aware, often saying that "she only knew how to read her prayers."

She was devoured by a thirst to see all her children

saints, and whether she addressed them by letter or by word of mouth, this was the ever-recurring theme on which she spoke. "The only way for us to go to heaven," she would say, "is to be saints, and very great saints." When St Dominic's Convent was being completed, she made some allusion to the subject in one of her chapter addresses, and concluded by saying, "And now, if this house is not going to be a nursery of saints, I would like nothing better than to light a match and burn it to the ground. . . . If I had the choice given me, I would rather bury you all to-morrow than know you would live on without any attempt to become Saints."

It need hardly be said that her ardour often found expression in strong and burning words, and in one of her letters she asks the pardon of her children for any harshness of expression which might at times have escaped her through excess of zeal. "Eagerness for your perfection," she says, "and a great desire to see you perfect imitators of our sainted parents, may often cause me to speak strong things that may give pain ; but with truth I can say, it comes from a heart that loves you all in God and for God, and that would go to any risk to save and perfect your precious souls."

There were many to whom this language was equally familiar in their private intercourse with her. One of her children relates the following touching incident: "Having once incurred our Mother's displeasure," she says, "she had for some time used towards me a severity of manner, which was beginning to make me too much in fear of her. Perceiving this, she came to our cell, and going down on her knees, she begged my pardon, saying, 'My child, forgive me, I have been too severe to you. I thought it would be the best way to guide you, but I see I was wrong;' nor would she rise from her knees till I lifted her up. Then she pressed me to her heart, and said again, 'Forgive me, I was too harsh, but it was all in love.' And as if by way of making it up, for some time after that she used to put small boxes of sugar-plums into our cell, and would say to me, 'Here are some sweets to make up for the bitters.' I cannot express the effect caused on my soul by this act of humility, to see our dearest Mother at my feet; it did more for me than all the penances I ever had. It shed a new light upon my soul, and obtained for me a special grace. And her humility will seem the greater when I add, that I was then only a child of nineteen."

One who knew Mother Margaret well was accustomed to say of her that no one possessed equal power of consolation or desolation. Some who approached her were no doubt more conscious of her desolating than of her consoling power, for not the least remarkable feature in her character was what we must call its *many-sidedness;* its aspect varied according to the various dispositions of those with whom she was brought in contact, or the degree of her own familiarity with them. With all she was not equally at home, and where this was the case, imperfect sympathy would produce a kind of shyness on her part, which manifested itself in restraint of manner. Yet on the whole, her power of attraction largely preponderated, and made itself felt on characters the most opposite, whether by nature or education; converts or native Catholics, young or old, simple and learned, alike were conscious of the charm ; so that it was often said, she was like a "master-key, which opened all hearts alike."

That such a soul as we have attempted to describe, so mighty in its will, so fervid in its passions, should have possessed the charm of a childlike simplicity— that it could be winning in its tenderness and its genial sympathy, and that what was so great could make itself so little—here was the wonder and the grace of Mother Margaret's character. To know her aright, it would not be enough to have listened to her in her graver intercourse with seculars, or even with her own Religious, to have read her letters, or have studied her works of active benevolence : you must also have known her in those hours of familiar relaxation, when, sitting in the midst of her children, she threw off the pressing anxieties of her many cares, and was exclusively the Mother. Her notion of recreation was, that it should be real recreation. Gossip of all kinds she rigidly excluded, whether it were worldly or Community gossip ; the families of the Religious were never spoken of ; she disliked the affairs of the schools, the hospital, or the poor, to be made a subject of conversation ; and, in particular, she would never permit the faults and tiresome ways of children or patients to be idly tattled over. She desired that all things should be to edification ; but, provided that the bounds of religious modesty were never overpassed, she had no objection to innocent merriment. She knew that minds engaged all day in the labour of teaching, or in other active cares, require at times to be wisely unbent, and she often urged on her children the duty of exerting themselves to make the hour of recreation agreeable and profitable to their Sisters. She liked some instructive book to be read aloud during a portion of the time, and never was there a better listener than herself. She listened with her whole person. If the book were of graver interest, the deeper chords of her spiritual nature were ever responsive to the slightest breath, and it needed but a word, or the name of Almighty God, to elicit that sigh and that upward glance, which showed how true her soul was to its centre. The "Life of Père Lacordaire" was almost the last book read in this way during the recreation-hours, and every one will remember how she hung upon its pages, how word by word seemed to pierce her very soul, and how her tears flowed over that touching narrative of his last hours—too soon, alas! to be brought back to the minds of her children as they watched her own.

She was quite as good a listener to a story as to a book, and at recreation-hours often called on one or other to exert their skill for the general amusement. If the story were pathetic, it readily drew her tears, while, if it touched on the horrible, her extreme tenderness could not endure to listen, and she would put her hands to her ears, saying, " If it is going to be dreadful, don't tell me ; I shall not sleep all night." Her simplicity displayed itself on these occasions in a thousand ways. One of her Religious, for the sake of giving her a few moments of distraction from weightier thoughts, once produced " Jules Gerard, the Lion-Killer," and entreated her to listen to the killing of his first lion. She listened with more than her usual interest, and at the critical moment of the sportsman's danger, forgetting that he had lived to tell the tale, repeated, in a tone of breathless anxiety, "The lion won't eat him, will he?" When at last the lion was killed, every one laughed at her sigh of relief, and exclamation of "God be praised!"

She was too true a Catholic to be insensible to the instinct of loyalty, and among her other characteristics must be noted the peculiar affection and respect which she always bore to the person of the Sovereign. She possessed that genuine sense of loyalty which is, or ought to be, native in a Catholic heart, and often expressed her dislike of the tone which a certain section of the Catholic press of these countries allows itself on this subject. A flippant remark about royalty having once been made in her presence, she severely rebuked the speaker, who was a convert, saying, "You converts will never learn reverence ; you do not know what a real Catholic feels for those in authority."

She could never bear certain forms of expression to be used, which, common as they are on English lips, grate discordantly on Catholic ears, and convey the idea of murmuring against Providence. If any one complained of the weather as too hot or too cold, too wet or too dry, it displeased her, and she always took care to remind them that "it was God Almighty's weather, though not perhaps His very best." Lamentations over temporal losses were equally repugnant to her deeply Christian sense. Some mischievous boys once took it into their heads to set fire to the convent hay-rick ; it was somewhat mortifying to see it smoking away in the meadows across the canal, and was one of those small events of domestic interest which are apt to furnish forth more than their due amount of notice. But the least approach to a grumble at such a casualty, inspired Mother Margaret with a kind of horror, and she silenced it with one of her strongest reprehensions.

The gleeful simplicity of her nature was manifested in her love of children, and even in her tenderness towards the brute creation. Children and young people were always at home with her; she had been used to them from her early years, and perfectly understood how to win their confidence. Nor, as we have hinted, could she exclude from her capacious heart even the dumb animals. It would be hard to say whether the cats in the convent, or the birds in the garden, most shared her benevolence, and as their interests were liable to clash one with another, she was sometimes perplexed to adjust their rival claims. Under the apple tree, already mentioned, a daily breakfast of crumbs was provided in winter-time for the robins and sparrows, who took full advantage of her hospitality, and gathered there in great numbers. One morning, a Sister entering our Mother's room, found her standing at the open window, looking into her apple-tree, up which the grey cat had just climbed in search of prey. In her zeal to protect the robins, Mother Margaret had seized the first offensive weapon that came to hand, which chanced to be a broom, and had thrown it with no weak arm at the four-footed marauder. Unluckily it failed in its object, missed the cat, and only stuck in the branches, and a little abashed at being thus discovered, our Mother entreated the Sister to find some means for recovering the broom, " or Sister ——," she said, " will be in a sad way when she misses it."

Nothing distressed her so much as the notion of

anything, whether man or beast, not having enough to eat. Hence the lean appearance of the sheep on the Roman Campagna was quite a trouble to her as she journeyed from Civita Vecchia to Rome, and she insisted on throwing them pieces of bread, in spite of the representation of her companion that sheep do not eat bread. The half-starved flocks of turkeys daily driven through the streets of the Eternal City likewise moved her to compassion, and she every morning provided herself with crumbs, and stationing herself at the window, watched for their approach, that she might throw them some provision as they passed.

In her daily intercourse with her religious children, there was the same mixture of strength and simplicity. Those who were most sensible of her maternal tenderness shall describe it in their own words. " The care and thought which she had for each," writes one of her Religious, " was something that could not be told. With all her business, there was nothing too little for her to remember. She knew in the most trivial circumstances what each one would feel, and would be sure to say or do something to put the soul at rest. If any family trial befell any of us, she felt it more than if it were her own ; specially was she distressed if she had to break to any the death of a relative. On our feasts, she always had a picture or some other little present for each one, and if absent, she was sure to write on feast days or anniversaries of our holy profession." Her maternal kindness to her religious children in times of domestic trouble is recorded by many who experienced it in almost the same language. " You would have thought," they write, " that we were the only people in the world she had to think for."

Her singular quickness of perception frequently gave her an insight into the interior of others, which enabled her to read their very thoughts. A young novice confessed that being once engaged in sweeping some matting, she was tempted to murmur at the hard work when our Mother passed by on her way to her room. Her quick glance had probably discerned the feelings expressed on the countenance of the other, for she presently opened her door, and, calling her in, gave her a little picture of the infant Jesus sweeping the house of Nazareth, saying, "Here is something that if you look at will make all your work easy." The same young Religious had received directions to do a particular piece of work, and the thought how she should set about it was occupying her mind in choir, and causing her distractions, when our Mother came up to her as she stood in her stall, and said, "Child, why are you letting that work distract you and keep you from the presence of God?" Another Religious had been changed week after week from one employment to another, till her patience became somewhat tried, and she more than once found herself giving way to the thought that she was being made nothing but a *stop-gap*. Going one morning into our Mother's room, she was saluted by the words, "Well, Sister *Stop-gap*, what a good thing it is to have some *stop-gaps* in the house," and she was obliged to acknowledge how exactly our Mother had read her thoughts. The same Religious was very desirous to go to Holy Communion on a day which was not a general communicating day, but feeling a hesitation about asking permission to do so, she contented herself with praying to her angel that if it were the will of God something might happen to enable her to go. Just as the Mass began, our Mother touched her on the shoulder, and whispered, "You can go to Communion to-day, if you like." And incidents very similar to this are narrated by other Religious.

In a general way the experience of most would probably be, that her manner of guiding others was rather by act than by word. She was not an advocate for very minute and burdensome direction, which might hamper the freedom of the soul, or interfere with the action of God. She contented herself with inculcating a few great principles, such as purity of intention, and the habit of acting for God alone. One of her Religious, after an interview in which she had opened her whole soul to our Mother, expressed her regret that such opportunities of speaking heart to heart were of such rare occurrence. "It would be waste of time;" she replied; "better to speak heart to heart with our Beloved." Most will be able to recall some powerful word of this kind said from time to time, leaving behind its indelible impression : such as that frequent exhortation to "begin with fidelity," and that as constant reminder to "do all for love." "Try and do everything for love," she writes; "speak for love, think of love, work for love, sigh for love ; never seek any other love than that of our Beloved Jesus. Oh, Name of love, may we all have no other love than His ! "

When visiting any of the smaller convents, she seems to have pleased herself by occasionally taking part in the ordinary work of the house, and practising various acts of humiliation, with greater freedom than she could do at Stone. Thus a young Religious was once distressed by her presenting herself as her aid in the refectory; and letters from the other houses frequently allude to similar incidents. No doubt she felt it a recreation to be occasionally released from the far more wearisome duties which devoured her time at Stone. There, her days were divided between the guest-house and her writing-table, and subject to the incessant interruptions of business. Her correspondence was prodigious; nor can we venture on anything like an estimate of its real extent. She overlooked the affairs of her distant houses in their minutest details; and to read her correspondence with the local Superioresses, you would gather the idea that she was personally present in each house, and that she had each member of the Community—we had almost said each article of furniture—distinct in her mind's eye. In addition to the daily intercourse which she kept up with her own religious Sisters, she had to answer the demands of friends, and few persons possessed a wider circle of friends than Mother Margaret. Of course, a very large portion of necessary correspondence was carried on by others, but there were certain letters which Mother Margaret always wrote with her own hand. One day, at a time when much important business was awaiting settlement, the Religious who acted as her confidential secretary observed that the first letters which she despatched were addressed, one to an old woman whom she had known in Belgium, and to whom she wrote offering her a home in the hospital; and the other to a person also in distress, whose sick boy she

M

was going to receive into the Orphanage, free of expense. Having made some remark on her writing these letters with her own hand, when so many others were awaiting reply : "Yes," observed Mother Margaret, "there are plenty more to be written, *but I always like to put the unfortunate first.*"

The thought and attention which she bestowed on what some would consider minor points of detail, would hardly be credited. Every subject connected with the government of her five Communities, and the particular requirements of each Sister, were made the subject of anxious reflection and earnest prayer. She never decided on the least thing, such as the removal of a Religious from one house to another, without recommending it to God. On one occasion, when a change of this sort had been determined on, she exclaimed to her companion, "How I have prayed to know who to send! Truly prayer is my light!" And circumstances often occurred which proved in how marked a way she was guided by God in these apparently indifferent matters.

Mother Margaret's singular influence over others was quite as much manifested in her intercourse with seculars as with her own religious children. Some of those who have been on intimate terms with her described her loss as "something gone out of their life." "She seemed," says one, "to belong especially to each one, and always to make one's interest her peculiar care. I have often thought how wonderful it was how she found time for everybody's needs. I have many times written to her about things purely personal, or relating to friends, or persons in trouble, and almost without exception have received answers with-

in a few days, often by return of post. I used to
wonder how it could be that she could at once enter
into it all, and advise and help as if it were the
only thing in her mind, knowing, as I did, all the
cares and wide interests which claimed her attention."

This last observation finds its echo again and again
in the letters of her secular acquaintance. One who
knew her only by a single visit writes to thank the
friend who introduced them to one another, saying,
"I have so often thought of your words, 'You will
feel at once that you have found a mother who will
take you to her heart;' it was exactly what she
seemed to do, and the kind, loving letters I have from
her will now be most precious to me." "I have no
one now left," says another, "who will take the same
kind interest in me or my children as she did; she
was everything to them, and always advised me what
to do for their interest, body and soul." Words like
these might be quoted to weariness; and it is not too
much to say that her relations with those outside her
own Community made her loss as much felt in the
world as within the walls of her own convents.
"Who shall tell the number of persons in the world,"
says Bishop Ullathorne, "whose minds or whose
course of life have been happily settled by her wise
and judicious counsels?—gentlemen as well as ladies,
priests as well as seculars, rich as well as poor. And
how many of them have been able to trace some turn
in the tide of their life to her searching or encouraging words! Not that she sought them, but they
sought her, and could not resist giving her their confidence. And when once a person had given their con-

fidence to her, she never lost sight of them or forgot
to pray for their necessities."

These remarks apply equally to persons of all
classes who were wont to consult Mother Margaret,
not only on spiritual matters, but on their personal
and domestic affairs, applying to her as to a real
mother in all their troubles and concerns. Her compassion for poor tradesmen was very great, and she
would never allow them to wait for their money. She
once gave a considerable order to a carpenter who had
recently set up in business, expressly to help him
through his first difficulties. He himself, after her
death, related that, being sent for to the convent one
day, he feared he was going to be dismissed, as he
knew he had been dilatory over the work. To his
great surprise, Mother Margaret said to him, "I know,
B——, you must be short of money, and the wood
will be an expense to you ; so I will advance you part
of the price at once." He was so overwhelmed he
hardly knew what to say. This timely assistance
enabled him to buy his materials and finish the work
quickly, and with greater advantage to himself. But
it was the *kindness* of the act which especially struck
him. "I felt that she thought of me and cared for
me," he said, "and that is what no one else ever did."

There remains for us to notice one feature in
Mother Margaret's life and character which stands
apart from all the rest, and by which the world best
knew her, though to the world it was never more
than partially revealed—we mean, of course, her
spirit of active charity. It sprang from the same
source as her munificence towards God, from that instinct of liberality, namely, which manifested itself in

her early days of poverty and dependence, no less than when she had the alms of a Community at her disposal.

With her, generosity almost seemed at times to be the indulgence of a natural instinct. " What a pleasure it is to *give !* " she would say. " I fear I shall have no merit in it; how can people help giving ? " But more than this, the passages we have quoted exactly depict the character of her liberality. She habitually regarded all things as God's, and as such to be returned to Him again, either directly, in the service of His sanctuary, or indirectly, in the person of His poor. She never looked on what she disposed of as her own, but dealt with it as with something which the Master of the household had placed in her hands, simply to be dispensed in His service. She often used to say that money was the very least of God's gifts, and invariably acted on the principle that, as a matter of course, He would provide what was to be spent for His glory. It cannot be denied that some of her principles of conduct on this point were amongst those things which are more to be admired than imitated, and belonged to the romance of disinterestedness. Superiors often found it difficult to enforce the most obvious rules of prudence, for when the community was in actual want, she would often give away the money received in alms to others less necessitous, perhaps, than herself. She felt a bashfulness in receiving pensions for her orphans. " If I could," she would say, " I would keep all the poor children for nothing, and never ask one penny for them: it is such a pleasure to give to Almighty God." She often took in entire families of orphans, both boys and girls, free of charge, and her character in this matter was so well known, that applications were continually being made to her to receive cases, which the applicants would hardly have ventured to present in other quarters. "Send them to Mother Margaret," said one gentleman, speaking of some such perplexing case of charity; "she is the refuge of the destitute." In the same way she felt a reluctance to receive payment for any kind of work done in the convent, if it were for the Church. When remonstrated with on one occasion for having offered to make a vestment for £30, and then causing it to be so elaborately embroidered as to be worth more than double the sum, she replied, "I can't help it; I am so ashamed of asking to have money given me. Even when a servant I was just the same. I could not bear doing things for gain, but of course that was pride."

It was her practical experience of the generosity of Almighty God which made her so constantly reiterate the maxim, "Never be stingy with our Lord: He will never be outdone in generosity; He, the Giver of all things, alone is grateful." She so knew and trusted to the liberality of God, that, as we have elsewhere said, her favourite resource when in difficulties was to undertake some fresh work of charity. "She rarely had recourse to begging," writes the Religious who enjoyed her closest confidence; "partly because it was seldom successful, and partly because, as she said, she always seemed to hear a secret reproach from Almighty God, who whispered in her heart, 'Have *I* ever failed you?'"

"I could not trust in man if I tried," she would say, "for this is the way I see it—If God help you, who can hinder Him? and if He will not, who else can ? " On one occasion, a person who had promised a considerable sum to a certain charity, not only refused to pay it, but used the most insulting language. Mother Margaret had always felt an interior conviction that the promised aid would never come, and when the painful scene was over, during the course of which she had herself remained perfectly calm, she sent for the priest to whom the promise had been given, and, stretching out her hand to him, said, " There, Father, is your £200 gone. You will come to my way of thinking, and find out what the promises of creatures are worth." Then addressing her Religious, " Mind," she said, "if ever in time to come you are tempted to count on human help for carrying on a work, you will find *it will all go smash*. It has begun in confidence in God alone, and it must go on so to the end. You will all come to my way of thinking: *In Te, Domine, speravi*."

As has been already said, her favourite charity was towards orphans. Remembering her own early desolation, her heart flowed out towards them with peculiar tenderness : she would never have them dressed in a way to stamp them with pauperism, or allow their food to be weighed out and measured to them, but given according to the appetite and requirements of each. Yet, though she did not wish her orphans to be treated as paupers, she always desired that they should be brought up to labour, and not be unfitted for the position they were to fill in after-life. Her strong practical sense was apparent in all her directions on this head. " Be sure," she writes, " to look to the cleanliness of the place ; to see persons 'speaking fine and looking dirty is something dreadful." And again : " The best education you can give these children is to make them clean, orderly, and industrious." She showed them a mother's tenderness, yet for serious faults she would have them severely corrected. Yet, at the time when she was herself in charge of children, whenever she imposed a punishment on any of them, she made it a rule to perform some penance herself, which might be equivalent. "It is because I was an orphan myself, and ill-treated," she said, " that I always made myself suffer something when obliged to punish a child."

The number of those whom she rescued from destitution and raised to respectability was very considerable, and the records of these charities are not without beauties of their own. Two of the Religious, returning one day from visiting the sick, reported that there was an orphan child in the town without a home, living on the charity of the neighbours, now in one house and now in another, and sometimes sleeping in the street. "And did you know that, and leave the child there ? " said Mother Margaret, with flashing eyes; "go out again, this moment, and bring the child to my room." Her orders were gladly enough obeyed, and we well remember her look as the motherless child was brought to her. She found a home for her in the hospital, where the little orphan was known by the soubriquet of " Polly Providence."

Our limits forbid our adding more on this subject, of saying all that might be said of Mother Margaret's charity to orphans ; but we must add that it was a charity that partly met with its reward in the affection of those on whom it was bestowed. "Oh, what a tender Mother she has been to me, and to hundreds of others!" wrote one who had been reared from infancy under her care, and who heard of her death on board a Queen's ship at Plymouth; and the sorrow and devotion of her orphan boys at Stone was evinced after her funeral in a touching manner. They contrived to purchase some choice flowers, and requested to be allowed to lay them, with their own hands, upon her grave. When the flowers were afterwards removed by the sacristan, a letter was found concealed among them, which, as the genuine expression of children's love to a good Mother, shall be here transcribed :—

"DEAREST AND REVERED MOTHER,—It is almost impossible to express our gratitude to you, but will you accept the flowers we lay upon your grave? though we well know the far better flowers that now form your heavenly wreath. Dear Mother, to the honour of God we will also beg Father A. to offer the Holy Sacrifice of the Mass for you.—Your grateful and loving children,

"THE ORPHAN BOYS."

The foundation of St Mary's Hospital at Stone has already been spoken of; its inmates were always made to know Mother Margaret's sunniest side. She reserved for them her heartiest and most cheering words, and her brightest smiles. If anything arose to try the patience of those in charge, it was hopeless to appeal to her for any help that involved the necessity of a reproof; she never appeared in the wards except as a gleam of sunshine to the inmates. The thought of their comfort and happiness occupied her even at a distance, and in her letters we find her sending them her Christmas gifts, and reminding her Religious "to make the dear invalids happy." From time to time she contrived to give them little feasts and holidays. "We have had two great *fêtes* in the meadows," she writes to a friend, "one for the hospital and one for the schools. The hospital one would have pleased you. They were carried there in the cart, and the tea-boilers went in a wheelbarrow. We were *primitive Christians*, and went to the fields without cloak or bonnet." In the August of the year 1867, only a month or two before she was laid prostrate by her last illness, she took the opportunity of the holidays to give her hospital patients a grand entertainment in the garden of the young ladies' school. In spite of her extreme weakness, and the bodily sufferings which were then gaining fast upon her, she devoted herself to their amusement during the whole afternoon, saying, when it was over, "I am as tired as a dog, but it has been a happy day."

Mother Margaret's benevolence flowed out in other channels besides those we have named. One severe winter she observed a canal boat fast bound up by the frost, and something prompted her to pray earnestly for the poor people who might be there. That night two rough-looking girls presented themselves at the convent, and asked to see the Sisters. They were found totally ignorant of religion, and received instruction. When questioned what had put into their heads the idea of coming to the convent, they replied that they did not know, but "something seemed to draw them. " Some years later a great many boats were frozen up for several weeks, and the people on board were reduced to great distress. Mother Margaret entertained them with her usual liberality. A general invitation was given to all the children of the boats to come to school, with the promise of food and fire for the day ; whilst the elders came in also for their portion, and twice a day were served with it in the convent porch. On this occasion, also, Christian instruction was given for the first time to many who, until then, had been living in a nominally Christian land as simple Pagans. One of the boys so instructed had never heard of our divine Lord, and was filled with astonishment when first he listened to the story of His birth in a stable. He repeated the tale to a younger brother, and complained of his incredulity, saying, "He wadna believe me when I told him !" But when he heard the history of the Passion, and of our Lord's death on the Cross, his feelings broke out in language like that of the royal Clovis under similar circumstances: "If I had been there they should na ha' done it."

In general, however, Mother Margaret preferred supporting the charities which were administered within her own convent to indiscriminate alms-giving out of doors. Indeed, a little address was sometimes required in presenting a case for consideration. Often enough the applicant received a rebuff at first, and had to thaw our Mother's good-will by a course of judicious diplomacy. But on such occasions it was amusing to see the struggle between prudence and compassion, and the gradual steps by which the latter feeling was made at last to triumph. A Religious, who at that time had the charge of some external charities, was interested in two poor persons whom it was desirable to get married, but who were too poor to pay the registrar's fee of five shillings. She took the case to our Mother, and received only a sharp reprimand for meddling with such affairs. With great difficulty she extracted permission to beg the required sum of a charitable friend, and having succeeded in her quest, ventured, on next meeting our Mother, silently to exhibit her two half-crowns. Mother Margaret, however, thought fit to behold them with an air of grave disapprobation, but next morning, sending for the Religious, she addressed her something as follows: " Have you married those people yet? Not till to-morrow? I suppose they have not got a ring? There is one that will do. And has she got a good dress? Nothing but rags, do you say? That is not proper respect to the Sacrament. I have got something up-stairs that will do; you can have it for her. And I suppose they must have their breakfast here. There, off with you, and none of your thanks: and mind, child, you never make up any more matches."

But what was her charity for the temporal relief of her neighbour compared to her zeal for their souls? It consumed her like a fire. " I go up and down the cloisters," she once said, " saying, Lord, what can I do to save souls?" She writes from Walthamstow, " Forget yourselves, my dear Sisters, and think only of God's interests. *Souls, souls, souls*—let that be your one prayer day and night. Prayer alone will do it. Aim at the perfection of your state by prayer, humility, and penance, and God will hear our sighs and give us

what we ask." In comparison with what she longed
to do for this great end, all that she had effected seemed
in her eyes as nothing. " Whenever I enter the choir,"
she said, " it seems to me as if our Lord reproaches
me for having done nothing yet."

And another time she expressed her wish that she
could turn all her Religious into Friars Preachers, and
send them through the world like so many St Vincent
Ferrers. Strong expressions of this sort sometimes
led to the very false impression that she sought to
usurp the functions of the priesthood, and that she
imagined the active work of her Communities could
supply for the want of priestly ministrations. But
in point of fact, lofty as were her desires, she sought
to carry them out by the very humblest means. If
from time to time she reminded her Religious that
" they were called to the apostolate as far as any
women could be," she never failed to let them know
that the only scene of their apostolic labours lay in
the hospital or the poor school. Some kinds of active
work she deliberately refused to undertake, such as
the charge of reformatories, believing that the vocation
of her children was rather to preserve the innocent
than to rescue the fallen. And she declined taking
part in several other undertakings which, had publicity
and a great name been her object, would certainly
have offered better opportunities for attaining it than
the very unpretending labours in which she preferred
that her children should be engaged.

It was one of Mother Margaret's principles to
secure *first* the objects of her charity, whether children or sick people, and place them where she
could, leaving it to time to provide suitable accommo-

dation. The consequence of this was, that the beginnings of all her charitable institutions have been rough in the extreme, and a most admirable exercise of the virtue of *longanimity* to all concerned. Moreover, her ardent desire to gather under her wing all who were in need, made her over-estimate the stretching capacity even of her *gutta percha* walls; perhaps, even to the detriment of health. But, notwithstanding many trials, there were also great advantages in getting a certain small number trained under difficult circumstances, who were able to give a tone to the after-comers before the institution attained any size; and, in the only instances when she acted otherwise, and made her preparations beforehand, she always remarked that the institutions did not thrive like those that had begun in a garret or a cellar.

She was ingenious in her plans for adapting such offices to new and unheard-of purposes; and when she had located her Religious in these premises, she expected them to do their work there cheerfully until such time as Providence should send them something better. Many of her letters are addressed to those engaged in the very arduous duties of the kitchen. "Have courage," she writes; "and when you are hot and weary, offer it all for the suffering souls in purgatory, or to save some soul ready to perish in mortal sin." And again: "Remember our dear Lord is with you in the kitchen as well as in the choir. He sees and blesses all. Have courage and patience— that is the necessary thing for a cook. Our seraphic Mother St Catherine will help you. She was cook and maid-of-all-work to her family. You are somewhat higher; you are cook to the spouses of Jesus Christ!" And never did she omit to remind those whom she addressed, that no amount of anxiety or hard work, or intercourse with seculars, was ever to be suffered to efface the religious character, either interiorly or exteriorly. "When conversing with seculars," she writes to one much engaged with the external world, "never forget that you are a spouse of Jesus, and that you are to kindle the holy fire of love in the souls of all with whom you converse; with your eyes, your ears, and your tongue : for remember that the eye of God is never for one moment from you."

What has been said will perhaps suffice to give some idea of Mother Margaret's spirit of universal benevolence, and the principles on which she carried out her works of active charity. She often quoted Olier's words, "If God loves you He will humble you, and while he raises the work He will abase the workman." Her charitable institutions had no pretension about them to be greater or better than those or others. Often enough the want of means and other providential circumstances hindered her from bringing them to completion in her own lifetime, and she could but bequeath to her children the rough outline of her greatest designs. But the outline, however rough, was sketched by the hand of a master; may all those on whom the duty falls of finishing and perfecting it preserve unmarred its noblest features, and hand on to future generations the principles which Mother Margaret left stamped upon all her works— generosity to God and man, self-sacrifice and self-annihilation, the absence of all human views and interests, and the simple and single purpose to accomplish all things for God and for *God alone !*

* * *

CHAPTER XI.

VISIT TO ROME.

WE must now return to the thread of our history, passing over a year or two during which the annals of the Community present few incidents of general interest. Year by year it grew and developed, but its very development rendered it more and more imperative to provide for the future security of an edifice which was rapidly assuming proportions unlooked for in the days of its first foundation. The Papal Rescript obtained in 1851 had not proved sufficiently explicit as to the degree of exemption thereby granted to the Religious from the jurisdiction of the Ordinary, and questions had arisen in the diocese of Clifton which manifested the necessity that the powers of the Ecclesiastical Superior should be more exactly defined. Moreover, as the number of convents increased, it became desirable that their union as a Congregation, under one general Superioress, should receive some more authoritative sanction. It was therefore at length decided, by advice of Bishop Ullathorne, and with the approval of the Master-General, that Mother Margaret should herself proceed to Rome, in order that the whole *status* of the Congregation might be laid before the proper authorities, and a definitive decree obtained for the settlement of its future government.

This important step was finally determined on in the autumn of the year 1858, and on the 14th of October Mother Margaret left Stone, in company with one Religious, and under the escort of the Rev. J. S. Northcote. On the 21st of the same month they arrived in Rome, where their first night was spent at the Hotel of the Minerva, close to the great Dominican Church of Santa Maria *sopra Minerva*, which they visited the following morning ; and Mother Margaret's spirits, which had been before at a very low ebb, quickly revived after she had heard Mass at the tomb of our Holy Mother St Catherine.

By the kind exertions of Monsignor Talbot, the three travellers were able to take up their residence in the Palazzo Antonelli, part of which belonged to an English lady, who resided there with her chaplain, and who generously placed three apartments at their disposal.

The Most Rev. Master-General was still absent in Naples, and the first Dominican Father who visited our travellers was Père Hyacinth Besson, who had formerly been for several years prior of Sta. Sabina, the French Novitiate House, but was now engaged in painting the restored Chapter House of San Sisto.

Monsignor Talbot having made an appointment to meet Mother Margaret and her companion at the Vatican, they proceeded thither a day or two after their establishment in the Palazzo Antonelli, and after having transacted their business, they paid their first visit to St Peter's, the glory and magnificence of which more than equalled Mother Margaret's anticipations. The following day an English friend drove them to the Basilica of St Paul's, then fast approach-

N

ing completion. The vast size of these buildings, and their costly materials, seemed to give Mother Margaret's soul breathing space, and yet her general impression was one of disappointment. Her first letter to her children in England paints her feelings in a characteristic manner :—

" MY VERY DEAR CHILDREN,—It seems seven years since I left Stone, and nothing makes up to me for our happy convent home. I know it is a great grace and favour to be where the blood of so many martyrs has been shed, and so many saints have lived and died, and where their bodies repose ; still all this does not awaken in me the one only happy thought I have in our convent home—*Our God with us.* Could I make our churches as beautiful as they are in this Holy City I would gladly do it, to honour our Hidden God, and to increase the love, faith, and devotion of the people ; as it is, we must do our best. I am disappointed ; I expected more than I find here, in many ways. Had I never been out of England, it would have struck me more ; but I certainly like Belgium much better. Cleanliness and holiness do not go together here. Pray much for our affairs to be forwarded. I long to see you all again. I beg God to bless and love you at every holy place I go to, and I ask the saints whose shrines I visit to pray for you all."

The petition of the Congregation, which had been prepared in England, was presented to the Prefect of Propaganda, by the Rev. Mr Northcote, on the 26th of October. His Eminence received it kindly, and gave every hope of a favourable issue; but he explained that the course which the affair would have to go through would necessarily be tedious. Two days later, by appointment of his Eminence, Mother Margaret and her companion had an interview with him at the Propaganda, and were most kindly and graciously received. After this the necessary business was put in hand; and, pending its completion, and the return of the General from Naples, the travellers occupied themselves in visiting the various holy places of Rome, especially those most interesting to the children of St Dominic and St Catherine. Through the kindness of Padre Sallua, they were admitted within the enclosure of the two convents of Dominican Nuns, those, namely, of San Domenico e Sisto, and of Santa Caterina da Siena. In this latter convent they spent the Feast of All Saints of the Order, and were received with most sisterly affection and hospitality. An equally hospitable reception was given them by the Community of San Domenico e Sisto, where they had the happiness of venerating the hand of St Catherine, and the other precious relics which are there so carefully preserved; and were presented with a Vesperal and Processional—rare treasures in those days, before the late reprint of the choral books of the Order.

Another letter describes their visits to the churches of San Sisto and Santa Sabina, the scenes of so many incidents in the life of our Holy Father. The Padre Sindico of Santa Sabina showed great interest in the two English Religious, and regarded their appearance as a sort of miracle. Taking them to a spot whence they could look into the enclosure and behold the famous orange-tree planted by St Dominic, he pointed to its new young shoot, which he was pleased to interpret as a symbol of the English Dominicanesses.

Two visits to the Catacombs of Sta. Agnese and San Callisto were among the incidents of their pilgrimage, of which Mother Margaret cherished the most devout remembrance. She visited the latter on the Feast of St Cecilia, whose body formerly reposed there ; a grand subterranean *festa* being celebrated at her tomb. Another day the letters record a visit to the *Scala Santa*, which the two pilgrims ascended on their knees, for Mother Margaret would not be deterred from accomplishing this act of devotion, although the effort was exceedingly distressing to her ; large callosities having formed on her knees, which rendered the act of kneeling at all times most painful. Her greatest treat, however, consisted in her long visits to St Peter's. She liked to go there when all was quiet, and spend the morning, saying her prayers, and walking about that noble Basilica, the vastness of which so well corresponded to the greatness of her conceptions. On the Feast of the Dedication they attended the High Mass, and venerated the great relics exposed on that day, and the sight of the great golden candelabra " made our Mother quite happy." They were also able to visit the subterranean crypt, hearing Mass and communicating near the tomb of St Peter. " The oftener we go to St Peter's," they write, " the better we love it, and we promise ourselves some more quiet hours there before we leave, for there is nothing to compare with it." But the great event of the month of November was their audience with his Holiness, Pius IX., who received

them with his usual benevolence—Mother Margaret's
heart overflowing with joy as she bent to kiss the
foot of "the Christ on earth." For what other words
could rise to the lips of a daughter of St Catherine,
as for the first time she paid her homage to the Vicar
of our Lord? The interview was of course short and
ceremonious, but on taking leave Mother Margaret
begged for a blessing for her whole Community, which
his Holiness gave with all his heart, pronouncing the
words, "*Benedictio Dei Omnipotentis, Patris, et Filii, et
Spiritus Sancti, descendat super te, et super omnes
sorores tuas,*" in that deep, sonorous voice, which rests
so ineffaceably in the memory of all who have ever
heard it.

The memorial, or petition of the Congregation, had
meanwhile been drawn up, and through the kind
assistance of Father Mullooly, the Prior of the Irish
Convent of San Clemente, translated into Italian.
But before any answer could be given to this memorial
by Propaganda, it had to be transmitted to England,
and the opinion of all the English bishops taken regarding it. This of course involved a considerable
delay, and, moreover, great doubts were entertained
as to the final result ; for the main object of the
memorial was to petition the Holy See that the houses
of the Congregation should be placed in perpetuity
under the government of the Order, and not under
that of the Ordinary, and it was well known that this
kind of exemption was rarely to be obtained. Mother
Margaret, however, did not allow herself to be discouraged. Even when letters arrived from friends in
England, who seemed to regard the whole business as
a failure, her confidence never gave way. " I have no

human motive in this wish," she writes. "I know it
will bring its difficulties and its crosses, but this must
not make me unfaithful to the Order to which God
has deigned to call me, and to the strong impression
that has ever urged me to aim at this. Everything
has gone so contrary to what I expected, and I feel
so sure that Rome will do as it thinks best, that I find
the only peace for my soul is to be abandoned to God,
and pray and force my will to be ready for all that
God wills. All I can do is to pray and trust in God,
and our Divine Mother Mary, that, as all hitherto has
been done by His Almighty hand, He will not fail to
bring it as He wills. . . . I cannot reason on the
subject ; few here would understand me, and when
asked what I want, I only say, 'Not to be separated
from my Order, and to be a Congregation.'" Prayer,
as usual, was her one resource, and on the 10th of
November she began a Novena to our holy Mother
St Catherine, every day visiting her tomb at the
Minerva, and commending to her intercession the
issue of the whole affair.

Her faith and patience, however, had both to be
tried. Week after week passed by, and no answer
was received from England ; and the Feast of the
Immaculate Conception found them still in Rome,
with no present prospect of return. A ray of hope
presented itself just before Christmas, when letters
from England were received by Mgr. Talbot, which
appeared to promise a favourable answer. This
circumstance was not of much value in itself, but
Mother Margaret felt so thankful for it, that to express
her gratitude, she immediately sent out and hired
two *Pifferari*, to pipe a Novena of thanks before

the picture of the Madonna at the corner of the
street.

On Christmas Eve the two pilgrims obtained
admittance into a little tribune over the choir of St
Peter's, and assisted, from their retired seats, at the
Matins and Midnight Mass. The exact ceremonies of
the choir, the exquisite pastoral music, and the sight
of the little Seminarists—the *Pietrini*, as they are
called—communicating at the Midnight Mass, filled
them with devotion and delight. They assisted at
the grand function of the Papal Mass in the ladies
tribune, wearing the Belgian hooded cloak over their
religious habit, three Sisters of Charity being seated
near them. The emotion which Mother Margaret
felt in beholding Almighty God served with so magnificent a worship,—in seeing, as she said, "the
greatest man of the earth say Mass,"—was so powerful
and absorbing that at the time she was wholly
unconscious of fatigue. It was to her the supreme
moment of her life, and one to which she often afterwards referred. "I am afraid of saying what I felt
about the Pope," she once remarked, "lest I should
scandalise people. I wanted to kneel there and look
at him for hours. There was all that was most grand
and powerful on earth—the man before whom kings
were as nothing! And when I heard him sing Mass I
cannot express what I felt; *it was the god of the earth
prostrate in adoration before the God of heaven.*" She
wrote to the same effect a few days after Christmas:
"I could not put into words what I felt on Christmas
Day. It was like one long spiritual dream. We were
in St Peter's almost eleven hours. I really was
there and nowhere else, and I took all I loved in

England in there with me ; and what with making intentions, and trying to offer you all with the Pope's offering, I exhausted nature too much, and that I think has made me ill ever since. I cannot see the Pope without emotion. He seems so truly to represent God upon earth." In fact her health was sensibly affected, and during the whole of January she continued seriously ill.

By the beginning of February Mother Margaret was sufficiently recovered to be able to accompany some English friends on a visit to a little Community of Dominican Tertiaries established at Morlupo, a little village about three hours' drive from Rome. Mother Margaret was greatly interested in her visit to this Community. Everything she saw reminded her of her own beginnings at Coventry. The Community at that time reckoned but four members, very poorly lodged and provided for ; but in spite of their small numbers, engaged in all the active works of charity, and conducting a day-school of one hundred children.

The following week they accompanied the same friends to the Dominican Convent of the Second Order at Marino, in order to be present at a clothing of four of the Religious ; the ceremony being performed by the Master-General himself.

After the function was over Mother Margaret and her companion were summoned to the refectory, and afterwards joined the Community in their work-room, receiving from them the same kind and fraternal welcome that had been given in all the other convents of the Order. In spite of the long fatiguing day, Mother Margaret declared it had done her good rather than harm ; and, on returning home, her spirits were further

raised by the intelligence that a letter from his Eminence Cardinal Wiseman, relative to the affairs of the
Congregation, had at last been received at Propaganda. They began to see the end. The letter, containing the replies of the English bishops, proposed
certain conditions under which the petition of the
Congregation might be granted. These conditions
would have to be taken into consideration before
submitting the petition to the decision of his Holiness ;
and as all this implied the necessity of negotiation
between the authorities of the Order and Propaganda,
and possibly further reference to England, it was
decided that the two Religious should proceed home
without further delay, and that Mr Northcote, after
escorting them back, should return to Rome to act as
procurator of their cause. Preparations for their departure were therefore at once begun.

Before taking leave of the Eternal City they were
desirous, if possible, of obtaining the favour of another
interview with the Holy Father, in order to receive
his parting blessing. Having been so lately presented,
a formal audience could not be procured ; but Mgr.
Talbot arranged that they should take their places in
a hall of the Vatican through which his Holiness had
to pass. On his appearance, the two Religious presented themselves for his blessing ; and his Holiness,
who was acquainted with the object of their journey
to Rome, addressed them some remarks on the subject,
which did not sound encouraging as to its likelihood
of success. As he spoke in Italian, Mother Margaret
was entirely ignorant of the tenor of his words, and
knelt, gazing with a smile of delight on the countenance of the Holy Father, unconscious of the misgiv-

ings which were making themselves felt in the hearts of her companions. When they had descended the Scala Regia, and once more found themselves seated in their carriage, Mother Margaret had to hear their report of what had passed, and the doubts which it had suggested; but nothing was capable of shaking her composure. " I don't see it as you do," she said ; "you will see it will be granted all the same."

They left Rome for Civita Vecchia on the 16th of February.

Mother Margaret's impressions of Rome were of a mixed character. With its externals, as we have seen, she was disappointed. Her taste had been formed in another school, and she could not divest herself of preconceived ideas sufficiently to estimate at its full worth a form of beauty so totally at variance with them. But if material Rome only partially won her heart, so that she repeated again and again, that "she was in love with nothing but the Pope and St Peter's," there was another sense in which she rendered it the full tribute of her admiration.

" I have been delighted," she writes, " with seeing the works of the Church, and how sure one is that it is God's Church, and that the Pope and the Cardinals are really God's legislators on earth, and that their one end is God's glory and the soul of man, although we know that in other respects they are but weak, frail men. If I could, I love the Church more and more, and our Order also, for it seems here like a part of the Church herself."

It was on the 14th of March that the travellers reached Stone, where they were joyfully welcomed by the united Communities of Stone and Stoke. The

five months of their absence had been a weary and
anxious time to those at home : one Sister, whom
they had left in the last stage of consumption, had
departed to God, and there had been much sickness
and trouble of various kinds ; but all was now forgotten in the happy prospect of reunion.

It had been arranged to give them a solemn reception ; so the carriage which conveyed them from the
station, and which was decorated inside with flowers
and inscriptions of welcome, drew up, not at the convent, but at the church door within the enclosure, in
order that they might pay their visit of thanksgiving
to our Lord before meeting the Community. The
Religious were all assembled in the choir, and intoned
the *Te Deum* as soon as the travellers entered the
church. Both of them declared that they had not
heard any music half so sweet since they left England
as that *Te Deum*, and the Sisters in choir were of
opinion that the angels joined with them in singing
it. When this was concluded, mother and children
met together in the Community-room, and gave free
vent to their joy. Mother Margaret's next visit was
to Our Lady's chapel in the dormitory, which had
been painted and decorated in her absence, and
proved a welcome surprise. She had not forgotten
her favourite image during her absence, but had
obtained from his Holiness, among other privileges,
the grant of three hundred days' indulgence for any
prayers recited before it, under the title of " Refu-
gium Peccatorum."

So soon as he had safely conducted home his
charges, Mr Northcote returned to Rome,—whilst
prayers were offered unceasingly for the success of

the business with which he was charged.   The
result was in every respect favourable to Mother
Margaret's wishes.   On the 26th of May 1859, being
the Feast of St Philip Neri, in a special audience
granted to the Cardinal Prefect of Propaganda for
that purpose, his Holiness gave his assent to the proposed arrangement, and ordered that a decree should
be drawn up, embodying the substance of the petition, and certain conditions which had been agreed
on between the Cardinal Archbishop of Westminster,
on behalf of the English Hierarchy, and the Master-
General of the Dominican Order.   According to the
terms of this decree, the houses of the Religious
founded, or hereafter to be founded in England, are
formed into a Congregation, having one general
Superioress, and one Novitiate house.   They are
placed immediately under the jurisdiction of the
Master-General of the Order, who exercises his
authority through a delegate, nominated by himself,
his Lordship, Bishop Ullathorne, being confirmed in
that office for his life.

The good news was received at Stone on the 4th of
June, being communicated in a letter from Mr Northcote, beginning with the words of happy augury, *Deo
gratias et Mariæ et S. Philippo Nerio!* In thanksgiving for this favour the *Te Deum* was sung on three
successive days in all the convents of the Congregation.   Mr Northcote at once set out on his return to
England ; and on the 11th June, being Whitsun Eve,
he reached Stone, where, on Whit Tuesday, he sang
a solemn High Mass of thanksgiving.

Six months later the Master-General of the Order

forwarded to England the diploma by which Mother Margaret was appointed first Prioress Provincial, such being the title which his Paternity had selected for the Superioress-General of the newly-formed Congregation, which has since received the title of "the Congregation of St Catherine of Sienna."

CHAPTER XII.

LAST FOUNDATIONS.

THE latter years of Mother Margaret's life were occupied by those extensive undertakings at Stone and Stoke which have been spoken of in a previous chapter, as well as by the establishment of new foundations at Leicester, Rhyl, St Mary Church, and Bromley St Leonard's, near Bow. Two of these foundations, those namely of Leicester and Rhyl, were afterwards withdrawn ; and the Community now established at Bow was originally fixed at Walthamstow, in Essex, whence it was removed in the November of 1867.

The arduous business of establishing a new foundation was precisely one of those occasions which brought out some of Mother Margaret's special gifts. Her practical sense, and the genius she possessed for methodical arrangement, were never displayed to greater advantage than when she had to begin a new work in a strange place,—to adapt some secular habitation to the purposes of religious life,—and to set in motion the whole machinery of a Community, to be worked in the first instance by some devoted little band of six or seven members. It was wonderful how few modifications of the ordinary Rule she allowed under these circumstances, and how few were ever required; how she contrived that all the regular exercises of the Community should go on, in spite of every disadvantage, as steadily as at the mother-house; and how happily the difficulties and drawbacks of the situation were wont to call into activity the capabilities and good-will of all concerned.

The choir was always the first thing thought of: the most suitable room in the house was selected for the purpose, and its arrangement was always reserved as Mother Margaret's exclusive share. She contrived to give so devotional a character to these room-chapels that many were found to lament the day when they were exchanged for choirs of greater pretensions. As much care and expense were bestowed on the decoration of the altar, and the correct carrying out of every ceremony, as if the Religious were in possession of a church; nor were their slender numbers ever suffered to be a hindrance to the celebration of the greater feasts with all due solemnity.

The foundation at Leicester was begun in the Lent of the year 1860. A small number of Religious took up their residence in a house occupying the site of part of the old Lancastrian College, called the New-ark. A great field of useful labour seemed open to them among the women and girls employed in the woollen manufactories, and their night-school was soon crowded. Mother Margaret took great interest in this work, and in one of her letters she announces, with a certain amount of glee, that she is once more mistress of a class, and is teaching *b, a, ba,* to some full-grown scholars. Difficulties, however, presented themselves in the way of securing the property at Leicester, and the Community was obliged to be withdrawn in the August of 1861.

Extensive additions to St Dominic's Convent were begun about the same time, the first steps being taken towards commencing the choir by the demolition of "Job's" and the adjacent cottages. The choir and chapter-room, and the sanctuary of the church, were completed early in the year 1863, and on the 4th of February took place the solemn rite of the Consecration. Invitations had been sent to every priest in the diocese, and in addition to the secular priests who were present, fifteen of the Dominican Fathers assisted at the ceremony. On the following day, being the Feast of St Agatha, the church was opened for public worship in the presence of their Lordships, the Bishop of Birmingham, the Bishop of Shrewsbury, and the Bishop of Clifton. It was naturally an occasion of deep and solemn interest to all the Community, but to Mother Margaret herself it was overpowering. What she felt in it all was the goodness of God to His unworthy creatures. "It was no work of mine," she said; "I sat at my desk and wrote my letters and the church rose." And she was heard murmuring to herself words that remind us of some of those on the dying lips of St Catherine : "Not a bit for self; all for the honour and glory of God."

The same year which had witnessed the opening of St Dominic's Church was rendered further memorable in our annals by the visits of some illustrious guests. The Most Rev. Master-General of the Order made his second visitation of the English province in 1863, and on the 11th of July he visited St Dominic's Convent, in company with the Most Rev. F. Louis Gonin, O.S.D., who had just been appointed to the archbishopric of Trinidad. The Father-General spent part of three days at Stone, and expressed himself gratified at the progress of the Community, which, at his previous visit twelve years before, had numbered but twenty-five Religious, occupying the single convent of St Catherine's, Clifton, and had now expanded into a Congregation, with three convents actually established, and two in course of foundation.

On leaving Stone, his Paternity proceeded to Ireland, visiting the convent at Stoke on his way thither, and again on his return passing a day at Stone, which he left on the 1st of August. Between these two visits the Community had likewise the honour of entertaining his Eminence Cardinal Wiseman, an event which must be reckoned among the pleasurable remembrances of this year.

This was the last visit which his Eminence ever paid to any of our convents. A few months later the proposal was communicated in his name to Mother Margaret, that she should make a foundation in London, for the purpose of taking charge of a Refuge for Females discharged from the prisons. The project led to a mature consideration of the question how far work of this nature was compatible with the object and spirit of the Congregation. The result was that Mother Margaret determined on respectfully declining the proposal of his Eminence, and the grounds on which this determination was based were fully confirmed and approved by the judgment of her ecclesiastical superiors.

It was in the October of 1863 that Mother Margaret paid her first visit to Rhyl, in North Wales, where the prospect of establishing a convent had presented itself. She was pleased at the thought of working for Wales, and recalled her dream in Belgium, often repeating that St Winifred had saved her life, and that she was bound to do something to honour her in return.

A house was purchased at Rhyl, in which a small Community was established on the 5th of June 1864. But the hopes that had been entertained of finding an opening there for the labours of the Religious proved fallacious, and they were finally withdrawn in the August of 1866, when the necessity presented itself of providing members for a more important foundation in London. Another foundation, begun in the same year with that at Rhyl, enjoyed a more prosperous destiny. In the spring of 1864, Mother Margaret was invited by the Right Rev. Dr Vaughan, Bishop of Plymouth, to found a house on some part of his diocese, and the village of St Mary Church, near Torquay, was proposed as suitable for the establishment of an Orphanage for Girls.

A house, with some ground adjoining, was purchased at St Mary Church, and six Religious were sent to form the little colony in the month of August, Mother Margaret herself accompanying them.

Since that time a beautiful church and presbytery have been built on the property of the convent, through the munificence of William Chatto, Esq., and the erection of conventual buildings has been commenced by the Community at their own expense. Attached to the convent is an Orphanage for the

o

Catholic orphan girls of the diocese, capable of containing eighty orphans.

One other event of a joyous and festive nature remains to be noticed before entering on the narrative of that closing period of Mother Margaret's life which was so deeply marked with the character of the cross. By a Pontifical decree, dated April 13, 1866, the Holy Father was pleased to declare St Catherine of Sienna Secondary Patroness of the city of Rome. This auspicious event was announced to the Order by the Master-General in a circular, wherein he likewise made known that his Holiness had raised the Feast of St Catherine to a higher dignity, and that it would henceforth be celebrated in the Order with a Solemn Octave. Mother Margaret immediately petitioned the Bishop for leave to celebrate a solemn Triduo of thanksgiving at St Dominic's, and, permission being granted, the Triduo was appointed to take place between the Feast of the Stigmas of St Catherine, which that year fell on Sunday the 17th of June, and the 21st of June, the anniversary of the Pope's coronation. The Triduo (which in reality lasted five days instead of three) was a solemn and splendid festival. An indult had been obtained from his Holiness, granting the same indulgences to those who should attend the devotions as had been attached to the Triduo celebrated at the Church of the Minerva, in Rome. The publication of these indulgences would, it was hoped, induce many to attend, and to profit by this occasion of approaching the Sacraments. Nor was this hope disappointed. Hundreds approached the Sacraments, some of whom had for years neglected their duties ; and it seemed as though St Catherine herself was on earth again, and at her favourite work of converting sinners.

Their Lordships, the Bishops of Birmingham, Shrewsbury, and Clifton, assisted at the services of the week, together with a large number of clergy, both secular and regular. The devotions were opened on Sunday the 17th, by a Pontifical High Mass, sung by the Bishop of Clifton, and in the afternoon, after Vespers, a solemn procession of the relics was made round the garden. Throughout the five days the relics of St Catherine were exposed on a lofty throne, erected in the central aisle, and were likewise offered to the people for veneration every evening after the Benediction. These relics, which are very considerable in quantity, were presented to our Congregation by the Master-General, on occasion of the translation of the body of St Catherine from the Rosary Chapel of the Church of the Minerva to the High Altar of the same church, which took place in 1855; and when the cloister of St Dominic's Convent was completed, a chapel was built for the express purpose of receiving these precious relics, which must ever be regarded as one of the great treasures of the Community.

In addition to the devotions specified above, there were sermons morning and evening, and afternoon catechism for the children—five confessors attending in the confessionals until a late hour every night. On Thursday, the last of the five days' devotion, Pontifical High Mass was sung by the Bishop of the diocese, assisted by the Vicar-General and the cathedral chapter. An additional interest attached to the ceremony, from the fact that it was the twentieth anniversary of his Lordship's episcopacy, and a special Votive Mass was therefore sung. His Lordship preached in the evening on the public life of St Catherine, and the Triduo closed with another procession of unusual splendour.

One circumstance connected with this great solemnity was equally a cause of surprise and of gratitude to Mother Margaret and her Religious children. The desire which Mother Margaret had entertained from the first of establishing in her Community the daily recitation of the Divine Office had increased rather than diminished with time.

Before, however, again urging on superiors her request for this great privilege, she thought it prudent to test the possibility of undertaking so great an obligation in a Community devoted to active works by a practical experiment. It had long been the custom in this Community to recite the Divine Office throughout the entire Paschal season, and this year it was agreed to continue the longer office* for a given time, in order to prove whether or no it could reasonably be undertaken. Meanwhile she herself made it the subject of earnest prayer, that she might live to see the accomplishment of this wish, so dear to her own heart and to that of all her children. Her prayers were unexpectedly granted, and that by a spontaneous act on the part of his Lordship, Bishop Ullathorne, who, at the close of the Triduo, announced his consent for the recitation of the Divine Office by the entire Congregation.

The yearly retreat, which took place in August,

---

* The Dominican Office for Matins throughout the Paschal season consists of one Nocturn only.

was this year given by Bishop Ullathorne, and was entirely based on the teaching of St Catherine. "It was like no retreat we ever had before," writes one of the Religious, "and made us feel that we never before knew the treasure we possess in the writings of our holy Mother." Others in like manner wrote describing it as "a time of great and special grace," and "something that would last them for their life-time." This spiritual consolation came at a moment when Mother Margaret was enduring unusual bodily suffering. A severe attack of illness in the spring of this year had undermined her general health; in addition to which, the affection of the skin, to which she had always been subject, had now reached a height which made it all but unbearable. "I often feel ready to cry with it," she said; "it is as if the evil one had peppered me from head to foot." Various temporal losses sustained at this time by the Community affected her but slightly, and in spite of them she was meditating a second foundation in Wales. To the prudential arguments urged in opposition, she only replied, "God has never failed us, and He never will. If it were to spend on ourselves that we wanted the money I should be afraid, but He knows we could not spend less than we do on our food and clothing, and that we only want it for His own work."

It was the will of God, however, that not Wales but London should be the site of Mother Margaret's last foundation. In the month of August 1866, a proposal was made by his Grace, Archbishop Manning, to place under the care of Mother Margaret and her Religious an Orphanage, destined for receiving the

Catholic orphan girls who might be given up by the workhouse authorities. He had secured a large house at Walthamstow, in Essex, for the purpose of receiving a certain number of the orphans, and this he now offered to Mother Margaret, rent free, for three years, a certain allowance towards the support of each orphan being expected from the Poor-Law Board. Mother Margaret was most desirous to meet his Grace's wishes, and the work contemplated engaged all her sympathies; she entirely overlooked the fact, obvious as it was, that the acceptance of Government money necessarily involved the acceptance of Government inspection also: and she therefore willingly consented to give the services of her Religious on the proposed conditions. On the 20th of August, therefore, she went to London, with one companion, to inspect the house, and come to a final agreement regarding the whole undertaking. After their interview with his Grace, they proceeded to Walthamstow House, a spacious mansion, capable of containing a hundred children, with five acres of garden ground. Its agreeable aspect, however, did not seem to inspire Mother Margaret with any pleasurable sentiments. Her drive through the eastern quarters of London had impressed her with painful thoughts, and she could not bear the idea of being located in a fine house, far out of the way of those masses of perishing souls for whom she longed to work. She had been told by some Protestant ladies that the parish of Stepney was one specially remarkable for the spiritual destitution of its Catholic population, and though there seemed but little chance of its being possible to undertake any additional work in that part of the world, she determined before leaving London, to pay it a visit of inspection. In her second interview with the Archbishop, Mother Margaret gave utterance to her feelings in her usual simple way. His Grace having inquired what she thought of Walthamstow, she replied, that it was a beautiful place, and very suitable for an Orphanage, and that she and her Sisters would be happy to begin there as soon as he wished. "But oh, my Lord!" she added, "can't you send us to *some dirty place?*" The Archbishop smiled, and hearing her attraction towards Stepney, advised her to go and make the acquaintance of Father M'Quoin of Stratford, who was most anxious to find some Community to assist him in the infant mission of Bow, a quarter of the world which was supposed to possess all the required qualifications. To Bow, therefore, Mother Margaret and her companion proceeded.

A boy from the school directed them to Father M'Quoin's house, and having delivered the Archbishop's letter of introduction, they were a little surprised to hear him say, on glancing at the name, "Mother Margaret! Oh, I have been thinking of you a long time, and wishing you would come to Bow!" He then proposed to take them to the school-chapel at Bromley, dedicated to St Agnes, after first showing them the rising walls of the church at Stratford; and having inspected the premises at Bow, Mother Margaret expressed her willingness to come to his assistance, provided a suitable site for a convent could be procured. And so she returned to Stone, pledged to undertake two foundations involving the gravest liabilities, at a time when the finances of the Community were more than usually embarrassed.

On the 3d of November the first colony of Religious was sent to take possession of Walthamstow House, and begin the necessary preparations for receiving the children, and Mother Margaret herself followed three days later. She was more than usually depressed and anxious. Something of this she always endured before beginning any new work, but there are indications in her letters of a sense of failing strength, and a longing for rest, that was rare for her to express. "Pray for me," she writes; "you know how dark I always am before beginning. I wonder I ever do begin; but it is not I, it is our dear Lord who pushes the birch broom along, and does what He wishes. It will be nice when all the work here below is done." A little later she writes, "*I am getting tired of work;*" and again, "I hope we shall both work on till our work is done, and our dear Lord is satisfied with His poor creatures; may He give us a resting-place when we have satisfied for all our shortcomings!" Her stay at Walthamstow did not tend to cheer or encourage her. Arrangements had been made for receiving one hundred children, but it soon became apparent that great difficulties would have to be overcome before the Poor-Law authorities would give them up. The consequent state of inaction was exceedingly trying to Mother Margaret; she would walk about exclaiming, "Oh, if I could but go and get the children out of the courts!" If the sound of wheels was heard in the road, she thought it was a conveyance bringing orphans to the door. At last she could endure it no longer, and determined on the Feast of the Presentation to make a present to Our Lady of some children to be supported at the sole charge of the Community. "No children come yet," she writes, "so we intend to take some *gratis* to offer to Our Lady on the Presentation. *L. s. d.* is certainly the god of the English : it does not suit me." She therefore entreated the priest to find her some children, and in the afternoon he brought to the house two destitute little girls. Her delight was unbounded, and turning to one of her Sisters, she said, with a bright look, "Now, don't be afraid, you will see our Lord will feed His own." About six that evening the butcher called at the door with a leg of mutton, which, he said, he had orders "only to give to a Sister." The same Religious having gone to receive it, he said, "Please to open the cloth, and put down on a bit of paper that it is all right." When the cloth was unfolded, a paper was found fastened to the leg of mutton containing a sovereign. Both meat and money were carried to Mother Margaret, who exclaimed with effusion of heart, "How like our good God ! These poor children have procured us the first offering we have had since we have been here ! "

But weeks went by and things appeared no nearer a settlement ; the small Community remained alone in their great house, the very quiet and solitude of the situation increasing Mother Margaret's impatience to be at work. Moreover she began for the first time to realise the necessary sacrifice of independence which must follow on her acceptance of Government aid. " I am quite unfit," she writes, "to deal with clever worldly people. I wish they would leave us alone to work in our own way, and not in the way of the Government." On the Feast of the Immaculate Conception, how-

ever, when the Blessed Sacrament was exposed in
their little chapel, she had what she called "a joy."
"I had one joy yesterday, I nearly went into an
ecstasy. We had our Divine Lord quite to ourselves,
which I was regretting, when about four o'clock nearly
twenty of the boys from the industrial school came
in, and sang four or five of Father Faber's hymns.
It was just our Lord's own. I was delighted, and
when they went away we gave them some biscuits."
Her heart warmed towards these poor boys, and she
often had them up to work at the convent, and showed
them a rather excessive amount of kindness. One lad
actually ran away because he had not been chosen for
the envied office of "scrubbing" at the convent. In
all Mother Margaret's troubles at this time, one thing
cheered her, and it was the hope she entertained of
ere long establishing herself at Bow. "That is the
place for us," she would say; "it is really a place
to save souls in. This place is too grand for us.
We want poor children, not trees." And then she
would go into the chapel and spend hours before the
tabernacle, and would say, "I never prayed so hard
as I have done here; I keep saying to Our Lady,
Give me Bow, give me Bow." The Religious who were
with her at this time also speak of her being in the
chapel long before the usual hour in the morning.
"At whatever time we might come down," said one,
"we were sure to find our Mother there. I believe
she spent half the night before our Lord."

She returned to Stone at the end of December,
after an absence of nearly two months, to spend the
last day of the old year among her children, a year
which one of them truly characterised as one "of

temporal losses and spiritual gains." Many causes had combined to awaken in the Community a great and general increase of fervour; the recitation of the Divine office commenced during this year, the unusually valuable retreat which has been already spoken of, together with examples and bereavements which had found their way to many souls.

It cannot be doubted that the close of this year, and the opening of the next, was a period of extraordinary spiritual grace to Mother Margaret, and that her soul was granted some special preparation for the excruciating sufferings which preceded her departure from this life. "Pray for me," she writes, "for lately there has been a great change in my soul, and God seems to require more of me in every way. May He perfect me as He best pleases, and give me humility, love, and (what will you say to my third request?) *money*, that I may be able to buy souls, to build hospitals, schools, churches,—everything that will win souls to God."

It is the custom in the Community, on the 1st of January, for the Religious to draw their patron saints for the coming year. On New Year's day, 1867, Mother Margaret drew for her patrons the Martyrs of Gorcum, whose canonisation was fixed to take place in the ensuing June, and the practice annexed ran as follows: "Prove your love of God by your love of suffering." And as she afterwards observed when lying on her sick-bed, everything at that time was continually preaching the cross, every book she opened seemed to tell her to prepare for the cross and for suffering, whilst at the same time both her interior trials and her exterior difficulties appeared to increase.

A great consolation had been afforded her in the autumn of the previous year by the appointment of the Rev. Father Procter as chaplain at St Mary Church. She felt his presence there a protection to the young and distant Community, and had been gratified by the hopeful terms in which he expressed himself regarding the rising mission in a letter written shortly after Christmas. On the 9th of January, only a few days after the receipt of this letter, the melancholy news was received by telegram of the sudden death of the writer, which had taken place at St Mary Church on the day previous. The telegram arrived in the evening, and early next morning Mother Margaret set out for Devonshire, performing the long journey in a single day. She found the Community in sad trouble, for the unexpected loss of this good pastor seemed to threaten a severe check to the work he had so solidly begun.

Mother Margaret remained at St Mary Church until after the funeral, and on the 21st of January returned to Stone, where she soon afterwards made a private Retreat of eight days. She appeared to be moved by an urgent and unusual longing for this period of prayer and solitude, as she said, in order to prepare herself for death. Most of her children were far from entertaining any apprehensions that the need for such a time of preparation was indeed so close at hand; but a few, who watched her more closely, were filled with sad misgivings as they beheld a change in her appearance, which indicated more than passing indisposition. Yet, in spite of her increasing infirmity, she not only gave herself no relaxation, but imposed on herself many acts of penance, for which her strength was quite unequal. Even the ordinary prostrations and *venias*, which occur in the daily ceremonies of the choir, could not be performed by her without great physical pain and exhaustion, yet to the last she persisted in all these observances. Nor was this all; during her Retreat, which every one remarked to have been a season of profound and extraordinary recollection, she solicited and obtained permission to make a general confession of her whole life to her ordinary confessor; and those only who are aware of the anguish which any exercise of self-introspection occasioned her, can appreciate the distress to which she thus voluntarily submitted for her own greater humiliation.

Meanwhile the arrangements connected with the reception of the orphans at Walthamstow were beginning to cause many harassing anxieties.

Mother Margaret had by this time become fully aware of the various liabilities incurred by her acceptance of this work, and a correspondence was opened with the Archbishop for the purpose of explaining her difficulties. As soon as his Grace became aware of her feelings, he most kindly consented to set her free from the engagement into which she had entered without a sufficient comprehension of the conditions involved; only requesting that the Sisters would remain at Walthamstow until he was in a position to place the house in other hands.

Mother Margaret's joy at finding herself free from the burden, which had weighed on her in so distressing a manner, was unbounded. "Truly," she observed, "Almighty God does bring us out of our difficulties in a wonderful manner. He knows our simplicity of intention, and that we only sought to serve Him. He brings down to the grave, and makes alive again;" and a large candle of thanksgiving was immediately lighted before Our Lady's image. On the 19th of March she left Stone for Walthamstow, where she remained nearly seven weeks.

The Forty Hours, and the Christmas Festival, and now also Lent, and Passiontide, and Easter, were all to go by, and her place in the midst of her children still remained empty. Though absent in person, however, she was present by letter, and at no period of her life is her correspondence so full as during the last weeks of her residence at Walthamstow. And still through all of them runs one unvarying note: *the Cross, the Cross!* "It is a painful, anxious life," she writes; "and if our dear Lord did not sustain me with His all-powerful hand, I should sink under it. . . . God is truly founding us in the Cross. . . . He has blessed us with many crosses this year; may He be blessed for ever! . . . We are children of the Cross, conceived and born at the foot of the Cross, servants of the Cross by our own free choice. We have chosen it for our inheritance; so we must bear it willingly and cheerfully. Pray for our work here: it is not yet begun, as we cannot get the children. The evil one is very busy, and, like all God's works, it is marked with the Cross; but that, no doubt, is its best security."

Towards the close of April negotiations were opened for the purchase of a piece of ground at Bow, and their favourable issue formed the principal intention in the devotions offered during the month of May.

Mother Margaret had never testified the same ardent desire concerning any of her former foundations, but her whole heart seemed bent on this, and again we find her writing that she can do nothing but go about asking Our Lady to give her Bow. She returned from Walthamstow to Stone on the 3rd of May, and the Fifteen Mysteries of the Rosary began to be recited, going processionally in the early mornings to the Chapel of Our Lady of Victories. On the 11th of May she proceeded to Clifton, where another trial awaited her in the illness of one of the Religious, who had to undergo a painful surgical operation. Only those who were familiar with Mother Margaret's extreme tenderness of heart, and her peculiar dread of surgical treatment, can realise the distress and anguish which she underwent on this occasion. When she reached St Mary Church a few days later, the traces of what she had gone through were plainly discernible on her countenance, and indeed at this time her own health was beginning visibly to fail, and her children were in constant dread of a recurrence of the dangerous malady which had attacked her in the previous spring. At St Mary Church she received one great and unexpected consolation. The generous benefactor already named made known his intention of building the church to be attached to the future convent, and this welcome intelligence was communicated to her on the Feast of Our Lady, Help of Christians, under which title the Convent of St Mary Church is dedicated. But the many emotions which Mother Margaret at this time underwent greatly shook her failing strength, and on reaching Stone her appearance indicated an unusual amount of suffering and exhaustion. On the eve of Corpus Christi, which that year fell on the 20th of June, she found herself obliged to keep her room, and to her great regret was unable to take part in the preparations for the coming feast.   The illness of one of her Religious at the same time caused her much distress, and increased her own indisposition, so that when Sunday came, on which day the great procession is annually made at Stone, Mother Margaret could only watch it from her window.

It was about this time that she was one day seized with a sharp pain in the left side, which seemed to transfix her; and though the acute paroxysm was for the moment relieved, yet the pain in the back and side never afterwards left her, and were alleviated by no remedies.   It was, in fact, the beginning of her fatal malady, and during the remainder of the summer her health continued visibly to give way.

By the beginning of October, she became so seriously ill as to be obliged to remove to the infirmary, and submit to medical treatment; and during the Rosary Week, the whole Rosary was offered daily for her recovery.   On Rosary Sunday intelligence was received that arrangements had at last been made which would enable the Community at Walthamstow to remove thence to Bow.   As possession had not yet been obtained of the house purchased in the latter place, it was resolved to rent another, and to lose no time in establishing the Religious in this temporary dwelling. A small house was accordingly hired, and this first step towards the foundation at Bow filled Mother Margaret with such delight that it quite revived her. " I do not feel a pain," she said, " when I think of Bow.   It is a place after my own heart; and as to the rent of the house, the blessed Virgin will be sure to pay it."

On the 22d of October she left Stone for London, for the purpose of personally superintending the removal of the Sisters from Walthamstow, and their establishment at Bow. At the time when she undertook this painful journey, she was struggling with severe illness, and was in reality fit only for a sick-bed. The transfer of the little Community from Walthamstow to the hired house in Clarendon Terrace was accomplished three days later ; and the little chapel having been got ready, Mass was said in it for the first time, by one of the Dominican Fathers from Haverstock Hill, on Sunday the 27th. On this day, then, may be said to have commenced the foundation at Bow, Mother Margaret's last work on earth, on which some special blessing must surely rest, established and cemented as it has been in the Cross.

Her state of suffering, increased by the fatigues unavoidable at such a time, had now attained a height which rendered it a matter of doubt how she would be able to bear the homeward journey. But she revived sufficiently to make the attempt, and reached Stone on the 30th, bringing with her a most precious relic, which had been presented to the Community by J. V. Harting, Esq., namely, the incorrupt hand of St Etheldreda, the abbess and foundress of Ely. In spite of her pain and weakness Mother Margaret's heart was occupied with sanguine hopes regarding her new foundation. "I never felt such trust as now," she said, "that God would help us. If I had the money, I would build a beautiful church at Bow directly. It is Our Lady's own place." And on the

P

Feast of All Saints, when she saw the church at Stone decked for that great solemnity, she repeated more than once that it was like heaven, and that a church like that at Bow would convert thousands.*

On the 5th of November she assisted at the clothing of two novices, the last ceremony of the kind at which she was ever to be present. She went through it with difficulty, owing to the intense pain she was then enduring. But by this time she was obliged to own herself unable to stand erect, and at the urgent solicitation of the Bishop and of the Community, she consented to give herself a fortnight's entire rest. On the 7th of November, therefore, she took to her bed, and from that couch of excruciating suffering she was never destined to rise again.

CHAPTER XIII.

HER LAST ILLNESS AND DEATH.

THE fortnight of rest which Mother Margaret would have fain believed was all she required passed away, and found her at its close entirely helpless to rise.

* Since the death of Mother Margaret, her ardent wishes on this point have been realised in an unexpected way. A Church, which is to be attached to the convent, and dedicated to St Catherine of Sienna, is now erected at Bow, by a generous benefactress, who, at the time of her undertaking this pious work, was wholly unknown to the community. The foundation-stone of this Church was laid on St Margaret's Day (July 20, 1869). It was solemnly opened by his Grace Archbishop Manning on the Feast of All Saints of the Dominican Order, (November 9th, 1870).

Only four days after she had taken to her bed the bursting of a large lumbar abscess seemed to declare the nature of the complaint, and to afford an explanation of the pain that had gone before. Sanguine hopes were therefore entertained that the malady might have reached a favourable crisis, which would be followed by a recovery of strength; but by the end of the month the pain had become more acute, and those who had hitherto cherished the most confident hopes began to see that her illness, under its most favourable aspect, must be long and tedious, and that there was a manifest loss of strength and power, which increased from day to day. On Advent Sunday, which fell on the 1st of December, commenced a Triduo for the Holy Father, which had been ordered to be made throughout the diocese, and of which we have elsewhere spoken. It did not interfere with the celebration of the Forty Hours, which commenced as usual on the Feast of the Immaculate Conception. Mother Margaret, who up to this time occupied a room on the ground-floor, had to the last indulged the hope that she might be wheeled on her sofa to the church, and might thus be able to satisfy her devotion. She had directed certain alterations to be made in the usual decorations, and for some days beforehand spoke of her coming visit to the church, and of the pleasure she anticipated in once more beholding the beauty of the sanctuary. But when the feast came, the attempt proved beyond her strength. The usual procession at the beginning of the devotion was this year made round the cloisters, passing by the door of the room which Mother Margaret occupied. The sound of the bell indicating the near approach of the Blessed

Sacrament, quite overcame her, and, to use her own expression, she cried, like the blind man in the Gospel who sat by the wayside as our Lord passed along, " Jesus, Son of David, have mercy on me ! "

At this period of her illness Mother Margaret was suffering not merely from bodily pain, but from extreme desolation of soul. " I could bear all the rest," she sometimes said, " if it were not for this. Even Our Lady seems to have forgotten me;" and she would add, with tears, " God has done so much for me, and I have done nothing for Him in return." At other times she said, " I dread looking forward, it seems all such a dark void. How often I think of our Lord's agony in the garden, and use His words ! I have never once asked absolutely to get well, only that God's will may be done. It seems such a long, dreary prospect, *but I shall coax our Lord to make it short!* If only I *knew* that I should be saved ! " And this fear regarding her ultimate salvation caused her a severe interior trial. To her energetic mind the long inaction was itself a severe penance. " If it were our Lord's will to raise me up, and let me work again," she one day said, " I should be glad ; but if I am not to recover, I would much rather He took me to Himself, than let me lie here like an animal, eating and drinking, and thinking of nothing but the body. But when I say this, I always add at the end of it, ' God's will be done ! ' " In fact, her most plaintive words were ever mingled with expressions of entire abandonment to the will of God, and, to use the words of the Religious who was constantly at her side, " her acts of resignation were unceasing, mingled with prayers to endure to the end, without offending God."

Great as were the sufferings of Mother Margaret's last illness, they were not, however, unmixed with consolations. It may truly be said that God gave much in return for all that during life she had given to Him. The words had ever been on her lips that "He was a *grateful* lover," and that "He was never to be outdone in generosity," and on her sick-bed she experienced their truth. The reader may perhaps recall one incident of Mother Margaret's early life, when, having been left a legacy of considerable amount, she expended the whole sum in Masses for the soul of her deceased benefactor. Those Masses were repaid with interest. During her six months' illness, no fewer than eleven Novenas of Masses were either offered spontaneously, or procured by friends. Seventeen other Novenas of Masses were at various times procured by the Community to be offered for her, of which some were said in England, and others at Notre Dame des Victoires in Paris, at Our Lady of Assabroeck, at Loretto, and other holy places. Besides these Novenas, she had the unspeakable consolation and support afforded by a multitude of other Masses offered for her almost daily. Three priests, with extraordinary charity, persevered during the whole of her illness in giving her almost every one of their Masses not otherwise appropriated by obligation. Some offered the Holy Sacrifice for her every other day, others again, every week ; and on examining the list preserved of these benefactions, we arrive at the astonishing conclusion that during the last six months of her life she must have had as many as a thousand Masses offered for her intention; a very large propor tion of which were said gratuitously.

Mother Margaret's establishment in the room on the ground-floor which she had hitherto occupied, had been arranged under the idea that her imprisonment would be of short duration, and that she would be less separated from the Community than if removed up-stairs. But as all hopes of a speedy cure were now relinquished, she began to feel a scruple at not being in the infirmary, and became so desirous of removing thither, that though fearful of the risk, her children could not refuse her.

An arm-chair was prepared in such a way as to admit of her reclining backwards, for she was unable to bear the least approach to an erect posture, and on the 7th of January she was, with extreme difficulty, conveyed up-stairs to the infirmary.

In spite of the steady and manifest progress of her malady, its precise nature remained to the last obscure. The seat, however, was evidently in the spine, and she often said that her back was breaking. In the midst of the most excruciating pain, her countenance remained singularly tranquil; the features were not drawn or contracted, so that a casual observer would hardly have detected any change. Yet she described herself at this time as "lying on a bed of fire." "I am a soul in purgatory," she said. "May God help and sustain me! My patience depends more on others than myself. It is your prayers that keep me up; my own are worth nothing;" and to all who visited her she addressed the most earnest and touching entreaties that they would *pray, pray, pray,* that she might "persevere to the end, and not lose patience." "The last time she was ever moved from her bed to the sofa," writes one of her devoted nurses, "she expressed a great wish to die, and said, ' Oh, when will our Lord come for me ! How long I have to wait, and then I get so frightened of losing patience, and losing Him.' She was reminded that God sent these great crosses as a sign of His love. 'Ah, that was to the saints,' she replied ; 'but they were patient. They did not call out as I do ;' and then, in the midst of her sobs and tears, she broke out into exclamations, saying, ' But I *do* love Him ! He knows I love Him! O Love, I *do* love Thee! I love nobody but Thee !' She often repeated that she was a sinner, suffering for her 'great, great sins.' Her most frequent ejaculations were, ' Thy will be done !' and 'My God and my all!' and she used to tell us that those words were her Litany. Sometimes we heard her saying half aloud, ' A little ease, dear Jesus ! a little ease ! My Lord and my God, I unite all my sufferings to those of Thy Divine Son ;' or again, 'My sweet Mother Mary, O Divine Mother, my more than Mother, pray for me!'" " She was grateful for everything that was done for her," writes another, " and as simple as a child, but the simplicity was of a kind that constantly excited your reverence. She blessed God's goodness for everything which we gave her. If we gave her part of an orange, she would say, ' How good of God to make this orange for me ! I have everything He can give. He has given me all of you to wait on me. How good He is !' " Another time, when a Sister gave her a glass of water, she heard her murmur, " From His blessed Hands !" and the same Sister observes, " What most struck me in her illness, was that she was so exactly the same as when in health." No one could fail to remark the studied manner in which she sought to teach and to practise detachment. Far from seeking to fix the thoughts of those around her on herself, to make claims on their sympathy, or to cherish that clinging of children to their dying Mother, which would seem to some too natural to reprove, it was apparent to all that in a thousand nameless ways she was striving to loosen the tie, and to prevent the hearts of any from being absorbed in herself. Every one observed how strict was the guard she kept over herself in this matter, not certainly from any want of natural tenderness, for she owned to one who shared her closest confidence, that it cost her no slight effort to avoid exciting the sympathy of the Sisters. She was afraid of her own natural feelings, no less than of theirs ; and when giving leave for any Sister to visit her, bid her be told that "she must not cry."

Yet her tenderness of heart was at the same time constantly manifesting itself. "My poor children !" she would say, "they are suffering for their Mother ; it is a cross to you all, but *fiat, fiat.*" This tenderness of heart was also evinced in other ways. She forgot no one. If a Religious came to see her, she would ask after the children, the orphans, the servants in the house, or whatever else might fall under that Sister's peculiar care. She remembered the absent relatives of each one, and sent kind messages to them, and would show her usual maternal interest in the little affairs or troubles of that large circle outside her convent walls who called her "Mother." When she heard of the innumerable prayers offered for her by priests or other friends, she would reply, " I cannot think how they come to remember me. It must be that God has looked on the lowness of His handmaid, for He could see nothing viler ! "

For a short time after the beginning of her illness she persevered in reciting the Divine Office, until, through the increase of spinal pain, her arms became unable to support the weight of the book, and she was forced to substitute the little Office of Our Lady, which she recited as long as she was able to use a book at all. A Religious having one day read her the Prayer of St Gertrude, giving thanks for sufferings, which begins, " O most loving Jesus," * &c., she said, " You must read this to me every day ; " and her request was complied with (though it was difficult to read it without tears) until she became too weak to listen. " Now," she said, " I must say it in desire." The Rosary was constantly in her hands, and the very day before her death she made an effort to say it by way of preparation for Holy Communion. She did not like any one to sit and watch her, as it hindered her freedom for prayer and aspiration. About six weeks before her death, being asked what prayers she still felt able to say, she replied that she said the whole Rosary every morning before Mass, and the Litany of Our Lady about twenty times a day. "Then I say the Act of Resignation, beginning ' May the most just, most holy, and most amiable will of God,' I don't know how often. I try to pray all the time I am not speaking, but they are odd sort of prayers; only 'Our Fathers' and 'Hail Marys,' and I fall asleep between." Once she let fall the remark, " Oh, praying is like breathing ! " and the Religious to whom she spoke, adds, that they knew she was engaged in

* Prayers of St Gertrude, p. 174.

continual prayer by the movement of her hand, which she raised a little and let fall again as she made her aspirations.

The beginning of February brought a torturing increase of pain. Yet all remarked that the countenance of the sufferer gave no indication of this; there was no writhing or contortion of the features, only the eyes cast up towards heaven, as she uttered brief aspirations for " patience to the end." " I can see," she one day said, " how God has been preparing my soul for all this for the last two years. I felt something was coming, and I had such a reluctance to suffer ! and yet all the books I read were about suffering, and all my prayers were for generosity to suffer. I used to be so weary sometimes, and say to myself, ' How I long for a holiday !' and something always seemed to answer, ' God will give it you in His own way.' "

The Catholic congregation of Stone offered a touching tribute of their respect for Mother Margaret, by begging for a Novena of Masses to be offered on their behalf for her recovery ; but before the termination of the Novena, Mother Margaret's state became so critical, that although no immediate danger was apprehended, it was judged prudent to administer the last Sacraments. She received the rites of the Church, therefore, on the 14th of February, with great peace and tranquillity, and perfect possession of mind ; humbly begging pardon of all the Religious who were assembled round her bed, for any pain or scandal she might ever have given them, and answering the usual questions proposed by the priest in a tone of intense fervour.

A few days later a letter was received from Rome, conveying to Mother Margaret the blessing of the Holy Father, which had been obtained for her by Monsignor Talbot, immediately on his hearing of her illness, and which, when read to her, she desired as a mark of veneration to be laid on her head. Other letters, also, from the Master-General of the Order, brought the consoling promise of Masses to be offered up in her behalf at the tomb of St Catherine, together with some words of sympathy and encouragement to her afflicted children. It was apparent from many circumstances that by this time Mother Margaret had altogether withdrawn her mind from temporal affairs. She appeared to consider the government of the Congregation as a thing in which she was no longer concerned, and if consulted on any matter, would show an unwillingness to give an opinion which might bind those who had to act. To the Religious who had assisted her for so many years in all the cares of superiority, she from time to time gave a few simple words of counsel, which all spoke the one lesson of *God alone.* " Lean on *God alone*—God and yourself ; that is what I have always found. No one else can help you. Never decide on things in a hurry. One should pray and say the hymns of the Holy Ghost, and then God tells you what to do." Once, having referred to the many years they had worked together, her companion replied, " And now, you leave me to work alone." "Don't say that," replied Mother Margaret ; " see how many you have to help you, compared to the little help I had when we began. God will help you if you are faithful ; and as to temporals, I don't like to hear you make an 'if' or a 'but' about them.

It is sure to be right.   How could you doubt it when God has done so much out of nothing?"

She was now entirely confined to one position, and could only relieve the pressure on the back by supporting herself by her arms.   This she did by means of loops at either side of the bed.   During the severe paroxysms of pain her hands were extended to grasp and hold by these loops, and by degrees this became her ordinary position, so that one beheld her day and night, lying thus on her back, with her arms extended in the form of a cross.   Sometimes, when she was wearied out and stiffened with cold, she would try and bring her arms down ; but she was soon obliged to raise them as before, and thus, as one of her attendants writes, she seemed day and night like a living image of the crucifix.   Her face began to show signs of emaciation, but there was not a line of suffering. It constantly wore the same expression of tranquillity, except when moved to tears by the sight of the crucifix, or in what she called "a frenzy of pain."   An ardent desire to go to God seemed to fill her soul, and even to the medical men who attended her she would address the plaintive words, "Do let me go to God!" If the crucifix was presented to her, she would kiss it with abundance of tears, saying, " My sweet Jesus, my Beloved, come and take me : I desire only to be united to Thee !"   A picture of Our Lady of Perpetual Succour was sent, about this time, by the Redemptorist Fathers of Clapham, and being taken to her, drew from her some ardent expressions of her love for the Blessed Virgin.   "I *have* loved her dearly," she repeated.   " And have fought her battles too, have you not ?" remarked one of the Religious.

"I have, indeed," she replied, "and I fear I have sometimes committed sin by it." And on other occasions she also accused herself of the many times she had been excited to anger in defence of the Blessed Virgin. She often spoke of Bow, the foundation on which she had spent her last remains of strength, and which lay so close to her heart. "I always think of Bow with joy," she said, "and never regret having gone there, though I do believe I am suffering for that place;" alluding to the saying in the Community, that there was always a victim for each new foundation. And in the midst of her severest agonies she made known her request that the convent should be dedicated to St Catherine, and opened on St Catherine's Feast, naming all the arrangements which she wished to be observed on the occasion.

During Holy Week it seemed as if our Lord had been pleased in a special manner to unite her sufferings with His own, for her pains were more than usually intense. Yet, on Holy Thursday, she was able to see and express her approval of some decorations prepared for the sepulchre, and as one of the Religious was leaving her room, in order to take her hour of adoration, Mother Margaret looked at her rather wistfully, bidding her "say everything to our Lord for me; but," she added, "He is here as well as there, that is my comfort." During the night she spoke several times of our Lord's agony and betrayal, and of all He had suffered for us. No doubt, this lover of the Passion of our Lord was able to offer all things in union with His bitter sufferings; and how close she kept in spirit to the Cross of Christ was manifested by the words she was heard murmuring to herself when Holy Saturday came at last, " *How glad I am He cannot suffer any more !* "

On Easter Monday she would seem to have thought her end approaching, and seeing beside her the Religious who had for years been her chief companion and assistant, she attempted to console her, saying, " Pray for a happy death for me ; if God is satisfied, why should not you be ? I have felt it a great favour of God that you were not taken before me : I was getting old, and could not have done without you." Then she added, " My prayer has always been that I may retain consciousness to the last ; but if I should lose it, *you* know that I·have always believed in the Father, Son, and Holy Ghost, and that I die in the faith of the Holy Catholic Church." To her confessor she expressed her thanks for all he had done for her soul, promising to pray both for him and for the Order. "I have always loved the Order," she said ; " it has been almost an *irregular* affection with me. Not that I cared so much for any individual in it, but it is an Order of Saints, and I desired to see it flourish. I wish I could have done more for it. I would if I could." Then she begged the confessor to express to the Father-Provincial her regret if she had ever said or done anything to give pain to him or to any of the Fathers ; adding, " If I have, it has been the head, not the heart, and a warmth of temper I could not always control." And then she spoke of herself, and the work which God had suffered her to do. " I know some people think I have done much for God, but I could never see it so. Oh, it is God who has done much for me. To me it was•all gratification ! I have had only to ask and have. It is

wonderful what God has ever done for me in all the
works I have undertaken for Him. It was too much.
I always felt there must be some great suffering to fill
up the measure on the other side."

On the 23d of April she spoke much of the arrangements she wished to be made regarding her burial,
and being told that the Bishop had already regulated
that she should be laid in the choir, "Oh!" she
exclaimed, "impossible; you would all be frightened!"
Then after a minute she added, "Well, I like it, and
I don't like it." She concluded by begging that she
might be laid in the centre of the new cemetery, with
the cross at her head, and her feet towards the convent. "Of course I am nothing now," she said,
"but if I have a wish, it is this, and let it be written
down in my name;" and she added more than once,
that "she was not worthy to be buried in the church."
The Bishop, to whom the matter was referred for
decision, overruled the scruples suggested by her
humility, and decided that her children should have
the consolation afforded by the hope that their Mother's
venerated remains would repose among them in the
choir.

This conversation took place on the day when a
solemn Novena to St Catherine was begun in preparation for her feast. The effort of speaking so much
caused Mother Margaret some exhaustion, and so
marked a change manifested itself in her appearance
that the priest was called, and gave her the last blessing. At this very moment the Community were
beginning their procession round the cloister, bearing
the relics of St Catherine, and singing the hymns of
her Office. The distant sound mingled with the voice

of the priest as he pronounced the prayers and blessing, and deeply moved those who were present, and
who almost dreaded lest the Novena now commencing
should be the immediate preparation for the end.
The remainder of that evening was spent by all in
prayer before the Blessed Sacrament, and the following
morning, the 23d of April, Mother Margaret appeared
in such imminent danger that all the Religious were
summoned to her room, where the Litany of the Saints
was recited by the confessor. By the time he had
concluded, Mother Margaret had rallied considerably,
and the curtains at the foot of her bed being withdrawn, so that she could see all her children, she
exerted herself to address them a few parting words.
" May God bless you all, my dear children," she said ;
" I beg pardon for all I have ever done to offend you.
Ask of God the forgiveness of my sins. Sin is an
awful thing when you come to your last hour. Pray
for me. It is a terrible thing to fall into the hands
of the living God. God bless you all, my dear children. Keep close to Almighty God and to your Rule,
and whatever you do, do all for God alone." During
the remainder of the day she remained in a weak and
suffering state, with her mind often rambling. She
once asked that the Litany of Our Lady might be recited, and at its close made signs for the Sisters in
attendance to come near, and gave each what she
used to call her Belgian blessing, making the sign of
the Cross on their foreheads, and laying her hands on
their heads. The next day she continued in the same
state of partial wandering, yet through it all her aspirations were most moving and devout. Once she was
heard murmuring, " All bounty, all mercy, all love !"

Another time she seemed offering a long prayer for the pardon of sin, and the Religious by her side caught the words, "O my Father, pardon, pardon my many great sins!" And again, "How good God is! Who is like to God?" Once she missed her crucifix, and putting out her hand to feel for it, was heard saying, "O my crucified Love, where are you?" and when it was put into her hand, "That is right," she said; "I want nothing else." Her thoughts seemed often occupied with Bow. "May God bless and prosper it," she said; and sometimes she appeared to be giving directions relative to the removal of the Sisters. into their own house at Bow, and the opening of the convent, which had been fixed to take place on the Feast of St Catherine.

The weakness of her faculties was now increasing, and of this she herself appeared conscious, saying to the Religious whom she regarded as her second self, "Whilst I have my senses you must be my constant counsellor." She often asked those about her to help her to prepare for Confession or Communion, and to assist her in examining her conscience. "Be sure to tell me," she would say, "if you see the least thing in me that would detain me from the presence of God." The Feast of St Catherine was past, and Our Lady's Month of May had begun, and still the long agony went on without change or intermission. It seemed as if the sufferer's magnificent organisation was holding out to its last fibre. Every part of the body had to endure its own peculiar torture. The very tongue was hard and dry, and furrowed with deep cracks from the intensity of the internal fever. On Saturday the 2d May, she received Holy Communion, and

Q

afterwards, when the Crucifix was presented to her, she made an effort to kiss the Five Wounds, and then sank back exhausted, whispering, " I can do no more." During the days that followed, her intervals of entire consciousness were few, yet, from time to time, amid pain and wandering, the words were ever on her lips, " The Will of God, the Will of God ! " Her sufferings were intense, the very feet twitching and convulsed with the tension of the nerves. On the 6th of May, the physician in attendance having visited her, she herself asked him how long he thought it would last. He told her she was much weaker since his last visit, sixteen days before, and that he did not think it possible she could survive another sixteen days. " Thank God ! " was her reply, and then she begged to be left quiet, saying, " Sixteen days is a short time, I wish to be alone with God." On the 9th of May, she was seized with a paroxysm of pain exceeding anything she had yet endured. " God only knows what it is," she said. " My back is on fire. God's holy will be done. I have not murmured, have I ? " Hitherto she had always said, " My back will break ; " but now she used the words, " My back is *broken !* " marking some great crisis of the disorder. Her exclamations of suffering, however, were all mingled with prayers and acts of resignation. At intervals during the day, she spoke affectionately to all around her, expressing the comfort she felt in having them near her. She uttered the Holy Name repeatedly ; " God of God, Light of Light," she exclaimed ; " oh, if it would please Him to take me ! How happy I was this morning when I thought I was going ! " Occasionally she whispered, " I am so frightened!" and at one sharp pang, "O my dear child, pray that my faith may not fail!" but it was noticed that this was the only occasion when she seemed to fear the possibility of the last-named temptation. Her attendants were very desirous of making some alteration in the arrangement of the bed, and as they were consulting how this should be done, considering the impossibility of moving the sufferer, Mother Margaret overheard them, and said in an emphatic manner, "Now you let it alone; you can't mend it; leave it all to God, He will mend it—*wait till Sunday!*" Then after a minute or two she repeated, "Leave it to God! *He will put it right on Monday!*" They thought her wandering at the time, but the event seemed to show that she had a foresight of the time of her death.

Sunday, the 10th of May, the Feast of St Antoninus of Florence, came at last. It was also the Fourth Sunday after Easter, and the words of the Gospel spoke to the hearts of those who heard them with no ordinary power. "I go to Him who sent me; and because I have spoken these things sorrow hath filled your hearts. But I tell you the truth; *it is expedient for you that I go.*" Three of the Religious remained in her room during the night. She breathed with difficulty, but was comparatively quiet till about midnight, when, hearing by the sound that the oppression of the chest was increased, Mother Assistant came to the side of her bed, and observed that her eyes were very prominent, as though struggling for breath. Some remedies were applied without effect; she was, however, perfectly conscious and recollected, and asked if they had not better send for the medical man.

But the next moment, sensible herself of the approach of the last change, she exclaimed, "The priest, the priest!" and they saw that the end was come at last. The chaplain was accordingly summoned, and the Community were roused by the fatal death-signal,* the dismal sound of which, in the silence of the night, struck to their very hearts. In a few minutes all were assembled in the sick-chamber. On either side of the bed knelt the Superiors of the Community and the elder Religious, one of whom supported the blessed candle in her Mother's dying fingers, a large Crucifix being held before her at the foot of the bed. The priest knelt at her right hand, and began the commendatory prayers; the Religious answering aloud, their voices interrupted by their tears, and their looks fixed on the countenance of their dying Mother. She appeared to retain consciousness to the last moment. The last words she was heard to utter were, "Lord, into Thy hands I commend my spirit;" followed by a whispered ejaculation of the Holy Name. There was scarcely a struggle, only a few sobs and heavings and a gradual gentle failure of the breath, which lasted hardly five minutes, and then she drew her hand up to her cheek, like a child asleep. There were a few deep-drawn breaths, and all was over. Her words had been verified, for she expired between Sunday and Monday, about a quarter after midnight on the 11th of May 1868.

Early in the morning, before Prime, the body was conveyed to the chapter-room, and the doors of the

---

* Notice of any Sister being in her agony is given by a particular clapper only used at such times, and during those days in Holy Week when the bells are silent.

chapter-room and choir being thrown open, Mass was celebrated for the repose of the departed. The Religious watched by the body by turns, reciting the Psalter aloud, according to the custom of the Order. Towards noon the Bishop arrived, and arranged that the funeral should not take place until Thursday, and that on Tuesday evening the body should be removed from the chapter-room to the nave of the church, that the people might have an opportunity of beholding, for the last time, the remains of one who had so many claims on their affection and respect. During Monday and Tuesday the body continued in the chapter-room; every member remained flexible, and the countenance lost all appearance of suffering or emaciation, and assumed a beauty which rather increased than diminished as the hours went by.

On Tuesday evening the body was carried processionally to the church, and deposited on a bier in the central aisle, which was arranged as a temporary choir. A considerable number of the Catholic congregation were assembled to assist at the ceremony; and the Religious having taken their places in the seats prepared for them, recited aloud the Penitential Psalms, and chanted the *De profundis.* That night some of the patients from St Mary Hospital assisted the Religious in watching beside the body, and throughout Wednesday the church was visited by hundreds of all ranks, who came to touch the body with their rosaries, medals, and pious pictures. The Divine Office was recited by the Religious in the temporary choir which had been formed in the nave, and at seven in the evening the Dirge for the Dead was said, the Lauds being sung. On this occasion, the church was crowded, most of those present wearing mourning in token of their respect, and at the conclusion of the service, the body was visited as before by great numbers.

On Thursday morning the Requiem Mass commenced at ten o'clock ; from an early hour up to that time the church continued to be visited by hundreds who came to gaze at the body, and touch it with their pictures and rosaries. The features remained unchanged in their singular beauty, and the fingers of the hands were still perfectly flexible.

It had been intended that the body should be removed to the choir before the commencement of the Mass, but in order not to disappoint the people this arrangement was given up, and it was determined that the whole ceremony should proceed in the church, where all might satisfy their devotion. The last sad ceremony of closing the coffin took place immediately before the commencement of the Mass. All the Religious who assisted at it pressed a farewell kiss on the beloved features of their Mother, which they were to behold no more in this world, and fell on their knees as the lid was closed, and the coffin covered with a white funeral pall. At ten the procession entered the church by the cloister door. It included the Chapter of Birmingham, who all attended in their canons' dress ; the priests of the Conference ; nine Dominicans, three Benedictines, and one Oratorian Father ; in all about forty priests, with his Lordship Bishop Ullathorne ; the Right Rev. Dr Amherst, Bishop of Northampton, arriving before the conclusion of the ceremony. The Mass was sung *coram pontifice,* the Dominican Fathers alone forming the choir, and singing the beautiful plain chant Requiem with singular feeling and expression. The Religious occupied the temporary choir immediately surrounding the body, the remainder of the church being filled with a densely crowded congregation. The Bishop delivered a funeral oration, in which he gave a sketch of Mother Margaret's life, dwelling both on her labours of charity and on her more interior and spiritual gifts. At the conclusion of the sermon, which lasted an hour and a half, the ceremony of deposition began. The priest, deacon, and subdeacon, attended by the fathers who formed the choir, having descended from the sanctuary, the procession was formed, eight of the Religious bearing the body to the choir, preceded by the rest of the Community. The procession passed up the chancel steps, through the sanctuary, the grave containing the leaden coffin having been prepared just within the choir gates, and immediately below the spot where the Religious receive Holy Communion. The accustomed psalms and anthems of the Dominican Office were chanted around the grave whilst the wooden coffin was lowered, and the beloved remains were laid in their place of repose. Thus, like her great patriarch St Dominic, Mother Margaret lies "beneath the feet of her children." A wooden tablet, inlaid with her monogram, surrounded by a crown of thorns, marks the spot on the choir floor beneath which that great heart has been laid to rest ; and it is no little consolation for her children, when they assemble before the altar, or for the daily office, to feel that their Mother is in the midst of them still. May her spirit no less abide among them to the end! may a double portion of that spirit rest on those who are called to fill her place and carry on her work, and may one and all of the hundred souls whom she trained in religion be animated to follow in her footsteps, and to teach the lesson expressed in her entire life, " GOD ALONE, GOD ALONE, GOD ALONE ! "

THE END.